The Storyteller

The Storyteller

Kathryn Williams

HARPER TEEN

An Imprint of HarperCollinsPublishers

For Greg
and Teddy

HarperTeen is an imprint of HarperCollins Publishers.

The Storyteller
Copyright © 2022 by Kathryn Williams
All rights reserved. Manufactured in Italy.

ISBN 978-0-06-304939-0

Typography by Corina Lupp
21 22 23 24 25   GV   10 9 8 7 6 5 4 3 2 1

First Edition

"*To call a story a true story is an insult to both art and truth.*"

—VLADIMIR NABOKOV

"*Lying to ourselves is more deeply ingrained than lying to others.*"

—FYODOR DOSTOEVSKY
(apocryphal)

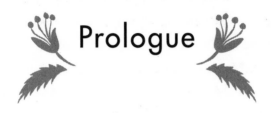

Prologue

I'm not sure when I became an impostor. It wasn't a conscious decision, more a slow, smooth slide into something that felt, just, easier. Maybe it was in sixth grade, when I told my mom that I wanted to take piano lessons, but she convinced me to play sports instead because it was more social. I've played soccer for six years. Truth is, I hate soccer.

Or it might have been in ninth, when Ms. Emery, the school guidance counselor, with an office the size of a broom closet, cocked her head to the side and asked, "You doing all right, Jess?" and I replied cheerily, "Yep, I'm great." It was simpler than explaining that Jenny Glocke had suddenly stopped talking to me for no apparent reason and that the tense exchanges that drifted from beneath my parents' bedroom door had started to become tenser. "Great" was what my mom crisply replied when we were visiting my grandparents in Florida and Gammy would ask, with narrowed eyes, "How are things at home?"

Or maybe it was the day Ryan Hart asked me if I liked to ski, a lone dimple winking from his right cheek, and I looked down at the hot dog in my hand and nodded and told him, "Yeah, sure." It was Labor Day 2003, and we were at a barbecue in the Harts' backyard. They'd just moved to Keene from Boston. Our parents were friends from their college days who hoped Ryan and I, both entering eighth grade, would be friends, too.

We sat on top of a picnic table under an oak tree whose leaves had yet to turn for fall. With honey-tan skin and boy-band hair, Ryan was certifiably, undeniably, trademark Cute™ in the charming, slightly aloof way of the love interest of an eighties movie. Late-afternoon sun filtered through the branches, making the fine blond down on his forearms glow. He appeared golden.

Even his name was made for doodling in the margins of a notebook or murmuring under your breath just to see how the syllables felt in your mouth: Ryan Olivier Hart. For the next year and a half, every textbook I owned, every diary, every scrap of paper that came through my hands bore some calligraphed form of his initials within a perfectly lopsided heart.

At school, a single "hey" as we passed in the hall—on Tuesdays and Thursdays after second block, and some Fridays if he was coming from Mrs. Cardinetti's—was enough to spin me into orbit. *What was the inflection of that "hey"? Was there eye contact? Sustained eye contact? When he asked if I was coming to the Harts' holiday party, did that imply he* hoped *I was coming, or was he just being polite?* I tortured myself—as well as my best friend, Katie—with the possibilities.

Ryan was everything I thought I was supposed to be: confident, popular, easy, *at* ease. Where I strained, he glided. Where my small clique of best friends was hard won, popularity seemed to come to him instantly. Our social circles overlapped in a thin, almond-shaped sliver, but Ryan Hart was nice to me. And sometimes, I suspected—*hoped*—he even sought me out.

The truth is, I do not ski. In fact, I hate the cold. Mummifying yourself in six layers of clothes in order to careen down the side of a mountain while someone screams at you about pizza slices and French fries is something I will never understand. Yet in that moment, when Ryan asked me on the picnic table in his parents' backyard if I liked to ski, it was so easy to say . . . *Yeah, sure.* Two little words. But words have weight.

The next fall, Ryan would go to Mountainvale Academy, a special boarding school in Maine for elite winter athletes. They had a really good ski racing team, and turns out, Ryan was a really good skier.

I never told him that, actually, I hate skiing. Even when our families went to Sugarloaf the following Christmas and I faked a stomachache so I wouldn't have to show him how bad I actually was at the thing he loved most in life. I'd rather Ryan Hart believe I had explosive diarrhea than know I don't like skiing—*that's* how devoted I was to my story.

Even when we started dating later that winter, I didn't fess up. It was too late by then, anyway, once I'd been kissed outside the arcade room in the basement of the ski lodge. My first kiss, the one I'm told I'll always remember, and I will: my heart exploding into a million tiny sucker-red pieces.

The following week, he called from the shared phone on his dormitory hall because he didn't have cell reception at school. We talked about everything and nothing: scary movies and funny videos, the virtues of fast food, our siblings' exceptional ability to annoy the crap out of us, and his coach, who'd once trained the Olympic team. Something I said made him laugh. We talked for an hour, through three different dormmates pestering him to give up the phone.

Our first date was to Athens Pizza V, home of the famous heart-shaped pizza. Mrs. Hart dropped us off, grinning from ear to ear. "You know she's calling your mom right now," he said, clearly embarrassed, as we watched the Volvo pull away. He held the door for me and paid for my pizza. It felt so adult, so much like wooing. Two months later, nonchalantly, in the middle of a conversation about our favorite breakfast cereals, Ryan Hart called me his girlfriend. And that's what I happily became.

I never told him that, actually, I hate mushrooms on my pizza. Or that concerts freak me out because I dislike big crowds—sometimes small ones, too. I did not share that I found the video games we played in his basement too loud and too violent, that they made me feel anxious but that I feel that way 99 percent of the time anyway. That I sometimes cry in the shower or that, although I like being alone, I fear being lonely. Ryan did not know that I filled thick notebooks with the stories I imagined and that, while I was too embarrassed to say it out loud, I wanted to be a writer when I grew up.

My boyfriend knew a different Jess—a laid-back, outgoing, adventurous Jess, ready for anything, whether that meant breaking into a neighbor's pool or nursing a skunky beer while watching three Fast and Furious movies in a row. This Jess was cool. She was girlfriend material. The Jess who lost sleep over grades, who often preferred books to people, whose body physically hurt when she was forced to try something new—Ryan didn't know that Jess. I made sure he never did.

It wasn't just with him, of course. I pretended, in ways, with everyone—my parents, my teachers, even sometimes Katie. The bottom line is that there were two of me: the Jess I showed the outside world and the Jess I knew on the inside. Every day a performance—laugh, smile, *engage.*

It's surprisingly easy to pretend to be someone you're not. Writers do it all the time; that's how they write a story—pluck a character from the air and try her on for size. What I know now is that we're all made up of stories, the ones we tell ourselves and the ones we tell each other. They're the masks we wear every day, the personal histories we write and revise again and again, the futures we imagine, the images we project online, the narratives we construct in order to fit in.

Then there are the other stories, the stories we don't tell, the ones we lock away within the hidden, dark rooms of ourselves—the secrets. Here's what I also know now: secrets tend to seek the light.

1

August 4, 2007

I'm stuck, fingers dancing above the warm keyboard . . . hovering . . . waiting for inspiration.

Sometimes the world around me disappears as I write. My vision constricts to a pinhole of light, only the page in front of me visible—"in the zone," I've heard athletes call it. But I've also heard of writer's block, and that's what I have now.

At the edge of the cliff, Iris watches waves throw themselves against the rocks. Behind her, suddenly, a voice.

Saying . . . saying . . . I can't decide: Is this a romance I'm writing, or a tragedy?

Endings are the trickiest part. Harder even than beginnings. This one I've been working on for weeks, the third act for an ambitious actress who falls in love with a roguish, backstabbing ship captain. Katie's always trying to get me to confess who my characters are based on, and this one is based loosely on her, but the thing is, I tell her, characters like to get away from you; they take on a life of their own.

She turns to face him. Wind whips her ha—

No. Delete. Delete. Deleeeeeeeete.

She refuses to turn.

Of course! She hates his guts; he's betrayed her. She won't pardon him. She'll punish him.

"Do you know the cost of telling lies?" Iris's voice is almost lost in the wind.

Yes! Gold. Words spill onto the screen like so much digital ink . . . and there's a knock at my door.

Ignore it.

"I know the value of telling the truth."

"Jess!"

The pinhole dilates. "Just a sec!" I call frantically, but the door has opened, and my mother is standing in it, back from her

8

eight-mile morning run. The world zooms into focus.

"Up and at 'em!" Her voice is as bright as a fluorescent bulb.

"I've been up since seven." I'm not usually an early bird, but sometimes I'm pulled from the quicksand of sleep by story ideas—nonsense that fills a small red journal by my bed: *She has a celestial twin. A snowstorm in July. Something about a walrus????*

Mom rips aside the curtains and perches on the edge of my bed. "Well, then, how about you get out and do something?" She's always saying things like this.

Midmorning light makes the walls of my room glow pale purple—officially "Lavender Cream," the paint color chosen when I got to redecorate for my tenth birthday. Actually, the color was my mom's choice. I don't love Lavender Cream; it feels kind of like living inside of a My Little Pony.

I close the laptop. Mom is already showered and dressed for the day, though not in her usual Ann Taylor Loft business caj. It's the weekend, but as a real estate agent, she works every day. Instead, in crisp khaki shorts and a collared polo shirt, her hair pulled into a neat ponytail, she looks like a camp counselor.

Her fingers run scales on the lid of my laptop, and my eyes drift over the stickers plastered on top: *Sierra Club.* A crimson *H*, for Harvard. A holographic avocado from Katie. *Ski Free or Die*—that one's from Ryan. I resist the urge to pick at the decals' peeling edges as Mom confesses to the real reason she's in my room now, other than to keep me from being a lazy bum: "I need your help today. I'll take you to lunch at Luca's afterward."

Luca's is my favorite restaurant, and I can't remember the last time Mom and I spent a Saturday together. *A bribe?* "Okay," I ask warily, "with what?"

She stands, neatly folding the sweatpants lying across my bed. "Aunt Anna's house is listing next week. I finally convinced your dad to sell it, but we need to clean out the attic."

I groan, duped like a rookie. "Can't Griffin help?" My gym-obsessed, six-foot, fifteen-year-old brother is far better suited to manual labor, but Mom knows I never say no.

"He doesn't get back from lacrosse camp until tomorrow."

Right. Since he hit puberty and developed the burning need to make fun of everything and everyone, my brother and I so carefully avoid each other that I'd almost forgotten he's been gone all week. The absence of slammed doors and toothpaste smeared across the bathroom counter should have reminded me.

"All right," I relent, sighing and throwing back the covers. "I'll help."

I haven't been to the house in more than six years, not since Aunt Anna moved to a nursing home when I was in fifth grade and my dad started renting it to college kids from Keene State. It's a sagging farmhouse at the edge of town that I remember smelling of baked beans and damp earth, but it was also filled with books—on mantels, on tables, stacked against the walls, bowing bookshelves. Like they owned the house, not her. There was something magical about this. There were paperbacks and

10

hardcovers and ancient encyclopedias that not even Goodwill would take when my mom cleared the house before the students moved in. She let me keep a few novels, but my stomach churned to watch her chuck the rest in the dumpster behind her office.

Maybe, I tell myself, this will be fun. Attics have been known to hold interesting things: long-lost heirlooms, family secrets, rare first editions.

"Do you want to shower first?" Mom asks.

"Oh." I look down at the baggy athletic shorts I've just pulled on. "Aren't we gonna get, like, dusty?"

"But if we're going to Luca's afterward. . . ."

"Right." I grab my towel.

She claps once. "Great! See you downstairs in fifteen." Then glances at her watch. "Actually, make it ten."

A fine layer of grit coats my arms, and the dust in the attic has triggered an allergy attack. As for family heirlooms, so far I've found a Keds shoebox filled with cheap plastic Mardi Gras beads and a box of cassette tapes promising peace through positive thinking.

Luckily, Mom keeps a small pharmaceutical operation in her purse, and I'm happy for a break from the attic's hot, mite-ridden updrafts.

In the kitchen, I pop an antihistamine from its foil bubble and wash it down with lukewarm Diet Sprite, then check my phone. Ryan is supposed to call after weight training, but I have no new messages. "Jess!" I hear my mother call from the attic. "Coming!" I shout, slipping the phone into my pocket and trudging upstairs.

Mom swipes a pale, freckled forearm across her chin, tiny

tufts of insulation clinging to her knees. My mother relishes chores, but even she seems to be regretting this one. From the floor, she hoists a cardboard box labeled, sloppily, *EASTER EGGS*, and hands it down. The box goes on the floor next to the others.

"Still sneezing?"

I try to sound as pathetic as possible. "I'll be better once the drugs kick in."

"Just a few more." She ducks again into the shadows, and from the gloom, I can hear but not see her. "Why on earth did Aunt Anna save all this junk? Can you imagine what buyers would think?" Something thuds to the ground. "'Hoarder,'" she mumbles, "that's what."

There's no doubt that my aunt was . . . different. Winter was the only season she dressed for, bundled in a scarf and coat even on days when the August heat glimmered from the sidewalk, and although her clothes were shabby, she always had a new pair of shoes. Beyond that, her movements were nervous and fluttery, as if she thought someone was watching her. When she visited, I got the feeling she was watching *us*, taking mental notes. She didn't talk much on these visits, but occasionally she'd smile at something someone said—a sad smile, more like the memory of a smile.

Maybe this was why I'd once overheard my parents argue about whether to invite her for Thanksgiving dinner:

"Why do we keep asking when all she does is sit in the corner?" Mom griped.

"She's ninety-seven years old, Valerie; what do you expect from her?" my father replied.

"She's weird, John."

He exploded, something he rarely did. "She's family!"

And so weird Aunt Anna came to Thanksgiving and to Christmas that year.

There were the trinkets she'd bring Griffin and me, cheap gifts like a sparkly rubber ball from a grocery store coin machine or a figurine clearly retrieved from a Happy Meal. She handed these over as if they were rubies. Typically, there was a book along with them, one from her own musty library. Though the books were often over our heads—*The Odyssey*, *The Great Gatsby*, *The Rise and Fall of the Great Powers*—she was the one who introduced me to *The Secret Garden*, which I read no less than a dozen times.

Then there was the Hello Kitty diary. It must have been Christmas, because I remember sitting on the living room floor, a light-strung tree behind me. The diary wasn't wrapped. She simply took it from her purse and handed it to me. "For—" she said, making a herky-jerky scribbling motion in the air.

"Thank you," I replied, acutely aware of how closely she watched as I opened the diary and flipped through its pale pink, lined pages.

I loved that journal, not because of its bright cartoon cover but because it had a tiny working lock and key, which I kept in my sock drawer. My first story, a "novel" about a horse named

Babbling Brook, was written in it. When the diary was accidentally left in a hotel room the summer we drove to Palm Beach to see my grandparents, I cried across two whole states.

So, yes, she was eccentric, Aunt Anna—and a pack rat—but "hoarder" didn't seem fair. I liked my great-great-aunt, maybe because she was strange.

"Earth to Jess."

My mom is holding another box. A peek between the flaps reveals a jumble of chipped porcelain tea sets, the kind a child might use to throw a tea party for her stuffed animals, even though Aunt Anna and Uncle Henry didn't have children. He died a long time before I was born.

She stands, stretching her back. "There's a trunk here. I'm trying to figure out if we'll give ourselves hernias trying to lift it."

My ears perk up. Picturing an old-timey steamer trunk straight off the *Titanic*, I scuttle up the stars and am not disappointed. At the back of the attic, beneath the shadowy eaves, is a beautiful old chest with leather straps and wood ribbing faded to a greenish gray. The leather has started to disintegrate, and the canvas covering is ripped in places, but I can tell it was once a fancy thing.

"What do you think's in it?" I ask.

"Commemorative thimbles?" Mom jokes.

"Should I open it?"

She shrugs. "Sure."

My mom isn't into old things the way I am. To her, "vintage" means reproduction apothecary jars and hand-distressed bird-cages from the Pottery Barn catalogs that clog our mailbox. New is good, and newer is better. But for me, old stuff is fascinating, a wormhole into the past.

Carefully, I work stiff straps through rusty buckles and flip open the trunk's corroded hasp. When the lid still won't budge, I worry it's locked, but with a little more effort, it gives with a satisfying creak. The trunk seems to exhale the musty, sweet odor of decay. My own breath catching in anticipation, I fully raise the lid.

Mom peers inside. "Great. More books."

Even I feel a ripple of disappointment. Not exactly the Heart of the Ocean. Still, the books look old—their pages swollen with time—and this intrigues me. Jumbled in a heap, they're an array of colors and sizes. Plucking one from the top, I turn it over, handling the brittle, powdery leather with care. Curiously, the book has no title. Its spine crackles as I open it. Inside, a stream of cursive flows across the pages in faded black ink—so, it's not a book; it's a journal. But a frown tugs at my lips, because the writing puzzles me. It's not a language, or even letters, that I recognize. It's not the English alphabet.

My mom is squinting at her BlackBerry beneath the attic's single bare bulb. She needs glasses but won't admit it.

I open a second book. The same foreign script stares back. I check a third. There are numbers at the top that seem to be dates and what appears to be a signature, or sometimes just the letter *A*, at the bottom.

A *for Anna.*

"I think," I say, "these are Aunt Anna's diaries."

"Hmm," Mom mumbles.

"But what language is this?" I raise the journal so she has to tear herself away from her phone and look.

"Huh." She frowns. "I'm not sure. Looks a little like Greek, actually." She and Dad went to Mykonos a couple of years ago for their anniversary. They brought back evil eyes and baklava but never talked about the trip.

"Aunt Anna didn't have an accent . . . did she?" I ask, searching my limited recollections.

"Not that I remember."

One particular memory plays in my mind, an old one I'd half forgotten, although the event meant something to me at the time.

"Weird!" Mom chirps, slipping her BlackBerry into her shorts. "Okay, first stop, Goodwill. Second stop, lunch."

"Wait, can I keep them?" I ask.

"These old books?" She looks confused. "Sure, but why?"

"Diaries," I correct her. "And I don't know, they're kind of cool, I guess." I run a hand over the journal's soft cover.

She sighs. "Okay. You know, the trunk might make a cute coffee table. Kind of shabby-chic?" She cocks her head, mentally staging the trunk in one of the homes she's selling.

I place the journal back in the trunk and close the lid.

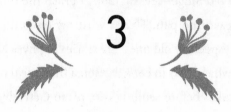

3

Katie doesn't like the fancy consignment store on Main Street. "House of Hipster," she calls it. Instead, she prefers the dirty, overstuffed vintage shop down the street that smells like air freshener and decades of dust.

Following the promised but rushed lunch at Luca's, Mom dropped me and the mysterious trunk at home. Still no word from Ryan, but Katie had texted for a fro-yo run so she could spy on her latest crush, a college student with ear gauges and a nose ring who works behind the register. Afterward, we find ourselves amid the vintage shop's congested, antique-carpeted stalls.

I can get lost in this palace of hand-carved decoys and rusted butter churners, green-hooded lamps and faux Chinese vases, *Conan the Barbarian* and *The Justice League*. Every inch of the space is crammed with the ephemera of bygone eras, bygone lives. Brittle maps curl from the wall. Atop a pyramid of nesting suitcases sits the giant tin trumpet of a phonograph.

From an old Singer sewing table, I grasp the rough, heavy handle of a cast-iron pan. This is what my mom doesn't get—that objects, especially old ones, are stories in physical form. I'll never know what it was to cook my son a final meal of salt pork and johnnycakes before sending him off to Gettysburg, but in the ache of my wrist holding that pan, I am momentarily transported into another life, another time.

Wandering to the books section, I'm distracted by a display of old postcards: *London! Paris! Essex Junction! Niagara Falls!* they shout in faded colors.

"J!" Katie calls. "Check me out."

On the other side of the store, she's posing before a full-length mirror. An elaborately beaded, canary-yellow gown hangs on her slight figure. She wears T-strap heels on her feet and satin gloves on her hands, her fingers decked in rings: fake pearls, chunky gold, and cubic zirconia. Pouting her lips, she mugs for the mirror. "I'm getting a Katharine Hepburn vibe."

"Really?" I tease. "I'm getting Miss Hannigan."

"Okay, your turn." She throws me a piece of clothing. The shop doesn't have dressing rooms, so I'm not sure how Katie managed to wriggle into her yellow number. I slip the dress over my tank top, then look in the mirror. The black-and-white gown has broad shoulders and ruching around a sweetheart neckline, down to a V at the skirt, which is made of black tulle. I have no idea what decade it's from. Nineteen thirties? Forties?

"Here." Katie tosses me a brown mink stole, and I squeal when I see two beady, dead eyes glaring at me from the unlucky animal's head, which is still attached. "Gross!"

"Glamorous," she corrects me. She's behind me now with a dark green cloche hat, which she pops onto my head. "And your finishing touch." A large, gaudy brooch of plastic pearls and green glass gets pinned to my waist.

"Dahling," she says, "you look fabulous. Wish Tyler was here to get a pic instead of playing house with Zach again." She rolls her eyes and sticks out her tongue.

"Tell me how you really feel."

Katie has been my best friend since the Great Curly-Fry Incident of second grade. Tyler was a crucial addition, turning our duo into a trio in ninth. He and Zach, a junior whose parents seem to travel for weeks at a time, have been on-again, off-again (currently on-again) since March, and to be honest, I think it makes Katie jealous. Not just of the boyfriend but of the drama.

Drama is Katie's "thing." This summer, she's playing Olive Ostrovsky in the local professional theater company's production of *The 25th Annual Putnam County Spelling Bee*. Adopted from China at six months old, Kathryn Samantha Weston has ambitions, and American theater's lack of imagination when it comes to casting outside traditional ethnic and gender lines is not going to hold her back. "This state is whiter than its mountains," she gripes, but Olive is her "big break."

She flops theatrically onto a faded velvet chaise longue. It's a mystery how I came to be friends with someone so insanely opposite from me. Sometimes I wonder if Katie realizes how hard I have to work to project even an ounce of the confidence she oozes.

Shy isn't the right word for me. It's just that being around too many people for a long period of time makes me feel like an hourglass, sand slipping through the gap until there's not much left—*introverted* is the word we learned when taking personality tests in ninth grade. But I can fake it; when no one was looking, I changed my *I* to an *E*.

Katie is eyeing me from her repose. "You look hot," she says, in her best Paris Hilton impression.

"Yeah, right," I say to the mirror, twisting my hair into a rope over one shoulder. The bell-shaped hat is meant for a shorter cut, a bob.

She bolts up. "I'm serious, Jess Morgan. You are an amazing, beautiful, incredibly talented young woman, and you of all people should know that. Also, you should buy that dress."

"Sure," I joke. "Maybe I'll wear it to church. Val would love it." My mom makes us go every Sunday, although sometimes I think it's more about finding clients than finding God.

Katie blows a raspberry. "Who gives a toodle? Does your mother still dress you?"

I roll my eyes. "Of course not. It's just more you than me, that's all." I shrug a shoulder out of the stretchy fabric and drop the dress to my feet. "Hey, I meant to tell you I found something cool today."

Katie's eyebrows dance as she removes the rings and then the gloves from her hands, finger by finger, like Marilyn Monroe doing a striptease. "Tell me more."

I tell her about my morning in Aunt Anna's attic, about the trunk and the journals, and before I can finish, her eyes are wide. "Wait!" Her voice is loud, and a guy browsing the men's section turns to look at us. "Jess, are you serious?" She grasps my shoulders.

"Yeah. I mean, they're really cool, but I have no idea what they say. They're completely unintelligible."

"What-what-what are you saying, my dear? You *have* to find out. Like, have to. Your aunt was hiding a trunk full of journals in her attic—"

"Well, I don't know if she was *hiding* them."

She presses a finger to my lips. "—that might reveal some super-juicy secret, and you're just like, 'Oh well! Guess that's that!' Jess, what if she was a spy? Ooh! Or maybe a famous ballerina, and the diaries belonged to her deceased but married choreographer lover!"

"Wow." I laugh. "Are you the writer, or am I?"

"Maybe they're a hot, steamy memoir. Or her unpublished manuscript! Jess, these were *meant* for you to find."

The memory that the journals stirred earlier comes back full force: I was twelve the last time I saw my aunt, four and a

22

half years ago, and she was over a hundred. By then, she was in the nursing home. Sometimes Dad took us to visit, but it had been a while. Griffin had a basketball game so it was just me, which seemed supremely unfair as the nursing home's automatic doors wheezed shut behind us. Looking back, my dad must have known this was goodbye.

When we arrived, Aunt Anna was in bed, propped against a pile of pillows, wearing a powder-pink bathrobe. She was so tiny she looked like a little girl, only her hair was as white as snow. It lay feathery and flat against her scalp, different from the cotton-candy helmets most of the old ladies at the nursing home wore. Wrinkles etched her face, and her mouth looked as if it might collapse in on itself at any moment. She smelled of VapoRub and urine, sweet and medicinal and tangy. I was slightly terrified of her that day but fascinated at the same time.

"Aunt Anna! How are you doing?" my dad shouted, which felt wrong in the hospital-like room. "You remember Jess." His hand was on my shoulder, and he used it to guide me forward.

"Hi." I waved meekly, doubting that my great-great-aunt remembered anyone.

"She's in seventh grade this year, can you believe it? Just won a prize at school." He beamed down at me. *Come on*, his smile said, *help me out here*.

I'd recently won a writing contest at school. Now my teacher wanted to publish the story in the school newspaper, and I was mortified; it felt like inviting the whole world to peer inside my brain. Katie was the only person I'd shared my stories with before. For me, writing had always been something private in nature, a thing done behind closed doors. One time I'd worked up the courage to submit a story to a magazine; it was a stupid one for little kids, but I was hopeful. I used a pen name with my initials: Jasmine Martin. Jess Morgan. The story was rejected.

That day at the nursing home, Aunt Anna stared into space. My dad persisted: "A writing prize."

Suddenly, her gaze seemed to focus, sun breaking through clouds. She turned, chin trembling, and smiled. "You're a writer." Her voice was watery, but it was a statement, not a question, and my heart skittered like a stone skipped over a pond. To write is one thing, but to *call* yourself a writer is another. "I'm a writer, too," she said.

"Jess's best subject is language arts."

"Actually, it's history," I corrected him. The A-plus on the report card my mom always tacked to the fridge confirmed that.

A cackle erupted from the bed, startling me. "History," my aunt croaked with giddy contempt, "is a story."

We waited for her to say more, but her mouth had clamped shut as her expression grew suddenly serious. Milky-blue eyes snapped to my dad's face and then mine. "History," she rasped again, "is a story we tell ourselves."

With the words, she sputtered and coughed and began to struggle for breath. Her chest heaved. "Should we call a nurse?" I asked frantically, terrified she'd die right in front of us, but just as quickly, the fit stopped. Her breathing steadied, and she looked at us, eyes widening, as if she was surprised to find us standing in her room.

A frown worked at her lips as a bony hand rose from the blankets and reached in my direction, the hand of a witch. It shook in the space between us. She wanted me to come closer, but I was scared, inching toward the bed. Finally, I took her hand, soft and light as paper.

Her eyes held mine. "Do you tell stories?" she whispered urgently, conspiratorially.

"How do you mean?" I asked. My dad had just told her about the contest. Maybe she hadn't understood.

Her eyebrows, pencil thin, arched in a look of surprise. When she laughed, it was the sound of dry leaves blowing down an empty sidewalk.

"Yes," she said, smiling and letting let go of my hand to pat it. "Yes," she said again. She lay back against the pillows and, as if resigned, folded her hands at her middle. "You're a storyteller, too." But her eyes were now sad, and we were gone again.

Shaken, I shuffled back to my father. *What did she mean?*

Moments later a nurse knocked for Aunt Anna's sponge bath. My dad apologized in the car, saying perhaps he shouldn't have brought me, that Aunt Anna was too agitated for visitors. Dementia, he explained, her brain failing.

The incident stuck with me for days, playing over in my mind like a movie clip. It felt as if Aunt Anna had seen something in me the way a fortune-teller sees the future. Only weeks later did the other meaning of *storyteller* occur to me: "Are you telling me a story?" my mom used to ask Griffin when he spilled his milk and blamed it on his imaginary friend.

A lie. *Had Aunt Anna been calling me a liar?*

I never got a chance to ask her. My aunt died six months later, while I was in Cape Cod with Katie's family. My parents didn't tell me until I got home. There wasn't even a real funeral, just a small graveside service with my parents and uncle. It wasn't a shock, really, but I was sad; no one I knew had died before.

"Is that you?"

I'm snapped from the memory. "Huh?"

"Isn't that your phone?" Katie's asking.

A buzzing emanates from my purse, next to the dress I left lying on the dusty floor. I scoop the dress up, brush it off, and fish the phone from my bag. Finally, a text from Ryan: *Party at Dougs. Meet u there?*

Doug Renfrew is one of Ryan's best friends in Keene, along with Josh and Josh's girlfriend, Lila. That Ryan's managed to stay close with them despite leaving for boarding school says something about him, I think. He's loyal.

"Ry-Ry?" Katie asks, voice sugary sweet. As talented an actress as she is, my best friend can't hide that this intrusion annoys her. In fact, I think Katie's so good at acting *because* her emotions flow just under her skin. Of course, they've also been known to erupt—when the test was unfair, when she doesn't get the part in the play, when I see the movie without her. "Hotheaded," my mom calls her.

K, I respond quickly, and slip the phone into my pocket. "We have plans tonight," I tell her.

"Plans with Central Casting?"

This is Katie's nickname for Ryan's friends, meaning the stereotypical rude, crude, beer-guzzling teenagers that populate a nineties high school rom-com. She usually says it jokingly, but when Ryan's home, he's with them, which means I'm with them, and this bothers her.

In eighth grade, Doug Renfrew told everyone he felt Katie up by the dumpsters behind Thai Garden. This was entirely untrue but launched Katie into the school spotlight for two whole days until Doug recanted. The bummer was, I think she'd liked him before the whole debacle; why, I'm not quite sure, except that Katie's never had a boyfriend and Doug paid her attention. Everyone moved on quickly—everyone except Katie, who, understandably, hates Doug like a cat hates water. Ryan is guilty by association.

"Doug's parents are out of town. He's having a party tonight."

"Of course he is." Katie's inspecting her nails, which are painted a glittery blue.

"You could come." It's an insincere invitation. She won't come, and we both know it, but this is where we've landed.

"I have rehearsal," Katie says, grimacing as she pretzels her arms behind her back for the yellow dress's zipper.

When it became clear a couple of months into dating Ryan that our relationship would stick, some invisible weight shifted between Katie and me. The three of us did hang out a few times, early on, but *awkward* was the only word to describe it. And this wasn't just green-eyed jealousy on Katie's part; it was as if I'd betrayed her. How, I'm not sure—it's not as if we swore a blood oath to never get boyfriends—but two and a half years in, it's still not worth the fight to ask what, exactly, her problem is with my boyfriend. It's frustrating. I don't need Katie and Ryan to be BFFs, but it would be a shit ton easier if I could at least *pretend* she liked him.

Mostly, we've arrived at an unspoken shared custody. If Ryan gets me New Year's Eve, Katie gets me New Year's Day; if Katie whisks me to Fun World for my birthday, Ryan takes me to dinner. The arrangement works, or at least it has until recently. The last two summers, Katie went to an eight-week theater camp in the Berkshires, which meant she missed two of the three months Ryan spent in Keene. Being cast as Olive Ostrovksy changed her plan, and this summer, balancing my relationship and my friendship has become as sticky as the zipper on Katie's dress. She huffs, giving up on opening it, and turns so I can try, but the zipper refuses to budge. The metal digs into the pad of my thumb.

"Actually," Katie says—she has one arm lifted, holding her

thick, dark hair out of the way—"maybe I will come to Doug's."

"Oh." My throat goes suddenly dry.

"He can help me run lines."

"Yeah," I force out. "Hey, I think this zipper's stuck."

She turns her head, so I can see, in profile, the smirk on her face. "I'm kidding, Jess. And I think we have a problem, because I gotta pee."

Katie's Beetle idles in the semicircular drive outside Doug's house, a newly built McMansion near the country club. The yellow dress lies in a puddle in the back seat. Katie's pretty sure her mom can sew it up where, giggling, we had to ask the shop owner to cut her out of it.

We are right on time, as Ryan's Blazer pulls into the driveway behind us. "'But soft! What light through yonder window breaks?' Your Romeo," Katie recites as we watch him jump from the truck. Last year, she starred in our school production of *Romeo and Juliet*.

Ryan's Hurley tee and frayed cargo shorts do an excellent job of showcasing the athletic build and chiseled calves he's worked hard for. On his head sit the Oakleys I gave him for his birthday. He strolls toward Katie's car, flip-flops slapping pavement, then abruptly stops, pauses, and turns back to the SUV before emerging from its back seat with a finger hooked through the plastic rings of a six-pack of beer.

"Ah, jackass juice," Katie says, watching from her sideview

mirror. The drinking at these parties makes her nervous. Truthfully, it makes me nervous, too. I find the skunky beer hard to swallow and dislike the swimmy, thick-tongued feeling it leaves me with. If Ryan gets caught drinking one more time, his coach says he'll have his ass handed to him along with a suspension—no Junior Nationals; I hope he's brought the beer for Doug.

"Ryan," Katie greets him as he rests his tanned forearms on the open passenger-side window.

"Katie. You coming in?" he asks, surprised.

"Alas, I have rehearsal." She keeps her hands at ten and two on the faux cowhide steering wheel. "Just needed to borrow this saucy strumpet for some fro-yo recon and retail therapy."

"You sure? Doug made a beer bong. Jess promised she'll try it." He grins.

Stepping from the convertible, I roll my eyes. "We'll see about that." I don't think it's crossed Ryan's mind that Katie doesn't like him, or that anyone might not like him. I marvel at what that kind of self-confidence must feel like.

"Well, I'm here if you need a ride." Katie makes an embarrassing point of meeting my gaze.

"Thanks, Mom."

She rolls her eyes. "Safety's no accident. . . . Text me later."

I agree, and she pulls away, fluttering her fingers in farewell.

The Handoff is complete.

~

"Natty Light?"

Lila dangles a sweating can of beer before my face as we wait in Doug's game room for people to arrive. "People" being the varsity soccer team, of which Doug is co-captain, plus a few hockey players—"for diversity," he says, and I can't tell if he's kidding. It's early still, but the horde is on its way.

Splat. A drop of condensation lands on my thigh. "Thanks." I take the beer, prepared to mime a few sips and then leave it as a floater.

"Ry?" Lila says. Ryan's playing pool with Doug, and she leans over the pool table, the dyed pink tips of her hair brushing the felt.

He's lining up a shot. "Training," he answers.

"Ooh, right." Lila pouts. "More for me, then!" She plops into a leather recliner, and I note with a touch of envy that her boobs jiggle within the black bra she wears beneath a white tank top. My mom assures me a flat chest will be an asset someday, but the first bra she got me was padded.

At the pool table, Ryan misfires. Doug sinks the final stripe and then celebrates by heaving his body onto the electric-green table and proceeding to hump it.

Ryan passes his cue to Josh and flops next to me. "That's fine," he tells a still-flailing Doug. "Get splinters all you want; I'll be over here making out with my beautiful girlfriend." Jokingly, he throws his body across mine, and I feel a tiny, effervescent pop of glee. He called me "beautiful"—not "hot" but "beautiful." There's a difference.

I'm not one for PDA, but when Ryan touches me around his friends, it cuts the Gordian knot of anxiety in my chest. Going into a night like this one, it's extra tight, extra Gordian. *Her*, Ryan's touch says. *This one. She belongs.*

At school, I do all right for myself—I have Katie and Tyler, and by extension the drama crowd, as well as a few girls I know from the soccer team—but I'm no Lila Craig, and I can't get over the nagging fear that one day Ryan will realize this.

It's been three years since we were at the same school, but even attending Mountainvale, Ryan is Keene High School royalty—his eighth-grade new-kid sparkle upgraded to high-school future-Olympian mystique. When word got out that *I* was Ryan Hart's girlfriend, people started waving to me in the hallways, people I had barely talked with before. Last year, on Tuesdays and Thursdays when Katie and Tyler had B lunch, I started sitting with "the Betties," a group of girls, led informally by Lila, who wear thick black eyeliner and spend their afternoons at the skate park on Gilbo Avenue. Jenny Glocke is one of them. It's an uneasy lunch. I don't say much, and sometimes I worry that Lila reports this to Ryan. *Why do we keep asking when all she does is sit in the corner?*

The messed-up thing is that I want Lila to like me, or at least to understand why Ryan does. Why he chose me, when there are at least half a dozen girls at school, including some Betties, who'd murder small, fuzzy animals for a chance with him. Maybe it's because I still haven't answered this riddle myself.

"Oh, shit!" Doug yells over the music. "I forgot to tell you guys. Guess who I saw yesterday in the condom aisle at Walmart."

Beside me, Lila is jiggling away to a Fall Out Boy song blasting from Doug's parents' speakers, the "emo" music of the kids she used to make fun of, that she now acts like she discovered.

"Why were you in the condom aisle at Walmart, Doug?" she asks coquettishly.

I might have asked the same thing. If Doug Renfrew needs to buy condoms, it's because the ones he's been carrying around in his wallet for three years have expired.

"Use your imagination, Lila."

She smirks. "You wish."

Josh sinks a solid in the corner pocket, and I wonder if it bothers him how Lila flirts with everyone.

"Mr. Austin," Doug continues.

"No way," Lila says.

Doug puts the pool stick between his legs, running his hands up and down its length in a raunchy approximation of an act I am sure he commits several times a day.

"Gross, Doug." Lila says what I'm thinking, but beside me, Ryan's body is shaking with laughter.

"Wait a minute." She turns to me, her eyes already with that glazed-over look they get when she's had too much to drink and gets mean. "Jess, weren't you, like, in his AP class?" They narrow to slits.

"Yeah," I say carefully. Most of my classes are Advanced Placement, but I don't exactly advertise it. "I basically flunked."

It's a fib. In fact, I got a B-minus in AP European History and a three on the AP exam—not an F, but for a straight-A student shooting for the Ivy League, it might as well have been. My mom insisted I talk to Mr. Austin, who agreed to reconsider my grade if I completed an extra-credit research paper over the summer: five thousand words with at least two primary sources, footnotes, *and* a bibliography. It's August, and I have sixteen pages of notes on the Protestant Reformation but not a single word written. I thought a rebel like Martin Luther might give me something to work with, but the dude was boring (and, it turns out, an anti-Semite). History is a story, my aunt said, but a writer needs a way in; I haven't found mine.

And there is no way in holy hell I am going to admit to Doug, Josh, and Lila—even to Ryan—that I'm working on a summer-long, extra-credit research paper to raise a B to an A.

He wraps an arm around my shoulder. "Did you know he was a perv?"

Even if I'm not fond of the man who single-handedly lowered my GPA, Mr. Austin isn't a perv, certainly not for being in a Walmart at the same time as Doug Renfrew. Still, I don't want to ruin the fun. "He did talk a lot about the Battle of the Bulge."

Crickets. Flames lick at my cheeks.

34

Outside, we hear multiple doors slam, loud music drift from a car radio, voices shout.

Lila jumps, breasts jiggling anew. She claps. "People!"

For once, I am grateful for a crowd.

"I mean, you're in a bathroom, but it's not like you're *going* to the bathroom." On the couch, Lila has a gaggle of freshman girls enthralled with a lecture on the art of the MySpace pic. By now, she's slurring her words.

The basement feels like an overcrowded elevator as I squeeze to the opposite side of the room, where a group of hockey players ricochet a quarter off the top of a toilet tank retrieved for the purpose (better bounce, Ryan once explained) and into a plastic cup. "Drink!" someone yells, and the room erupts into cheers as Andy DePalma retrieves the quarter by chugging the lukewarm beer. I slide in behind Ryan, but he doesn't seem to notice, as it's his turn to bounce the quarter.

By the bathroom, Whiskers, an overweight orange tabby, winds himself around the ankles of anonymous partygoers. Generally, I'm lukewarm toward felines, being mildly allergic, but I need an excuse not to interact with another human being for five minutes, so I make my way to the rotund beast and crouch to pet him.

My mind is not really here, in this standing-room-only basement. With Whiskers purring aggressively, it drifts to the journals in my bedroom, to what Katie said earlier, and to my aunt's mysterious words all those years ago: *You're a writer, too.*

Whiskers's claws knead at my thigh as a shadow appears above us. Ryan. "Hey," he says. "Where you been?"

Whiskers skitters off. "Here."

His arms reach above him into a stretch, and the bottom of Ryan's shirt drifts up to reveal the faint brown line of hair that trails below his boxers. My eyes follow it: "the treasure trail," he taught me, lying on the couch in his parents' basement. He sees me looking. "You wanna get a soda?" A grin hangs on his face. He doesn't mean a Coke; it's our code.

"Sure," I say, relieved to escape with him for a little while, so I'm confused when he really does lead me to the Renfrews' fridge.

He slides a caffeine-free Coke down the counter. "Sorry, all they got." But then he's coming around the island to where I'm standing, and I relax, because he sets his can on the counter and plants both hands on either side of me. Here it is: the tiny electric pulse.

"What did you do today?" I ask, smiling. He's so close I can smell the Right Guard. The pulse travels.

"I told you I had weight lifting."

"Yeah, but after that."

"Not much," he murmurs. "Helped my dad in the yard." The dimple flashes. "What did *you* do today?"

His hands go from the counter to my hips. "Helped my mom

clean out my great-great-aunt's attic. We found this trunk . . ."
Too late, I realize how unsexy a musty attic is.

"That was nice of you," he murmurs.

"Well, I'm a nice person."

"How nice?"

His leg nestles hard between mine, and my hips are pinned to the counter now. I'm not thinking about the journals anymore. And this is what I can't explain to Katie: the intoxication not just of wanting but of being wanted. It's far riskier than the warm Natty Light.

When Doug walks into the kitchen, we scramble to rearrange ourselves. "Whoa, dudes, get a room." He fishes in the cleaning supplies beneath the kitchen sink. "Just not my parents'. Or my sister's; that was messed up." It's rumored that Josh and Lila did the deed in his little sister's bunk beds—both of them.

I'm annoyed that Doug has interrupted us, but apparently Andy DePalma has puked in the washing machine. "What time is it?" I ask.

Earlier in the summer, my mom offered to extend my curfew to midnight. "You're a senior now; live a little!" she said. Much to her confusion, I declined, answering that eleven was still fine. On nights like this one, curfew is my only way out. Ryan thinks I have the strictest parents in Keene.

He checks the dive watch on his wrist. "Nine fifteen . . ." he says. *Dang it.* "Hey, Doogie, what're they doing down there?"

"I dunno, playing Bullshit, I think," Doug says. He's referring to another popular drinking game, one that involves bluffing. He has a bottle of dishwashing soap in his hands, and I almost—*almost*—tell him that's not what he wants to clean the washing machine before he jogs back down the stairs.

Ryan brightens. "You wanna play?"

Honestly? No. I want some peace and quiet and to look through my aunt's journals in my room. But no one likes a party pooper. "Sure!" I say. At least I'm good at bluffing.

"And that brings us to the Word of the Day . . ."

In the den, *The Colbert Report* blares from our television. It's Dad's favorite show, although he has to TiVo it because he always falls asleep before it comes on. "'Truthiness,'" the comedian intones in his fake news anchor voice.

In his sleep, Dad gently snarffles. Carefully, I pry the remote from his hand. When the screen flickers off, he twitches and wakes, blinking like a toddler roused from a nap. "Sorry," I say with a laugh at his wide-eyed confusion, "didn't mean to wake you."

"No, no! Just resting my eyes."

A swell of affection rises in my chest. "Well, I'm home."

"Thanks. . . . Mom's in her office. Maybe say good night to her."

I'm not sure how long it takes to prepare a house closing, but

Mom seems to be in her office a lot these days. I guess I don't need to point that out to my dad, though. "Hey," I say instead. "Can I ask you a random question . . . like really random?"

He leans forward in the old brown leather recliner. It's *his* chair. The recline mechanism squeaks, and the footrest bears permanent marker from when Griffin and I were kids, but it's the one piece of furniture Dad's fought Mom tooth and nail to keep over the years. "Shoot," he says.

"Aunt Anna . . . what was her story?"

Still bleary-eyed, he scrubs at his face. "Your great-great-aunt Anna?" He thinks for a second. "Well, she was married to Gram's brother, Henry. He was an interesting guy, taught at Keene State."

"Interesting how?"

"Well," he says, chuckling, "I remember he wore a monocle."

"Like Mr. Peanut?"

"Maybe 'eccentric' is more like it. He died in a car crash when I was really young—1961, I think." He pauses, as if sifting through Polaroid memories in his head. "Aunt Anna retreated after that, barely left the house."

"Do you know where she was from?"

"Originally?" He puzzles over it for a second, frowning. "You know, I haven't the faintest idea. That's sad, isn't it? She was . . . quiet, I guess. I felt responsible for her with Mom and Dad gone—we were all she had—but she was hard to know."

More questions buzz in my mind than did before, but my

dad stands and puts a hand on my shoulder, steering us out of the room. "Hey, thanks for helping your mom today," he says as we climb the stairs side by side. "She's got a lot on her plate."

An image pops into my mind, of my mother at a long Thanksgiving buffet, piling helping after helping onto an overflowing dish. *Jess*, she once told me, cupping my chin in her hand as we stood in the kitchen of the tiny house in the tiny Maine mill town where she grew up, a place we visited only once, *I don't ever want you to think you can't have it all.*

"I know," I tell my dad. "I just wonder when she'll decide the plate is full."

He nods, smiling sadly, I think.

At the top of the stairs, we say good night, and I check my phone. Doug's basement is a cellular black hole, and two missed calls and six text messages have just come through from Katie. It's drama drama; her director is sick and some guy named William asked her to run lines. Patience is not exactly Katie's strong suit, but she'll have to wait until morning for a response, and she has herself to blame—I can't stop thinking about what she said at the vintage shop.

The trunk hunkers under the far window of my bedroom, where my mom and I lugged it that afternoon. Cross-legged, I sink before it. No complaint from the rusty hinges this time. I pluck a random journal from the heap. Curiosity flutters in my chest.

The cover's brown leather is embossed with an ornate

41

double-headed eagle, and the edges of the pages are gilded. Very gently, I flip it open and am greeted with the almondy-sweet scent of library, the decay of paper and ink. Letters swim across the page in sharp slants and round loops. Some look familiar—a *K* here and an *M* there—but I have no idea what they say; it's nonsense.

Still, I can feel that these words hold meaning, the way a voice carries emotion even when you don't know the language being spoken. Underlined words suggest passion or anger. A splotch of ink spells the hesitation of nostalgia. Downward-sloping sentences show the frenzied rush to get thoughts down before they disappear.

Inspired, I grab the laptop from my bed and pull up a browser. Recalling what my mother said about Greek, I search that alphabet first. Some of the characters look similar, like the Φ and maybe the δ, but this writing definitely isn't Greek. Hope flickers when I remember the elaborate lettering of the giant Torah at Chloe Cohen's eighth-grade bat mitzvah, but I search Hebrew, and that's not it. Arabic? Definitely not. Hindi? Nope. On a whim, I Google *elvish scripts*, thinking maybe my bookish aunt was a Tolkien fanatic. Again, some similarities but no dice.

It finally comes to me in a flash, and when it does, it's so obvious that I feel like an idiot. *Russian alphabet*, I type. "Cyrillic," Wikipedia calls it, but while the capital letters at the top of the webpage are very similar, they're still too blocky and severe; the writing in the journal is fluid and elegant, like cursive. At the bottom of the Wiki page, I find a link to Russian handwritten letters. I click, and my heart stops. Back and forth, my eyes bounce between the computer screen and the journal's open page. Bingo.

Wait, I think. *Russian?* Aunt Anna hadn't spoken Russian, at least not in front of me. Like my mom, I don't remember an accent, but I search my memory for some small giveaway: the roll of an *R*, a "zee" for a *the*, a "w" where a *v* should have been. I come up empty. But people can drop an accent; actors do it all the time. Two years ago, for *Oliver Twist*, Katie affected a British accent for three solid weeks. "Going 'Method,'" she called it. By the third week, I told her, I was "going 'Bonkers.'"

Frustrated, I pull every last journal from the trunk. There are so many styles: red leather, brown leather, black leather, blue board, pocket-sized, oversized, lined, unlined, embossed, gold-leafed, plain. Some weigh heavily in my hand. Others feel like no more than a pack of playing cards. Neatly, I stack them back in the trunk and stare at them, hard. They are begging to be read, but how, if I can't read Russian?

Another quick internet search turns up a Russian translation site, but it requires a Cyrillic keyboard. A second one, however, lets me click on individual Cyrillic letters. I open a journal again and peck out the first word my eyes land on: корабль.

Enter.

Ship! The word means "ship." *What about a ship?*

43

I flip forward and try another: полиция. "Police." *Police?*

And another: люблю. *Love.*

Ship. Police. Love. Intriguing all right, but at this point, it would take months to translate even one journal, let alone a trunkful. Not to mention some of the handwritten letters in the diary look different from the font on the screen.

A toothbrush dangles from the corner of my mouth as the idea hits me. Spitting, I rush back to my laptop and pull up Craigslist. Keene is no United Nations, but it is a college town. Maybe someone at the school speaks Russian. My confidence is not high, but I click through to create a posting.

jobs > miscellaneous

posting title:

Russian Translator Needed

location:

Keene, New Hampshire

description:

Seeking person fluent in Russian to translate for personal project. Must be able to read handwritten Russian.

compensation:

I leave the last part blank. After the Oakleys for Ryan, I have around four hundred dollars saved from birthday gifts and babysitting, but the idea of blowing it on a Russian translator, no matter how curious I am about my aunt's journals, sounds crazy.

The job description takes several rewrites, but finally I settle on "personal project." Vague but true. I reread and post the ad, then close my laptop.

Slowly, my eyes adjust to the darkness. If I turn on my side, the trunk is visible in the moonlight creeping through the window blinds. "I'm a writer, too," Aunt Anna said. Maybe Katie was onto something; maybe these journals were meant for me.

5

August 16, 2007

KissMeK8E: i can't even

A bubbly blip alerts me to an IM. I resist. Or try to.

Real writers write every day—at least that's what I read once. During the school year, this feels impossible. Hemingway didn't have soccer practice, three AP classes, SAT prep, and weekly community service hours to strengthen his college applications.

If I'm being honest, though, it's not just about finding the time. I love writing. I feel the urge to write like I feel the urge to breathe or to sleep or to eat. Then why is it so damn hard sometimes to just . . . put . . . my butt . . . in the seat? I see the laptop sitting on my bed, and all I feel is dread. The thoughts don't even form anymore, not as complete sentences, at least; they're just there, in the background, like the hum of a refrigerator: *Who do you think you are? A "real" writer? Ha! No one cares about your stories, Jess. You have no idea where this one's going anyway! Why not just take a load off and watch TV? You can write tomorrow. Or the next day. Or—wait, was that a text message . . . ?*

So, this summer, I've made myself a promise: every day, I will write for one hour uninterrupted, no distractions. So far, it's working—when I'm not interrupted by a blizzard of instant messages from Katie.

KissMeK8E: The Saga of Zach
KissMeK8E: omgggggg
KissMeK8E: i. just. can't.

I break.

JesshireCat: then don't
KissMeK8E: i know, but THE DRAMA!!!!!!!!!!
KissMeK8E: and i luv drama . . .

At least she knows herself.

KissMeK8E: did u read the email? check ur email
JesshireCat: who uses email?
KissMeK8E: teachers and zach, that's who
KissMeK8E: just check it
JesshireCat: hang on. reading now. . . .

I pull up the Hotmail I use mostly for setting up user accounts. Katie has forwarded an email chain that Tyler forwarded to her from Zach. Another bubbly blip sounds.

KissMeK8E: sparknotes version: zach's a jerk. tyler's an idiot. the end.

Katie is nothing if not frank. I want to tell her I'm not sure it's so simple—Tyler and Zach are kind of cute together—but as I'm contemplating whether it's worth an argument, another email grabs my attention. Subject line: *Translator Needed?* It came in yesterday from a @keene.edu address.

Almost two weeks have passed since I sent my plea into the interweblactic void, and the only response I've gotten so far has been *three* messages from three separate pervs suggesting "personal project" meant something entirely different than I intended.

There have been a couple minor breakthroughs: when asked if there was any chance Aunt Anna had been Russian, my dad conceded that a lot of people from her generation had immigrated to the United States between the World Wars. "It would explain her fashion sense," my mom cracked. It was possible my aunt had been among them.

The second discovery was more concrete. I'd realized that the numbers at the tops of some pages were dates written in the backward European style my third-grade French pen pal used, where the day comes before the month: "1.10.16" for October 1, 1916. This placed most of the diaries in the 1910s and '20s . . . which was still useless unless I could find someone who could actually read them. I'd begun to lose hope.

Until now.

KissMeK8E: AAAAAANYway . . . we're seeing a movie later. gonna drown tyler's sorrows in butter flavored topping
KissMeK8E: u hanging with ry guy again tonight?
KissMeK8E: hellooooo?

I'm distracted by the email. *Translator Needed?*

JesshireCat: sorry. no, he's taking his grandma to dinner for her bdya
JesshireCat: her bday
KissMeK8E: awwwwww, wyan! model grandson
KissMeK8E: come with then! might sneak into a second one after

There's too much going on at once. I want to read the email. I also want to spend the night at home. My parents are going out, and Griffin's away again—football camp this time, an impromptu decision by my parents after my brother got himself grounded just two days after returning from lacrosse camp—so I'll have the place to myself. When Ryan said he was taking his grandmother to dinner, the evening, in my mind, had morphed into pajamas, slice-and-bake cookies, and a *Doctor Who* marathon.

I know I *should* hang out with my friends, but the truth is I don't feel like it.

KissMeK8E: please please please!!

JesshireCat: you're killing me with the exclamation points

KissMeK8E: that's the idea

Excuses rattle like train cars through my mind: a cold, a migraine, a power outage, an alien abduction, a paralyzing existential crisis . . . But how many excuses can I give before they stop asking me to join them altogether? My mom's voice echoes in my mind: *When all she does is sit in the corner?*

I cave.

JesshireCat: k. txt me deets

KissMeK8E: YAY!!!!!!!

JesshireCat: gotta run. ttyl

Before I can hear the *boop-boop-bleep* of her sign-off, I've clicked on the email.

Dear Madam,

I'm writing to inquire whether you are still in need of a

Russian translator. My name is Evan Hermann, and I am a rising sophomore at Keene State College majoring in Russian language and literature. What is it that you need translated?

Sincerely,
Evan Hermann

A tiny firework of hope goes off in my chest. I read the email again and then a third time. Oddly formal, but it seems legit. Reply. My fingers hesitate over the keyboard.

Dear Evan,

Delete.

Hi Evan,

Friendlier.

It's a little hard to explain. They're old diaries and they're handwritten, like cursive. Can you read that?

Thank you!

Delete. Too casual.

Best,

Jess

Send.

I am not expecting his reply to come immediately.

Yes, I am able to read handwritten Russian. Shall we meet at Brewbakers tomorrow at 2pm? We can discuss my rate then.

Brewbakers is a coffee shop on Main Street, not far from the college. I like it for its slightly shabby feel—scuffed pine floors and a cozy, worn leather couch. It seems like a safe-enough place to meet a stranger off the internet.

The primness of Evan Hermann's response—his "shall"— makes me chuckle, and the part about his rate worries me, but I'll deal with that later.

We shall, I reply giddily. *See you then.*

6

August 17, 2007

Evan Hermann is not hard to spot. In fact, he looks exactly as I imagined him, someone who says "shall": thin and pale with a brown riot of hair that stands at odd angles, as if he's just rolled out of bed. Even sitting, it's clear he's tall and—there's no other word for it—geeky. In the heat of summer, he wears a painfully unfashionable tan suede jacket over a shamrock-green shirt. He has that bookish look hipsters are going for, without any of the actual hipness.

What I am not expecting, however, is that Evan Hermann is attractive, with full lips and a lean face beneath chiseled cheekbones. His thick eyebrows arch dramatically upward, giving him a mischievous, elven look.

Evan has claimed a two-person table at the back of the long, narrow café. In front of him, steam curls from a porcelain mug. His head bends over a book.

I make my way toward him, a messenger bag carrying the three journals I've brought with me bumping awkwardly against my thigh. "Evan?"

Slate-blue eyes meet mine, startled and then confused. "Jess?"

I nod.

"I expected you to be older," he says, clearly disappointed.

"Oh, um, yeah, I'm seventeen?" *Why do I make it a question? Why do I feel uncomfortable when he's the one being rude?* "So . . ."

"Well . . . sit, please." He closes his book and pushes it to the side of the table. *The Brothers Karamazov*, by Fyodor Dostoevsky. A hulking tome.

"Some light reading?" I joke.

Evan frowns. "If you consider patricide and a philosophical struggle with the moral implications of faith and doubt . . . 'light,' then, yes."

O-key dokey, then. "Well, thanks for meeting me." I don't need him to have a sense of humor, just the ability to read Russian.

His eyes dart to my messenger bag on the floor. "You have something for me?"

"They're diaries." I pull the three randomly selected journals from the bag and place them on the table between us. One is simple: navy-blue leather with worn, rounded corners and a red spine. The second is similar but with the word *Diary* stamped on the front. The third is more ornate, brown with a gold border and a leather flap that fastens around the covers. Of course, I can read none of them.

"May I?" Evan asks. I nod, and he reaches for the brown diary, turning it over in his hands. His fingers are like a piano player's, long and delicate, with nails cut to the quick—the kind of fingers I'd once dreamed of having. He opens the journal to a random page. Behind him, the hiss of a cappuccino machine.

Closely, I watch Evan's face for a flicker of comprehension, but his expression is impossible to judge.

"So . . . can you read it?" I finally ask.

He doesn't answer, scanning. *Was this a mistake?* I have no reason not to believe Evan, but Tyler's brother bought his car off Craigslist and three weeks later found out it had been flooded and had to get all the carpet torn out. I want to be sure Evan can do what he says he can: translate the journals.

"Maybe you can read a page or two, like, out loud?"

For a second, his deeply furrowed brow makes me think I've offended him. *"Doveryai, no proveryai."*

He speaks in Russian; I have no idea what he's said.

"'Trust but verify'—it's a proverb."

"Oh," I say.

Clearing his throat, he bows his head and reads.

Snow again, but a great wind chased the clouds from the sky, a fox pursuing . . .

Frowning, he struggles for the word, or perhaps to decipher the handwriting.

. . . hares. And then the most dazzling blue sky! In the afternoon, walked with Maria. The sun threw sparkles across the snow, like a thousand brilliant gems, so much that it hurt our eyes. The geese agreed. They honked and honked, especially the mean one who lives by the marble bridge. This made us laugh. Tomorrow we'll go sledding.

The scene materializes before me like a paint-by-numbers. It's beautiful and, in my opinion at least, well written. Evan flips forward a few pages.

A parade in the morning. The new recruits. So serious in their handsome uniforms! Tea with Aunt Olga. Our friend comes this evening for prayers. Tomorrow is Easter. Paskha and kulich until my stomach bursts! Kisses and eggs in the afternoon.

Orthodox traditions, Evan explains: eggs dyed red with onion skins and three kisses exchanged on the cheek. He flips again and reads. Then flips again. He's reading fluently now, skipping between entries that catch his eye, and I'm swept in by his voice.

"Enough?" he asks eventually, an almost imperceptible twist to his lips.

He's satisfied with his performance, and admittedly, so am I. And embarrassed that I doubted him. My cheeks flush. "Yes, thank you," I say, a bit sheepishly.

Evan turns another page, scans it casually, and then closes the book. He stands abruptly. "Excuse me while I get another mocha." I'm left alone at the table to study the inscrutable journals, and I realize: I need Evan Hermann.

When he sits again, with another large cup of coffee, I ask how he found my posting.

"Student loans," Evan replies matter-of-factly. "I have them and need to pay them. You'd be shocked how few jobs there are out there for Russian literature majors."

When he sees my blank look, he adds, "I'm kidding," and slurps his coffee. "I do know what jokes are. Anyway, I saw this posting and thought it sounded perfect—assuming you can actually pay."

"I can pay," I say indignantly. The condescension in his voice irks me. In fact, I've brought fifty dollars from my babysitting stash. "Forty dollars," I say.

"Per journal?"

"All three."

Evan snorts. Loudly. "That's less than a quarter a page!"

Heat steals up my neck and cheeks. "Well, what do you propose?"

"Fifty dollars a pop."

It's my turn to snort.

"That's considerably less than I would expect to be compensated."

"All right, then," I challenge him, tossing my hair behind my shoulder in a way that I hope suggests indifference rather than the embarrassment and desperation I'm beginning to feel. "There's a whole Russian department at your school, isn't there? I'm sure I can find someone else."

"Not for that price, you won't."

I glare. He's suddenly less attractive, although I know he's right. "Thirty-five," I counter.

He combs his fingers through his hair, tugging at the ends, the kind of nervous gesture that suggests he's thinking. "Forty-five."

"Forty."

"Forty-five." His eyes narrow.

Quickly, I do the math. One hundred thirty-five dollars—a third of my babysitting savings—for the three journals I've brought. It's a start. "Fine," I say begrudgingly. "Forty-five a journal."

"Deal. I'll need a deposit of twenty-five dollars."

My eyes bulge. "For what?"

"So I don't do the work and then you skip out on me."

"Has that happened to you before?" I ask, voice dripping with sarcasm.

"Have you had someone respond to an ad claiming he can read Russian when he can't?"

I roll my eyes. "All I have on me is a twenty."

"That will do."

Grumbling, I fish for my wallet in the messenger bag and toss the bill onto the table. Evan smooths it before putting it into his own wallet and standing from the table. He gathers the three diaries toward him.

"Wait," I say, and instinctively, my hand shoots out to cover his, holding the journals. The unexpected touch seems to surprise us both, and my hand pulls back. My stomach does a strange somersault. "You have my deposit. How do I know I can trust *you*?" I say.

When Evan realizes that I mean he might steal them, his face opens into an annoying grin. "I guess you don't," he says, amused. "But," he counters, "how do you know they're not just some Russian housewife making grocery lists and complaining about her drunk husband and ten bratty kids?"

I'm losing my patience. "They're not some Russian housewife's," I snap, "because they were my dead great-great-aunt Anna's."

Unfazed by my outburst, he tucks the books under his arm.

The now-empty messenger bag feels disconcertingly light over my shoulder. "How long will it take?" I ask.

"Well, if you want it fast," he says, "it'll cost you more. . . ."

"Fine! The normal rate is fine. Just how long do you think it will take?"

He cocks an eyebrow, doing some sort of calculation in his head. "A week, give or take. I'll call you when I'm done."

"Do you want my number, then?"

For the first time, he appears flustered. "Uh—yes," he stammers, "yes, I suppose I will need your phone number."

"Okay . . . do you have your phone with you?"

His cheeks pinken, but whether it's because a girl is giving him her number or because he forgot he'd need it to call me, I'm not sure. He fumbles in his pocket to produce a flip phone circa Y2K. With difficulty, I punch my number into the keypad and press call. My phone rings, and I flip his shut and hand it back to him. "Now I have yours, too."

We weave our way out of the coffee shop. Out on the sidewalk, the sun is behind Evan, and I shield my eyes to see him, pointing to the journals tucked under his arm. "Just be careful with them, okay? I think . . ." I hesitate. "I feel like there's some sort of story there."

I'm not totally sure what I mean, but Evan grins, holding the books slightly aloft. "Of course there's a story; they're diaries. 'But how did you manage to live, if there is no story?'"

I squint. "Proverb?"

He smiles. "Dostoevsky. And I promise I will be careful. Nerd's Honor."

A blush creeps to my cheeks. *Have I been so transparent?*

Evan gives a two-fingered salute, clicks his heels, and turns in the direction of the college.

7

August 18, 2007

Music pounds from Ryan's speakers onto Washington Street. Warm air splashes through the Blazer's open windows. It's the kind of summer evening that can make you feel invincible, like August will never end, like you'll be carefree forever. Never mind you're not carefree, never mind being stuck sounds kind of awful, an ant trapped in teenage amber—in this moment, this is what it is to be alive.

Ryan moves a hand from my knee to shift gears, and we turn right, up a leafy, shaded street that winds toward Robin Hood Park. Opening night of *The 25th Annual Putnam County Spelling Bee* is in the park's grassy amphitheater. All week, Katie has been freaking out, sure that no one but the cast's parents will show. In order to get Ryan there, I've had to promise it isn't an actual spelling bee, just a play about one. "Oh, that sounds *a lot* better," he cracked, but agreed. Secretly, I'm hoping this show of support might thaw some of Katie's iciness toward him.

As we wind toward the park, the sudden chirping of crickets, my ringtone, sounds over the thumping bass of the music. "Dude," Ryan says, "tell Katie she needs to chill the eff out."

I rummage in the purse at my feet. It's the second time she's called. "She gets nervous," I start to explain, but my voice catches because it's not Katie's name on the screen but Evan Hermann's. I glance at Ryan—since the night at Doug's, I haven't mentioned the trunk of journals to him—but I'm too confused about the call to send it to voice mail. Evan said the translation would take a week; it's only been a day and a half.

"Hello?" I answer.

Ryan scrolls on his iPod.

"Yes, is this Jess Morgan?"

"Um, yeah?" *He called me, didn't he?*

"This is Evan Hermann."

"Yeah," I say, glancing again at Ryan. "I know. I have your number."

"Right," Evan says. I wonder if he's actually used a cell phone before. "Listen, is this some sort of prank?"

"What?"

"Did Amit put you up to this?"

"What do you mean—I don't know who that is."

The Blazer's tires whine on the pavement as Ryan makes a sharp turn into the parking lot. On the other end of the line, Evan is quiet.

"Hello," I say again.

"I've read the journals," he says warily.

"All of them? You said they'd take a week."

He pauses, as if he's still trying to determine whether I'm messing with him. "It went faster than I thought. I got into them and . . . well, I had to keep going."

Ryan has turned off the car and is watching me, confused; clearly, it's not Katie who called.

Evan's breath on the other end sounds like waves breaking on a shore. "Look, I think it's best if we meet in person," he says finally. "I'll tell you everything then."

"Why? What do you mean?" His agitation is making me nervous.

"I just think it would be best if we went through them together."

"Is it something bad?" A heavy lump forms in my stomach. This might explain why Anna hid the journals in the attic.

Are we going? Ryan mouths. I nod but place my finger in my ear so I can hear Evan's response clearly.

"No, definitely not. Or, not exactly," he says slowly.

Not exactly? If it isn't bad, then I don't understand why he can't just tell me. The phone vibrates against my ear with a text, and this time I know it's Katie.

"All right," I say. "Same place, four o'clock tomorrow?"

"See you there." He hangs up without a goodbye—apparently as bad at those as he is at hellos.

"Everything okay?" Ryan asks as I bring the phone from my ear. I shake my head to clear it, but I'm buzzing, as if Evan's call has switched on a big neon question mark. "Yeah, sorry. I'm meeting this person for a project thing."

We start toward the amphitheater. "A 'project thing'? Like, for school?" His tone makes me glad I didn't tell him about the paper for Mr. Austin, either.

"No," I say quickly. "Just this . . . family history thing." Essentially, this is true. "I'm helping my mom. It's not a big deal."

He stops, looks at me, incredulous. "A family history project?"

For a moment, I fear I've been busted. *Why* don't *I just tell Ryan about the journals?* I ask myself. The answer comes quickly: *Because hiring a translator for your great-great-aunt's dusty old diaries is not something he would understand, that's why.*

Then, just as I fear I'm going to have to explain, Ryan surprises me with a bear hug so tight my elbows jam into my ribs. My feet paddle the air as he lifts them from the ground. "You're too good to be true," he says.

He returns me to earth, and I flinch. "What do you mean?"

"Come on." He smirks, but it's an adoring kind of smirk. "Honor roll? Harvard? Spending your summer on a family history project? You're, like, every parent's dream, Jess."

Am I? I wonder.

And how does Ryan know I've made honor roll?

Over the sound system, someone is asking the audience to turn off their cell phones. "Please," I say, clasping my hands at the small of his back. "My mom would adopt you if it wasn't creepy."

His lips brush mine. "Oh, it would be creepy."

"So," Katie asks hopefully, "what'd ya think?"

The stage makeup she's scrubbed from her cheeks has left a clownish pink tinge. I've been sitting on the swings at the playground near the amphitheater, waiting for her to change out of costume. In the end, Olive Ostrovsky might not be the biggest break of her life, but Katie's performance was excellent. And as confident as she is, she still needs me to reassure her of that fact. The only problem: as my friend sang and acted her heart out, I was barely able to focus. I couldn't stop wondering why Evan had been so sketchy on the phone, and what was in my aunt's journals that had made him that way.

"You were fantastic!" I jump from the swing to present a plastic-sleeved bouquet of dyed-blue daisies Ryan and I got at the gas station on the way.

"Awww, thanks."

"Ryan picked them out." Actually, he'd pointed and mumbled, "Those look okay."

"Where is he, anyway?"

"Finding a bathroom, I think." The truth is he went to buy

beer for Doug and Josh, but Katie wouldn't approve of the fake ID he acquired at school.

She settles on a swing, hands tucked between her knees, flowers balanced in her lap. "It was good, right? I mean, people were laughing."

"A lot."

"You could hear us?"

"Totally."

"What was your favorite part?"

Shit. My mind scans for a scene I can name. I was so distracted. "The spelling bee was hilarious."

She looks impatient. "The whole thing's a spelling bee. Like, which scene?"

"Ummm . . . camouflage! The part where the girl had to spell 'camouflage.'"

"Yeah, that's a funny one." My answer seems to have satisfied her, and Katie pushes off the ground. We pump our legs in sync, slowly gaining air. "Sophie's super talented. She's the one who plays Marcy Park. Actually, she's having an opening night party—well, 'party' might be overstating it, but Caleb's gonna be there."

"Caleb?"

Katie stops pumping. "Caleb. He played William Morris Barfée? He wins the spelling bee? The guy I was texting you about?"

"Ohhhh. Right." I don't want to tell her that I'm pretty sure the guy I just saw onstage is not into girls. "But what about the fro-yo guy?"

"Derrick?" Since we don't know his real name, this is what we've taken to calling him, a name both hot and slightly ridiculous. "Derrick's a topping on the frozen yogurt of my romantic life," Katie muses. "He's . . . sprinkles. But, like, not even the good kind, compared to Caleb; he's, like, jimmies—"

I start to protest.

"—which, I don't care what you say, are not really chocolate! Anyway, you have to come. You can bring Ryan. Sophie has a pool; it'll be fun."

The chains squeak in their hooks as we both slow. "Shoot. Katie, I can't tonight."

She drags her heels through the mulch, coming to an abrupt stop. "Why not?"

"Andy DePalma's having people over." I suspect he's trying to redeem himself from the social suicide of puking in Doug's washing machine.

"You're going to Andy 'Axe Body Spray' DePalma's?"

"I have to go."

"Why?" she says sharply. "Why do you have to go?"

The last of the audience is filtering out of the amphitheater. A little kid runs over to the jungle gym, crying "*Aaaaaaagh!*" and scaling the playground equipment like Spider-Man on speed.

"I want to go," I correct myself.

68

"Do you? Do you want to go to Andy DePalma's?"

"It's just a bunch of people hanging out."

"Hmmm." She purses her lips. "And 'a bunch of people hanging out' has always been your thing."

"Katie, I don't get to see Ryan, like, ever during the year."

"Yeah," she says under her breath, "I used to think that was a perk."

The swing spins wildly as I stand to face her. The boy's mom is now desperately trying to lure him from the top of the jungle gym: *"Dashiell, come down, honey. Dashiell, honey. Dashiell. Dashiell. Dashiell. Dashiell."* It's almost funny, except neither Katie nor I are laughing.

I've known this conversation was coming, but I wasn't prepared for it tonight. "Katie, what is your problem? Why do you ha—"

She interrupts me. "Why are you with him, Jess?"

"What?" I ask, thrown.

"Why are you with Ryan?"

I glance at the parking lot; he's not back from his beer run yet. "Because," I scoff.

"Because why?"

The heel of my Puma grinds into the dirt. "Because he makes me laugh," I reply, "and because he's nice to be around, and because, I don't know, he's cute." I can feel that it's a weak answer, but I also feel angry that my best friend acts like it's a crime to like my boyfriend.

Katie cups a hand to her ear, as if she had trouble hearing. "Nice to be around?" she repeats, louder. "Is that the bar?"

"What's your bar? Unavailable?" I shoot. It's a low blow. I cover it quickly. "And because he makes me feel special, okay, Katie? Because he chose *me*."

She recoils a little. "You're not yourself when you're around him, Jess."

Now my blood boils. My nails dig half-moons into my palms. "How would you know?" I spit venomously. "You don't see it."

"Huh. I wonder why."

My nose is running with the effort not to cry. Katie's arms cross over her chest; she scowls into the middle distance. Why does she have to make this so difficult? Why can't she just play along?

I take a deep breath. Katie's hurt I can't go to the party with her, that I didn't remember who Caleb was, that I clearly wasn't paying attention during the play. "Look," I say, trying to appease her. "Can we hang out tomorrow?"

She's still mad, but her face is unscrewing itself, her arms relaxing. She plucks at one of the neon-blue daisies. "Maybe tomorrow night. You and Tyler could come over. . . ."

"Yes!" I say, and then remember. "Wait. Shit. Josh's brother is working." He's a waiter at the Chili's on Route 9; he serves the guys beer and Lila bright-pink cocktails.

Katie's glare could stop a bullet in midair. "Are you effing serious?"

"I told Ryan—"

"Enough," Katie says.

"What about earlier, during the day? Oh!" I say excitedly, remembering my meeting with Evan. "Guess where I'm go—"

She holds a palm to my face. "Enough, Jess. Or whoever *this*"—her hands wave over me as if I'm some kind of illusion—"is, because I don't remember befriending someone who thinks it's cool to ditch her best friend for a *dream* date night of Megaritas courtesy of Josh's brother." The disdain radiates off of her in waves.

"How am I ditching you if we didn't even have plans yet?" I protest, but she's already walking toward the amphitheater, where I can hear the tech crew shouting about lights. "Katie," I plead. The daisies lie in their plastic sleeve on the ground at my feet.

As if on cue, the boy who's been scaling the jungle gym runs by, sticking his tongue out at me. All of a sudden he gasps, and I turn to look. Katie's giving me the finger.

8

August 19, 2007

"We'll start with the first one I read."

No banter this time. Back at Brewbakers, once I've promised I have no idea who Amit and Russell are and this is not a prank, Evan has gotten down to business. He places the blue-and-red journal on the table between us. Perched at the edge of his seat, he keeps his voice low, so I have to lean in to hear him. He smells of Ivory soap.

"As we suspected, they are diaries." Evan turns the journal so it's facing me and opens to the first page. "This one is from 1913." He points to the numbers at the top of the page. "They're signed, mostly, with an 'A.'" His finger slides to the bottom, tapping one of the few letters I do actually recognize.

"Yeah," I say, a little annoyed, "I'd deduced that. But what's in them?"

If he hears my impatience, he doesn't show it. "Ordinary, diary-type stuff. It seems they were written by a young girl—a privileged one."

"What makes you think that?"

"She mentions tutors and nannies; Mass in a private chapel; fighting with her sisters; hating getting dressed up . . . you know, the inconveniences of a charmed life."

Do I know? Is that a dig? If so, I ignore it. My own finger traces the faded ink. "What does this one say?"

He squints at the upside-down handwriting. "It's about a trick she played on her tutor."

I flip to another page. "And this one?"

"That one's about getting in trouble for climbing a tree. She must have been mischievous because she says that her sisters and nanny call her 'Shvibzik.' It means 'imp.' Had to look that one up."

I smile to myself. "Sh-vib-zik," I repeat, mangling the pronunciation.

He winces. "Almost."

"Can you read it to me?"

Evan turns the book around. Bent over the page, his pale face glows like a pearl.

10.6.1913

Papa is cross with me, and it's all Olga's fault!

So rainy these last weeks, and then—finally!—

today the sun peeked out. After lessons, Maria and I walked in the park. Found the most beautiful maple tree to make our bower, like the Queen of the Fairies in the play Mr. Gibbes made us read. Only, Olga discovered us and demanded we climb down at once. Of course Maria obeyed, but I refused. Just then Papa came around, from a tour of the grounds. Olga told him I was being naughty, and he scolded me for disobeying. "You have no fear, little rabbit," he said, lifting me down. That's a good thing, isn't it? I asked. He laughed and said only God can know this. I told him Olga was only vexed because she's not heard back from her special "friend" Pavel Alexeyevich. Her cheeks flushed bright red, and Papa scolded me again for tattling. The injustice!

Reading the journals, Evan is animated. He takes on the writer's inflections, channels her emotions. He's so sincere in his performance, I almost have to suppress a giggle.

22.6.1913

A gay afternoon! Picnic by the beach. Took shore boats from the yacht to a small island. When we arrived, the sailors had built a pavilion with carpets and a banquet—milk and tea, fruits, candies. The most delicious bilberry tarts! I made Maria laugh by licking preserves from my nose till my eyes crossed.

After tea, played blindman's buff. Papa joined, and we roared with laughter—even the servants—as he stumbled about, almost catching the sash of T's dress. I wish we'd never return to Petersburg but sail the Standardt all around the world, a band of merry pirates. No more court with all its silly ceremonies.

Evan pauses to raise his eyes to me. *Ceremonies, servants, court . . .*

"So—" I say, clicking the puzzle pieces together, but he raises a hand to silence me and pulls another diary from the stack.

"This one," he says, "comes a little later. Nineteen fifteen."

Today Shura scolded me, but I am so terribly <u>bored!</u> She says there are hundreds of thousands of girls the empire over who would give an arm and a leg to be in my place. But those girls don't know the lonesomeness of our position!!! We never entertain, dear diary, except for Grandmama and the boring old aunts and uncles. Mama prefers it this way. She says the courtiers are nosy rodents who dislike her for her German blood and we must trust no one but Father Grigori, and of course dear Shura, but she is just a nursemaid.

Some days I am allowed to play with Glebe, the doctor's son, but a girl of fourteen needs friends! Who am I to trade secrets with?

So, because I have no one else to share it with, our little life here at Tsarskoe Selo, I shall describe it to you, my dear diary:

Maria and I share a room. In the mornings, she wakes me (the little swine). First, we greet Mama in her "boudoir," as Monsieur Gilliard calls it. This is the loveliest room in the apartments, its furniture and curtains and even the wall-paper a dusty mauve. Every day the servants fill the room with flowers. If I lie on the chaise longue and cloud my gaze through the fringe of my lashes, it's like reclining in a grove of lilacs. Mama says this is how the English decorate their homes, and she would know.

This is much better than the stuffy old Winter Palace or the Catherine Palace next door. There, everything is gold and precious stones and polished marble—perfect for making faces in your reflection, but cold and not at all inviting. It is lovely, though, like being inside one of the jeweled eggs Papa gives Mama for Easter.

I cut Evan off. "Palace?"

His eyes, sparkling, search mine as the word sinks in.

"Palace," I repeat. Slowly, he nods. "So, she was . . . these are the diaries of—"

Before my brain can fully form the thought, he raises his hand a second time. "Wait."

He opens the third journal to a page he's marked with a scrap of paper. "March ninth, nineteen seventeen," he reads.

Papa has arrived from the front. Mama wept to see him step from the train, and we all ran to greet him, hugging and kissing him. We feared we might never see him again. He is glad to be home, he says, but I am afraid the Tsarskoe Selo he left is much changed. There are sentries now, posted at every turn, and guards roaming the palace—as if it was <u>their</u> home! We've been instructed to stay within the fenced area of the park, but even then we are followed. Bodyguards we are used to, but these men are here to watch <u>us</u>. Sometimes I glare at them when Mama's not looking or imitate them behind their backs. Maria tells me I had better stop.

When we are alone, we try to pretend that all is normal, and almost we can. Mama says it is our responsibility to remain strong, to remind the people of who we are, but I know she is worried for Alexei since our Holy Friend was killed, and now that Papa has renounced the throne for them both.

Today, however, Mama is happy because we are all together again. I am happy as well. Perhaps the situation will improve now that Papa is back. I will put on a brave face and cease my naughty ways, as Mama said.

May God keep you,

"This one's signed," Evan says, "'Your Little Anastasia.'"

His gaze is the only steady thing in the room as my head wheels around names and facts that I remember from textbooks and multiple-choice questions.

"These were your great-great-aunt's?" he asks.

The coffee shop suddenly feels stuffy, the woman on her laptop next to us too close. "They were in her attic."

"And her name was Anna?"

"Yes." The thing my mind is trying to pin down is too large, too incredible. The eggs she was writing about, they weren't dyed in onion skin, they were crusted in jewels, they were Fabergé . . .

A sheaf of typed papers lies on the table between us. It's Evan's English translations of all three journals, and I place my hand on the stack. "Are these what I think they are?"

A twinkle dances in Evan's eyes, fire behind ice, the skepticism he'd shown earlier evaporated like mist off a lake.

A *for Anna.*

"These journals . . ." he says, voice measured but excited, "sound . . ." He's working out the sentence like a solution to a math problem. ". . . as if they were written by the grand duchess Anastasia Nikolaevna Romanova."

A *for Anastasia.*

"Anastasia Romanov," I say.

His voice is a conspiratorial whisper. "Jess, if your aunt was a daughter of the last tsar of Russia, she survived the execution the world believes killed them all."

78

9

My hands tremble in my lap. Sweat prickles my skin, and it isn't the closeness of the coffee shop. This is what Aunt Anna had been trying to tell me. *History is a story.*

"Maybe we shouldn't talk about this here," Evan says. The woman next to us has glanced over twice. "Shall we walk?"

Outside, I feel better, steadier. A breeze rustles the leaves of the elm trees that line downtown. It poured earlier, and the sidewalks smell like wet clay, a smell I love. A young couple breezes past us with a baby stroller, and Evan and I turn left, toward the gazebo at the end of Main Street.

I am still processing what he's said, but trying to focus my thoughts is like trying to find a radio station through static. I hug the journals and translations to my chest.

Evan, keeping pace beside me, is the one to speak. "I realize it sounds crazy. According to *nearly* everyone, Anastasia

Romanov died in nineteen eighteen."

We'd studied the Russian Revolution in European History, but the details are hazy now—maybe I'd deserved Mr. Austin's B-minus. Patiently, Evan reviews the basics: The First World War saw massive unrest in Russia. Poverty and food shortages on top of military losses had the lower classes pretty pissed at the monarchy.

"'Pissed' might be an understatement," I say.

"Indeed," Evan allows.

Radical socialists, who believed the country's resources should be controlled collectively rather than by the tsar, began to gain influence. Then, in February 1917, a revolution forced Tsar Nicholas II—Anastasia's father—to abdicate. A second revolution later that year brought the Bolsheviks to power under Lenin.

There's a name I remember. With his bald, shiny head and pointy beard, the notorious Communist always looked to me like a sinister elf. "It was Lenin who had the tsar killed," I say.

Evan nods grimly. "At first, the family was kept under house arrest—at their palace near St. Petersburg, then in Tobolsk, and finally in the Ural Mountains. They were executed in the basement of a house in Yekaterinburg in the summer of 1918."

"How old was she?" I ask.

"Seventeen."

My age. An icy shiver trails fingers down my back.

We've reached the roundabout that rings the square, where each October families and college students pack together for

Keene's "world-famous" pumpkin festival. Today, however, it's quiet except for cars circling. Evan waits for a gap in the traffic to jog across the road. I follow, waving apologetically to a BMW driver who honks his horn and points to the crosswalk we failed to use.

The gazebo's paint is peeling, but the wide stairs make a good seat and we settle on them side by side. Carefully, I place the three journals between us. There are more in my messenger bag.

"Who was she talking about when she said, 'our Holy Friend was killed'?" I ask.

"Rasputin, I imagine."

"The evil magician with a talking bat?" In elementary school, I saw *Anastasia* in the theater. The animated movie's pasty, pointy-nosed villain, all angles and shadows, was a sorcerer named Rasputin. How could it be this fairy tale was based on my aunt's life?

Evan grins. "Exactly—only probably with less singing and dancing.

"The *real* Rasputin," he continues, "was an Orthodox monk—either a holy man or a charlatan, depending on who you asked. Whatever he was, he wielded great influence with Alexandra, the tsar's wife. She was a deeply religious woman. Alexei, their only son, had hemophilia, a blood disorder that made him bleed internally; he was extremely frail. As the tsar's only male heir, you see, this presented a problem."

"No heir, no future."

He nods. "The family concealed his condition publicly, and the tsaritza was convinced Rasputin could cure him. He became her closest confidant, and the Russian nobility weren't too happy about that. They accused Rasputin of drinking and taking bribes and being, shall we say, something of a swinger."

"A swinger monk?"

"Believe me, I could not make these things up. Anyway, the Romanovs' relationship with Rasputin is one of the things that cost them the monarchy."

"She said he was martyred."

"He died before the revolution. A group of nobles poisoned, beat, shot, and drowned him."

"Geez. Talk about overkill." It feels like a small triumph that I make Evan laugh.

"They said he wouldn't die. It added to the *mystique*." He flares his fingers.

"How do you know all this stuff?"

"I read something once and remember it. My friends call me SpongeBob Smarty-Pants."

Across from the gazebo, there's a monument to fallen Union soldiers and two Civil War–era cannons. On the air is the smell of French fries from a nearby restaurant. The past and the future colliding. This is all surreal.

"There's something else," Evan says, striking my attention like a match. He rakes his fingers through his hair. "There *are* people who believe a Romanov survived. In the years after the execution, individuals came forward saying they were Alexei or one of the daughters. They turned out to be frauds, debunked by Romanov friends and family . . . or DNA. Your aunt," he adds. "When did she die?"

In 2003, I tell him, and, unfortunately, she was cremated.

"Any chance there's DNA in her house? A comb, toothbrush?"

"Not after my mom's band of Merry Maids got their hands on it."

We're quiet for a moment, watching the cars go around. "Let me get this straight," I say finally. "You think my great-great-aunt might have been Anastasia Romanov, that she survived her family's assassination, living in secrecy in *New Hampshire* all these years, and that I've found her diaries to prove it."

"'A hundred suspicions don't make a proof.'" He sighs. "*Crime and Punishment.* . . . But, yes, that's what the journals suggest. Though, obviously, I'll need to read more," he adds quickly. "I'll need to read all of them."

The messenger bag sits at my side. The books' mass couldn't total more than a pound, but as I lift the bag to my lap, there is suddenly the weight of history in them, and a thought runs through my mind: I've only met Evan Hermann twice. He's accused me of playing a prank, but what if he's the fraud, some twisted troll who gets his kicks pulling elaborate hoaxes? Or the alternative—what he's telling me is true, and these journals are priceless.

My instincts tell me I can trust Evan Hermann, but that doesn't mean I won't be careful. If we're working together, we'll have to work *together*. "You can read them at my house."

He scrambles to stand.

"I meant tomorrow," I say. He crouches awkwardly, halfway to his feet.

When I left this afternoon, my dad was cleaning the garage and my brother, returned from football camp, had glued himself to our couch. One thing I don't need as I try to unravel a potentially history-altering mystery: either of them hanging around asking questions. For now, I want to keep the journals my secret—and, I suppose, Evan's. I suggest he come at ten o'clock. On a Monday, my parents will be working, and with any luck, Griffin will be at Amanda's, the girl he refuses to call his girlfriend.

Evan is still frozen in his crouch. "I have oboe at nine thirty. Eleven?"

"Oboe?"

He rolls his eyes, straightening. "It's a very expressive instrument. Eleven?"

"Okay."

He sticks out his hand, and we shake on it.

"Right," he says, pumping vigorously. "See you then."

As I watch him play Frogger across the traffic circle, I realize the money Evan had negotiated so hard for is still in my pocket. He didn't even ask about it.

My first instinct, as always, is to call Katie—until I remember her interrogation the night before, and a bubble of anger rises and expands in my chest and I feel it pressing behind my ribs. What she said has me feeling like a mucky pond with its bottom raked up and swirled around, and this only makes me madder. I know better than to expect an apology so soon; experience tells me it'll be a couple of days before I hear from Katie. Maybe I could use a little time myself, to let the sand and silt settle.

Tonight, my mom has decreed one of her Forced Family Dinners, evenings where she tries to make up for how much she works by cooking four-course meals and peppering my brother and me with upbeat questions about our plans for the future while sparring with my dad over unimportant things like when the gutters need to be cleaned and the mercury content of swordfish. I hate these dinners.

I understand Evan's urgency to see the rest of the diaries— now that I know what's in them, my hands itch to hold them, too—but, while I can't read them, there's something else I can do. I buy myself a little time before dinner by veering down Winter Street. The Keene Public Library is my favorite building in town, slate-roofed and turreted like an old Parisian mansion. I haven't been here in years, since I started using the library at school instead. On the building's steps, memories from childhood come flooding back: the breathless anticipation of story time, the pride of finally reaching the return slot on my own, the comfort of all those books lined up nice and neat. Through the glass doors, it's the smell of books that hits me first, the same smell of the trunk, and then the soft blanket of silence.

Mr. Austin says the internet isn't a reliable source, but it's a place to start, so I head to the computers before the stacks.

A simple Google search shows that Grand Duchess Anastasia Nikolaevna of Russia was born on June 18, 1901, the fourth daughter of Tsar Nicholas II and his wife, Tsaritza Alexandra Fyodorvna, a German princess by birth and granddaughter of Great Britain's Queen Victoria.

There are hundreds of books, articles, and videos, and at least a dozen blogs not just dedicated to the Romanovs but obsessed with them, with detailed descriptions of their homes and palaces, dissections of their individual personalities and family dynamics, lists of their personal likes and dislikes, and scores of photographs.

I find a 1904 article from the *New York Times* that describes Nicholas as "a gentle-natured and constitutionally-minded man" who is "yet nominally a despot" suffering from "extreme, almost painful shyness." Alexandra, on the other hand, is a conservative stick-in-the-mud who dislikes court but loves her subjects and especially her children. In the library catalog, there are several biographies on the tsar and tsarina, and even a collection of their love letters.

I find a website dedicated exclusively to the Romanov girls (OTMA—Olga, Tatiana, Maria, Anastasia), and Anastasia's profile hits me like a dart: *Bright, if not especially studious, the youngest Romanov daughter was the clown of the family. Fiercely stubborn, Anastasia was gifted at getting her way, though she adored and mostly obeyed her older sisters and parents, reserving many of her pranks for her tutors and nursemaids.* It is, almost precisely, the girl I've just met in the diaries.

Anastasia's life was intriguing, and I jot down the titles of several more books. But what interests me most is what Evan shared, that on her death not everyone agrees.

I google the question blinking in my mind—*Did Anastasia survive?*—and am delivered into a digital forest of websites and blogs. *Unsolved Mysteries: Did Anastasia Live? . . . The Myth of the "Lost" Princess . . . Forgotten but Not Gone . . . The Romanov Lie.* In the silence of the library, the blood beats louder in my ears. Beneath the last headline is a photograph of the young Anastasia—glossy brown hair piled on top of her head, pearls, prim white dress, hand draped casually over the back of a sofa. A sly smile plays at her lips. What grips me, however, is the young princess's eyes. The image is black and white, with the softness of old photographs, but Anastasia's gaze is crystal clear, radiating an unsettling combination of wisdom and innocence.

I think back to the day in the nursing home with Aunt Anna and rewind the movie, rewind it all the way back, removing her wrinkles and age spots, fluffing her hair and thickening her lashes. I try to imagine her as the girl in the imperial portrait.

The dates are right. My aunt was 102 when she died, which meant she would have been born in 1901, like Anastasia.

I hesitate, then peck out a new search term, a decidedly morbid one: "Anastasia Romanov body." If I have learned anything from the cop shows Tyler forces us to watch, it's no body, no crime.

The third link down stops me cold: "Royal Remains Finally Confirmed." A click brings me to a British newspaper archive.

> British scientists say they have confirmed that the bones found in 1991, in a mass grave near Yekaterinburg, Russia, are the remains of Tsar Nicholas II and the Russian imperial family, missing since their reported execution in 1918. Five of the nine bodies have been identified as Romanovs. The remaining four are believed to be those of servants and the family's doctor.

Five Romanovs. My brain snags on the number. There were seven Romanovs: the tsar and tsarina, four daughters, and a son. My eyes scan farther down the article, and suddenly, the blood has stopped roaring in my ears, because it's frozen in my veins.

> The two missing bodies, those of the tsarevich Alexei and one of the younger sisters, Maria or Anastasia, are believed to have been buried separately. They are yet to be located.

Two missing bodies . . . Anastasia wasn't buried with the rest of her family . . . *yet to be located* . . . because maybe she wasn't buried in Russia at all . . . the idea shimmers like a mirage . . . because she died in 2003, in Keene, New Hampshire, as Anna Wallace . . . because she was my great-great-aunt.

10

"Remember," Mom says, lighting the candles we use only on these nights, "we have the family photo shoot next weekend."

Every summer, she dresses us in color-coordinated outfits and hires a professional photographer to make us look like we not only like each other but play Scrabble every Saturday night after a family sing-along. The photo will feature prominently on our annual holiday card, which is distributed to no fewer than two hundred people across the Eastern Seaboard, including my parents' college friends and business associates, Mom's clients, our teachers, and, I'm sure, the Harvard admissions department.

Hatred of this family tradition is one thing my brother and I can agree on, but he's more vocal about it. When I ask what time the shoot is, he rolls his eyes so hard I'm sure he strains a muscle.

"Ugggh. Are you friggin' kidding me?" Griffin whines.

"No," my mom replies, "and please don't use that language."

"I said 'friggin'."

She smiles at me. "Jess, may I pass you the steak?"

"I don't eat red meat," I remind her. In fact, I gave it up last year for environmental reasons.

"Saving the world one burger at a time," my brother adds snidely, and because he's talking with his mouth full, I get a front-row view of half-masticated steak.

My mother looks genuinely confused. "You've always loved steak. This is a lean cut. It's a little overcooked, maybe, but—"

"I wouldn't say *overcooked*," my dad grumbles from his end of the table. "You wanted medium."

Mom breathes deeply. "I said medium-rare. Medium ruins it."

"Is it ruined?" Dad asks, with an edge to his voice.

"I like it bloody." Griffin smiles.

My mom reaches for the wine. "No, John, it's fine; medium is fine." *Maybe I should have just eaten the steak.* "Jess, have some salad and asparagus, then."

Silently, Dad passes them down the table.

"Asparagus makes my pee smell." My brother. I knew he was going to say it.

Sometimes Mom calls Griffin her "work in progress." I know what she means—my brother is a half-formed cretin whose eventual release into society will no doubt wreak havoc— but I wonder what that makes me, then.

"Jess," she asks, "when does preseason start?" My mom was a relay swimmer in college. Athletic scholarships helped pay her tuition at Northeastern.

"Actually," I venture tentatively, "I'm kind of thinking of not playing this year."

"What? Why?" she asks, alarmed. "You love soccer."

Like I love steak? My fork glances off the undercooked asparagus I'm attempting to spear. "I don't know. I'm not that good, really." Last year, I warmed the bench more than I touched the ball.

"She's right," Griff says. "She sucks." My father gives him a look that says he's skating on thin ice.

"Sweetie," Mom says, sliding a hand across the table, "you know it's not just about field time."

I do know that. It's also about being co-captain, about painting your face for games and baking cookies for the team and selling more grapefruit for the booster club than anyone else. It's about making friends and putting it on your transcript and showing you're a "team player" and fitting in.

"Yeah, I know." *What's one more season?* But I add, "Guess I'm just worried about getting my applications done." One thing she can't argue with.

"True," she concedes, "but Harvard will want to see extra-curriculars, too. How's that history paper going, by the way?"

Griffin's jaw drops. "Wait. You're doing *school*work over the summer?"

I glare at him. "She's pulling her grade up," Mom says. "That's commendable, Griffin."

"Finding anything interesting about the Diet of Worms?" Dad asks. "How many calories *are* there in a nightcrawler?" He loves this joke.

"*Har,*" Griffin says.

"Actually," I reply, "I've changed the topic. To the Russian Revolution."

For a moment, I consider telling them about the diaries, but something stops me. If my great-great-aunt really was Anastasia Romanov, then the world will have her eventually. But not yet, not tonight.

"Interesting! Don't you think, Val?" My dad's staring down the table at my mom.

"Very cool!" She's been distracted by her BlackBerry, thumbs pecking at the keyboard like chickens in the dirt.

"Val," he repeats, because she's the worst offender of our no-phones-at-the-table rule.

"Sorry," Mom says but doesn't stop. "Melissa has a question about the walk-a-thon." Finally, she looks up. "What?" Sheepishly, she slides the BlackBerry under a napkin. Dad gives her a grim smile.

"Well, it was nice of Mr. Austin to offer you the opportunity—I guess he knows Harvard doesn't take Bs," she says.

The irony is that while my dad's the one with the Harvard degree, my mom's the one obsessed with me following in his footsteps. Boston's where my parents met. When asked where she went to school, my mom will say, "Boston." It took me a while to understand that this was a lie of omission, that even though Northeastern is a very good school, she wanted people to think she'd gone to the city's more famous university, Harvard (though it is, actually, in Cambridge). When I asked my dad about this once, he said something about a need for approval. I haven't had the guts to tell either of my parents that I'm far more intrigued by the college counseling office's sunny brochures from Stanford and UCLA.

"Griff," Mom says, after another sip of wine, "do you know what history class you'll take next year?"

"I dunno. Not AP European History. Probably civics."

"Why do you say it like that?" she asks. A light is blinking on the phone under the napkin, and I can tell it's quietly killing her.

"Because Butler teaches it, and she's a total chube," Griff replies.

"What does that mean?"

"'Bitch.'"

Mom's knife rattles to her plate. "Griffin Morgan!"

"What? She is!" In this case, he's right. Butler's notorious for sending kids to the office and even once denied Jonathan Hoover a bathroom pass for an entire period; he nearly peed his pants.

"Go." Mom's voice is dark. She points to the door. "You're dismissed."

He swipes his plate from the table. It clatters as he drops it on the counter. "You're the one on your CrackBerry!"

"It's for charity, Griffin. I'm thinking about someone other than myself."

Griffin looks like he's eaten a lemon. He shoves his chair under the table, hard. "I thought I was your charity."

My mom's voice shakes. "What is that supposed to mean?"

"Valerie," Dad pleads.

She snaps. "No, John. You don't hear Jess using language like that."

I do, on the regular, just not in front of her, and I don't understand why my brother can't just play along and keep the peace for once.

Griffin sneers at me. "Of course she doesn't."

He's ordered to his room. "I'll be there in a minute," my mom says, exhausted.

"Why, so we can have a heart-to-heart?"

"Griff," my dad says, and my brother slams the dining room door open, shoulder bumping against the frame so hard that I know it will leave a bruise. Sometimes I'm startled to see how much he can look like a man when he still acts like a little kid.

Silence settles over the kitchen. Mom empties the last of her wine. Red lace creeps up her cheeks, the same blush of emotion that I get, the curse of our pale complexion.

This quiet is different from the silence of the library a couple of hours earlier; a current of resentment runs through it. My father's chair scrapes tile, knife scrapes plate. "Dammit, Valerie," he says, "not everybody's perfect."

What does he mean by this? *Perfect like . . . you? Perfect like . . . Jess?*

Clearly, I want to tell him; some of us are just better at pretending.

By the time we leave Chili's, Lila's sloshed. She sways on the front porch of her house, at the end of a cul-de-sac behind the elementary school. "Bye-eeee!"

"You think she'll be okay?" Ryan asks. He sits shotgun. I've already dropped Josh at home.

After dinner, I called Ryan and offered to pick everyone up—anything to be out of the house immediately. As I pulled out of our garage, I could hear the rattle of doors slamming. At least amid the comfort of dry potato skins and Americana kitsch, of baseball on the flat screens and Ryan's warm thigh touching mine under the table, I could relax. . . . I could relax until Josh and Ryan started up a game of "Bartender," daring each other to drink disgusting concoctions of mustard, Sprite, and coffee creamer they mixed at the table. It was a game that Griffin and I used to play as kids—when Griff and I still got along.

Maybe it was funny at first, but when Josh started pretending to dry heave and the family in the corner booth complained to the manager, I wasn't laughing anymore. By the time an irate Daniel, Josh's brother, cut us off, I wanted to crawl under the table. As Lila, Josh, and Ryan headed to the car, I did just that, retrieving as many sugar packets and emptied creamer cups as I could. "Sorry," I whispered to a frowning Daniel. "You okay to drive?" he asked. I am; part of offering to be DD means I don't have to pretend to drink.

At her house, we watch Lila fumble with her keys. She drops them, retrieves them, drops them again. "I think she'll survive," I tell Ryan. "Although tomorrow she might wish she hadn't."

"Yeah," he says, tearing his gaze from the porch. "I guess Josh will check on her." The worry on his face is quickly replaced by a more familiar look, one that says, *Wanna make out?* "You want to come watch a movie?"

Watch a movie, like "get a soda." I glance at the clock. "It's after ten."

"Come on," he says, stretching the seat belt to nip at my ear. "Val will understand; she loves me."

"She does love you—that tickles." I nudge him away. "But she and Griff got in a fight."

"What does that have to do with you?"

"So, then my parents got in a fight," I say, annoyed—with Ryan or with my parents, I'm not sure, maybe both. Then, with a sudden realization, I'm even more annoyed—if Griffin was grounded, he'll be home tomorrow. But Evan is coming over, and I don't want my brother sniffing around.

The thought of the diaries sets my imagination whirring as Ryan continues to nuzzle my neck. How do I tell my boyfriend that, currently, there's a trunk full of journals in my room that suggest my great-great-aunt might have been Anastasia Romanov, and, right now, I'd rather spend the night with them? I don't. I blame my curfew.

When I drop him at his house, Ryan gives me a puppy-dog pout. "Sure you don't want to come in?"

In my mind, I'm already home, starfished on my bed reading the translations of the journals Evan typed up for me. "I can't."

"All right." He swings out of the car before poking his head back inside. "Call you tomorrow? We can watch that movie." He slurs a little bit, and I realize for the first time that he's more buzzed than I thought.

Katie's question swims up like a fish through the muck and the murk: *Why are you with him, Jess?* Once again, it sparks a small flame of fury inside of me.

"Yeah," I say, forcing a smile. "That'd be nice."

He grins. "Love ya."

"Love ya."

This is how Ryan always says it: not *Love you* or *I love you* or *I love you, Jess*—just *Love ya*. Two little words.

He taps the top of my car before I pull away.

Semantics, I tell myself. Only in my peripheral vision, I see that silver, glinting fish.

On the way to my room, I stop at Griffin's door. "You grounded?" I ask.

"No," he mumbles. "Get out of my room, nerk."

"Nice. What does that even mean?"

The video game he refuses to look up from gives his face a sinister glow. "Nerd and dork. 'Nerk.'"

"Ah, Griffin. If you'd only use your superior rhetorical powers for good instead of evil."

He throws a balled-up sock at the door. The *only* thing about me that impresses my brother is that I'm dating Ryan Hart.

11

August 20, 2007

The growling of a lawn mower wakes me, and I roll to check the time . . . 10:47. *Shit!*

Throwing off the covers, something heavy tumbles to the floor: my laptop—I fell asleep reading an article about life at the Romanov court. Cursing again, I check that the computer's not broken before making a beeline for the shower. I have a feeling Evan Hermann is the punctual type.

I'm right: at precisely one minute before eleven, there are three quick raps on our front door. From a laundry basket, I extract a rumpled pair of shorts and a T-shirt. My mom asked me to fold the clothes two days ago. Three more knocks.

I suspect Griffin's gone to Amanda's, but if he's still home, I don't want him answering the door. The stairs fly under my feet.

Evan stands on our welcome mat, fist raised for a third volley. "Hi," I say. "Sorry for the delay."

He takes in my wrinkled shirt, wet hair, red face. "We said eleven, did we not? After oboe?"

"I didn't hear a car pull up," I grumble, and step aside so he can enter.

"I travel on two wheels," he says, thumbing toward an old purple ten-speed leaning against the railing of our front porch.

The light fixture in our entryway is so low he has to duck. The dorky suede jacket, I notice, has been replaced with a blue striped crewneck—still not exactly stylish, but the color makes his eyes pop.

"Who was—" Someone nearly plows Evan over. My father. "Oh, hello!" He looks between Evan and me, confused by this young male stranger in his house. "I was just seeing who was at the door."

"Dad," I scramble, "this is Evan. He's helping me with that history . . . thing."

My father's grin hangs at an odd angle, as if he wants to ask questions but thinks better of it. An awkward moment passes. He continues to look between us. "All righty!" he crows finally. "Well, I'm off to the salt mines. Pneumatic retinopexy at noon."

I'm confused as he leans over to give me a peck on the cheek, something he never does. *O-kay.* "Is Griffin gone?" I ask hopefully.

"Indeedio!" *Indeedio?* "Nice to meet you . . ."

"Evan," Evan supplies.

"Helping with the . . ."

Evan looks to me. "The history thing," I answer, and pull him toward the stairs to my room.

"Door open!" my father calls after us, and I realize why he is suddenly acting like a 1950s sitcom dad: there is a boy in his house headed for his daughter's room, a boy he thinks I might make out with. I'm glad Evan's behind me, because my cheeks are suddenly bright red.

"*Bye*, Dad!"

Need I remind him that, even *if* I found Evan Hermann attractive—in a pale, frumpish, future-documentary-film-maker sort of way—I have a boyfriend? A boyfriend of two and a half years. A boyfriend who is funny and nice to be around and cute. A boyfriend who is Ryan Hart.

When Evan and I reach my room, I turn to try to explain, but he cuts me off. "Your dad's an ophthalmologist?"

"Umm."

His gaze slides over every surface of my room. I follow it to see what he sees: the Moleskin notebook on the nightstand; the photo collages Katie's made for my birthday every year, which my eyes intentionally skim over; the tangled duvet on my bed; the bra on the floor, which I surreptitiously kick under the bed. Evan is reading me like one of the journals.

"Retinopexy," he explains, "as in 'retina.' Your dad must be an eye doctor."

"Wow, Sherlock. Yes, he's an eye surgeon."

"Interesting. And your mom?"

His eyes pore over my life, and it's making me uneasy. Maybe inviting him here has been a mistake. "Real estate," I reply. "Why, are you in the market?" I'll distract him with humor.

"No," he says brightly, "just curious." Then he sees the trunk. His expression grows intent. "That's the rest of them?"

Two strides and he's across the room. As I watch him drop eagerly before the trunk, some of my impatience evaporates. It's exciting to watch someone else literally drawn to the diaries as much as I am.

Gingerly, he lifts the lid. "There are more of them than I thought," he murmurs, with what I think is a kind of reverence. "May I?"

Nodding eagerly, I kneel next to him as he selects a tan leather diary, turning it over and over in his hands, inspecting it, before thumbing the pages. They flutter like wings.

I'm dying to tell Evan what I discovered at the library. When I do, his eyebrows arch with piqued curiosity. But when I tell him about the article and the two missing bodies, all I get is "Oh. Yes."

"You knew?" I say.

"Well, the missing remains were part of the reason I came

to my hypothesis." Maybe he sees me deflate, because he adds quickly, "But it's great that you're researching—we'll need to corroborate the diaries with accounts of Anastasia's life."

"Right," I say flatly, feeling somehow like I've just been relegated to towel boy.

The journals are heaped in the trunk in no apparent order. Our first task, then, is to organize them by date—when we can find one; not all entries are dated. Some journals are only half full. A couple seem to end mid-sentence. When we're done, five neat stacks of books radiate in a semicircle around us. Thirty-two diaries in all. A life on paper.

The last journal we'd read was dated March 1917, around the time Tsar Nicholas abdicated the throne (he'd had to, Evan explains, as strikes and riots filled the streets, with some soldiers even joining in and the rest away fighting World War I). Russia's parliament, the Duma, had created a provisional government (it would fall soon enough to the Bolsheviks), and the entire family was placed under house arrest in the Alexander Palace at Tsarskoe Selo, "the Tsar's Village," south of St. Petersburg.

We agree to find the diary that follows. "This one," I say, waving a black leather journal with a simple gold border, when I find it. The date at the top of the first page reads March 30, 1917.

I hand it to Evan, and he reads.

Today stayed inside to play cards with Alexei. Poor monkey's not feeling well. Barely allowed to do anything these days. So sad, packed away like a crystal figurine.

I entertain him by making up stories about the guards, especially one with a pointy nose and large gray teeth who's prone to twitching. In my stories, he's a rat. This makes Alexei laugh.

Mama has one of her headaches and is resting. Papa went to the kitchen garden to chop wood. He says he must have split enough by now to heat the entire Winter Palace! But I suspect he enjoys something to occupy him. Earlier, he walked with T and O. It's not fair, I told Mama, that he always takes the Big Pair. She scolded me and said Papa loves us all, as God loves all His children.

This afternoon there was a funeral for "victims of the revolution." In our very own park! Through the windows, heard strains of the "Funeral March." I asked Mama if they would say prayers for the dead. Somberly, she replied that she did not know. I hate the revolutionaries, I told her. "We must not blame the people or the soldiers" was her answer. Whom must we blame, then? I asked. Can the people not raise their voices instead of guns? Already Papa has given them a Duma! She told me to eat my supper.

Of course I feel sorrow for the men who lost their lives, but are we to be blamed for ruin which they brought upon themselves? Papa has only ever wanted peace and prosperity for Russia's people.

It is not real. I refuse to believe it and shall pretend it is *happening to a different girl until it is over.*

May God keep you,

Anastasia

31.3.1917

Breakfast in the playroom today. Alexei's arm hurts him. It's swollen as a tree trunk, poor monkey.

In the past we'd have had one last ski on the hill, but it's no longer allowed. Pooh. Instead we will spend the day inside.

I am embroidering a kettle holder for Papa. It has a bright blue border and a happy kettle singing on the stove. Mama says he will like it. M is playing piano now (poorly) while T and O are reading. How they can read in that racket, I don't know, but at least the noise is welcome. Forty-six servants left today. Quiet without them.

God keep you,

Your Little Anastasia

1.4.1917

Breakfast again in the playroom, and English with Mr. Gibbes. I amused us all with impersonations, especially of that awful old governess, Sofia Ivanova, who spread rumors about Mama. Getting quite good at her. T says it's not kind to mimic others, but she laughs hardest of all.

Reading after tea. Papa says he will go later to clear ice from the bridge. Perhaps I will go with him. Sunshine on our faces will do us good.

> *Faithfully yours,*
> *Anastasia*

2.4.1917

Slept well. At eleven, Mass. Dreadfully long. Rear went numb on the pew, and Maria pinched me when I shifted to regain feeling—the little swine! Biffed her one as soon as we were out of the chapel.

Lunch boring but Papa surprised us with sweets in colored paper, like old times.

In a hurry, as Mama is coming soon for bedtime prayers. Until tomorrow.

> *Yours,*
> *A*

"The little swine." We laugh at this. It reminds me of a time when Griffin and I used to tease rather than torture each other. In fact, there's plenty I can relate to in Anastasia's diary; hers are the complaints of a lot of fifteen-year-old girls: too much school, annoying siblings, boredom.

7.4.1917

Sorry not writing past few days. Terrible sick. In bed three days. M too. Let's hope not measles or we'll have to shave our heads again. Have Jemmy to keep me company. Woke from a long nap to his wet little nose. Recovering.

Yours,

A

10.4.1917

Today, walking past Papa's study, heard urgent whispers. I know I am not supposed to but couldn't help myself and paused at the door. Mama asked where they will send us. Papa said there's still a chance that cousin George will have us in England. Or perhaps they'll take us to Sweden or Denmark. "Or Crimea," he said, "if we're lucky. Mother's already there."

"Yes," Mama replied, "how convenient for her."

Told Maria what I'd heard. "Well, you've always wanted to see the world!" she said. My sister can find the bright side of midnight.

After dinner, confessions in Mama's room. Suppose I shall have to confess to eavesdropping.

God keep you,

A

13.4.1917

M and I put on a little play today as we used to do at Spala. Spied even a guard laughing! In the evening, Bezique and reading. Tatiana is reading aloud The Count of Monte Cristo.

"What's Bezique?" I interrupt him, and for the first time, Evan doesn't have an answer. I find this mildly satisfying as we look it up: a French card game. A website details the rules. "Sounds complicated," I say after reading them.

"Nah." Evan sits in the rolling chair at my desk. With one foot propped on opposite knee, he forms a lanky, broken figure four. "Just a melding game."

I sit on the floor, leaning against my bed. "You play cards?"

"Mostly poker. And Magic."

"You do magic tricks?" The cringeworthy image of Evan wearing a top hat and cape dances before me.

"No, Magic: The Gathering. It's a world-building fantasy game of strategy."

"Like Dungeons and Dragons?" It's hard not to sound like I'm judging him, because I am.

He scoffs. "Way cooler. Similar motifs, but Magic is a competitive deck-building game, whereas D and D is a tabletop RPG."

I'm lost.

"These days, though, I'm more into poker and the occasional game of bridge." If he heard my judgment a moment ago, he clearly doesn't care. "Sonya's teaching me."

Sonya? A girl's name.

"That's my grandmother," he adds.

"Oh. Cool." *So, he plays bridge with his grandma.*

He holds the diary aloft. "Keep reading?"

"Yeah, but . . . there's something I've been wondering about." The thought's been bothering me as Evan reads, but I'm not sure how to phrase it. I try. "They're in captivity now?" I clarify.

Evan's brows knit together. "Yes, I'm sorry, I thought that was obvious; they're under house arrest at Tsarskoe Selo."

"Yeah, I know that. It's just that . . ." His eyes are really blue. "It's just that it doesn't sound so bad to me." I say it quickly, in case I've come off as a heartless jerk. "I mean, I know they're being watched, but they live in a freaking palace! When you said house arrest, I pictured them fighting rats for stale bread crumbs, not tutors and embroidery and card games. They seem nervous and bored, but . . . happy."

I'm glad my aunt wasn't in misery, but it's not the story I'd imagined in my head.

Evan considers this for a moment. "'Pure and complete sorrow is as impossible as pure and complete joy,' I suppose . . . Tolstoy." He's like one of those quote-of-the-day calendars my dad has in his waiting room.

He swivels in the chair and plants two faded Converse on the ground. When he leans forward, forearms on thighs, his gaze suddenly levels me. "Maybe it's not bad yet, but remember what happens to them."

The words hang in the air like the blade of a guillotine, and I'm reminded that, for all the plays and afternoon teas, it's a tragedy we're reading. Even if Anastasia did survive, her family—Tatiana, Olga, Maria, Alexei, Nicholas, Alexandra—were doomed, destined to lie in an unmarked grave for sixty years.

"You're right," I say sheepishly.

He looks at me, suddenly mock-serious. "Well, on behalf of the Romanovs, I accept your apology." He clears his throat and resumes.

19.4.2017

Mr. Gibbes tells us there was a parade in the streets yesterday—the first of May in other countries, Workers' Day. But what was the parade for? I asked him. For Marxists, he said. They sang songs and carried banners calling for the proletariat to rise up. Rise up against us.

Mama and Papa are no longer allowed to speak at meals unless an officer is present. They treat us like prisoners. I suppose we are prisoners.

God keep you,

A

23.4.1917

French in the afternoon with M. Gilliard. Weather improved greatly. Sun the last two days, but a storm in the distance—the smell of rain. Mama fears it's a sign.

Yours,

A

8.5.1917

To think this time last year we were preparing to head for the skerries. If we'd known then what our lives hold now, would that time have seemed more sweet? Hardly possible.

A bluebell day working in the garden. Afterward a frigid swim in the pond—perhaps not so different from Finland after all! Will tell myself this.

To chapel now.

Faithfully,

Your Anastasia

23.5.1917

A walk with Maria and Mama. Shouted at by guards for wandering too close to the fence. One called Mama a word I won't repeat. She says not to tell Papa. Lessons in the afternoon. Vespers, then dinner and bed.

Yours,

A

25.5.1917

Work today in the kitchen garden. Lessons with Mr. Gibbes and M. Gilliard. Tea together in the library. Bezique in the evening.

Yours,

A

26.5.1917

Same as yesterday.

27.5.1917

Same.

1.6.1917

Shall we ever be allowed out again? Rain, rain, rain. I should like to never play Bezique again.

2.6.1917

Bored!

5.6.1917

Today I am sixteen years old.
Yours,
Anastasia

Her birthday. This one in particular makes me sad.

8.6.1917

This morning walked in the park with Papa and O. Paused by the pond for Papa to show us the work he's been doing, clearing branches from last week's storm. Seeing us, a crowd gathered at the fence. "There they are!" they cried.

They wanted a better look at us, the animals in the zoo.

A woman, old and dirty, in a ratty brown kerchief, pressed her doughy face to the fence. "Murderer!" she screamed.

Blood ran hot in my veins. "Ignore them," Papa said, but I could not. "Liars!" I shouted, and thrust out my tongue. The woman again pressed her face to the bars and spat, phlegm quivering in the air.

It was rage that propelled me forward, but Olga held me back. "Nastya!" she hissed. "You do not help." The woman shook her fist, mumbling curses. Tears pricked at my eyes. A chant had begun: "Hang them."

"Come," Papa said. It's a wonder their jeers do not affect him. He simply bowed his head and turned toward the palace, hands clasped behind his back.

"How can you?" I asked Olga later. "How can you let them say such things about Papa, about us?" She spoke with seriousness. "Nastya, you've been a child too long. Now you must be a princess." But I'm not a princess, I told her, not anymore. "Which is why you must be one now more than ever," she said. And if I don't feel like one? I asked. She turned on me. "Do you think any of us do?" Her voice was more bitter than old tea. "Fake it."

Yours,

A

"You okay?" Evan asks.

I realize I haven't heard the last few entries he's been reading. Olga's words have been running on a track through my mind: *Fake it.* "Huh?"

"You have . . . a face," he says.

"I have a face?"

"Like, an expression . . . on your face." He waves his hand in front of his head.

"Oh." Anastasia's world was coming apart at the seams, and the only thread she had to keep it together was to act as if nothing had changed at all. "What kind of expression?"

"Just, like . . . never mind." He's grown exasperated and sighs loudly. "What does it take to get a glass of water around here?"

Downstairs, we make peanut butter and jelly sandwiches that we take on paper towels to the porch. Evan hunches on the top step, sandwich balanced on his knees, while I take the porch swing no one ever uses anymore.

The day has turned "bluebell," as Anastasia might have said. Not a cloud in the sky.

Methodically, Evan tears the crusts from his bread and piles them on the paper towel at his side. He munches along the edges of the sandwich the way a kid might. "So, Jess—short for Jessica, I'm assuming—tell me about yourself."

"Short for nothing," I say, covering a mouth full of peanut butter.

"How does one get 'Jess' from 'Nothing'?"

"*Har,*" I say, but I give him a begrudging smile. "What do you want to know?" The porch swing rocks gently.

"Well, your dad's an eye surgeon, your mom's a real-estate mogul, your brother's a jock—"

"How do you know that?"

"The scent of athlete's foot emanating from his bedroom."

"Observant."

"Always. And you are . . ." he continues.

"I am what?"

"You are a 'riddle wrapped in a mystery inside an enigma,'" Evan says. He isn't giving up. "'But perhaps there is a key.'"

"Poetic."

"Winston Churchill, on Russia, 1939."

I tear at my own peanut butter sandwich. If there's a key to my riddle, I might have accidentally lost it. "I don't know. Maybe I'm the black sheep," I venture.

He looks dubious. "How so?"

I sigh. "Maybe black sheep in white sheep's clothing?" Before he can correct me, I add, "I know the saying is 'a wolf in sheep's clothing,' but that doesn't really work in this case."

He studies me. "You mean you feel different on the inside but appear normal on the outside?"

I shift uncomfortably. "Forget it; it was a bad metaphor. Anyway, I'm the only Morgan who might spend her summer translating a trunk full of musty, old Russian diaries."

"To your credit." He doffs an imaginary hat. "And what led you to seek my services?"

Down the street, a car turns onto our block, and my eyes flick nervously in its direction, but it's no one I know. In answer to Evan's comment, I shrug. "I felt like there was a story in the diaries. I like stories. . . . Of course, I never thought it would be—"

"—a story of astronomical historical importance?"

I laugh. "Yeah, that."

Evan cocks his head. His eyelashes cast spidery shadows across his cheeks. "You like stories; does that mean you're a writer?"

I examine the last of the PB&J in my lap. "I guess."

"You guess a lot."

"I am." To say it confidently sends a shiver up my spine. *You're a writer, too.*

"Well, what do you write?"

"Mostly fiction."

"Could I read something you wrote?"

"No! I just met you."

"Whoa, whoa, whoa." He laughs. "I asked to read your writing, not stick my tongue down your throat."

"*Excuse* me?"

"What?"

"First of all, I have a boyfriend. . . ."

"Well, of course you do."

"What does that mean?" For a translator, he's awfully hard to make sense of.

"It means it adds up. Of course you have a boyfriend. You're attractive, intelligent, interesting . . ." He counts on his fingers, as if these are data points. "A little disagreeable at times, but overall fairly personable."

"You're the one who's been disagreeable!" I've crumpled my paper towel into a ball in my fist.

"In any event, a boyfriend would be the logical assumption. Also, there was a photo in your room." The one by my bed, of Ryan and me last summer.

I eye him. "You're kind of blunt, you know that?"

"It's blunt of you to say so." He grins rakishly. "I am sorry if I offended you, though."

"Don't worry, I'm hard to offend."

"I wouldn't say that."

The paper ball I lob narrowly misses his head before skittering off into the grass.

"See?" he replies.

His teasing has caught me off guard. The Evan Hermann I first met was icy and suspicious. Certainly, I've felt a thaw since our first meeting at Brewbakers, but the chatterbox across from me is unexpected.

"And what about you," I ask. His turn for the spotlight. "A girlfriend?"

"I don't have time for a girlfriend." I'm not 100 percent surprised.

"And why Russian?"

He smiles. "I'm glad you asked. The answer is because Russian"—he rolls the *R* like a Bond villain—"is brutally honest."

"A language has a personality?"

He feigns shock. "Of course!" And excitedly catalogues the characters of various foreign languages: German is exacting. Italian is extravagant. French is romantic. Chinese is efficient. And Russian is honest.

"You've read Tolstoy?" he says.

"I'm one fourteen-thousandth of the way through *War and Peace*—I've read the title."

"Well, you should," he says. "And *The Death of Ivan Ilyich*, and *Anna Karenina* . . . 'Happy families are all alike; every unhappy family is unhappy in its own way.'"

I wince. "Brutal."

"Brutally true. Also," he adds, "I'm Russian. Well, half Russian."

"Really? 'Hermann' doesn't sound Russian."

"Because it isn't; it's German. Hermann was my father's name."

Was. He reads the question on my face. "He died," he explains.

And I'm the jerk who brought it up. "I'm so sorry."

But Evan brushes a crumb from his leg. "Thank you for the condolences, truly, but to be honest, I was four, so I don't remember him much."

"So, your mom," I say, trying to change the subject, "she's the Russian one, then?"

"My grandmother." He replies with an odd briskness.

"Sonya," I say.

"Yes."

How have we been suddenly reduced to single-word answers? "I guess I don't even know where you grew up," I try. Evan goes to Keene State, but for all I know he was born in Saskatchewan.

"Here," he says.

"Here, as in Keene?" I think back to all the hallways I've walked, all the school bus rides I've taken; never once does Evan Hermann's face cross my memory.

He moved to Keene in fourth grade, he explains, but transferred in sixth to a small private school a few towns over that's known for taking rich screwups and disadvantaged geniuses; my guess is he was the latter. Keene State is a good school but hardly Ivy League. From what I've seen, Evan could have gotten into any college he wanted, even gotten a scholarship, so why has he chosen to stay here?

"It's just the two of us now," he says.

"You and your mom?"

When his jaw tightens, a vein jumps at his temple. "Shall we read more?" His voice constricts around the words. He stands.

I'm confused. Just a moment ago, we were joking around. Now *that* Evan is gone, and the one from the first day at the coffee shop is back. I've ruined something without knowing I was doing it.

"We shall," I say, but there's less fun in it now.

12

14.6.17

We are mice in a snake pit. Soldiers, now, everywhere we turn. Rough types wearing silly pointed caps with sewn-on stars. Yesterday there were gunshots outside the palace. Mama said they were shooting the goats that roam the park.

When they first arrived, the guards saluted Papa. Now they are cold and rude, refusing to look him in the eye or shake his hand. Papa is polite, but in private even he admits these men are slovenly and ill-mannered.

These are not the soldiers we once knew, not the sentries who patrolled the palace and parks, who'd happily pause their rounds to pluck a pear for Alexei; not the stately guards in shiny boots and handsome red pants who lined the streets on parade days, or the pink-cheeked sailors who manned the yacht and flirted with Olga and Tatiana. These men have rotten mouths and leering eyes.

The soldiers who convalesced within the Tsarskoe hospital were men of honor. "The Sisters Romanov," they called us. Of course, Maria and I were too young to be real nurses—we envied Olga and Tatiana their important red crosses—but we did our best to comfort these heroes and ease their pain. Nearly every day we visited the infirmary. Checkers was the soldiers' favorite game, or chess. Sometimes we'd read to them. For those who'd lost fingers or hands, we penned letters to families and loved ones. We plumped pillows and rolled bandages and darned socks. Back in my warm bed, their sacrifice haunted me. Once I told Papa I wished for one speck of their bravery. He smiled. "You are brave in your own way, Nastya," he said. I try to be now, but it's not the same.

If I am to be honest—and where can one be so, if not in her own thoughts?—then there is one soldier in particular who occupies my memories of those days. Never did I speak his name outside the hospital, afraid my sisters might tease me or, worse, tell Mama. Even from you, dear diary, I have kept this secret.

His name was Ilya Ivanovich. He was eighteen, four years older than me. Still young for a blood-soaked battlefield. Born in a copper mining village outside Yekaterinburg, he'd been wounded near Lutsk. Shrapnel mangled his left leg.

He was tall—feet nearly hanging off the cot!—and thin, though I suspect this had more to do with years of malnutrition. Set wide within a narrow face, his eyes were small, but when he smiled, how they sparkled! As if illuminated from within. Brown with a dot of green. My favorite feature, however, was his nose, long and straight with a tiny but distinct dimple at its tip. Unlike any nose I'd ever seen. I had the strangest urge to lightly place the tip of my pinkie on it—a silly thing!

The first words we exchanged are still fresh in my mind. Maria and I had arrived at the infirmary after breakfast. As usual, we drifted among the beds, acknowledging each soldier and thanking him for his sacrifice. I reached Ilya's bed. "Mother Russia thanks you for your service," I said, as I'd been taught.

"You speak for Mother Russia?" the boy answered. My eyes fell on his. Deep wells of sorrow in them, but a challenge in his voice.

At the time, I was stunned by this impertinence. I was a grand duchess of Russia, and yet he spoke to me as an equal. It thrilled me terribly. I must have flushed bright red because immediately he apologized for the familiarity.

This was the first time I visited with Ilya. He asked if I might come back to help him write letters; though his hands were unharmed, his head often ached and his vision was blurred. I returned the next day, and we talked, hours disappearing like minutes, until Maria came to fetch me.

Ilya's candor shocked and delighted me. Never had I been

spoken to in such an open way. He told me of the conditions in his village and others like it, about his father working twelve hours a day underground in the dark, risking rockfalls and explosions, and still unable to feed his family. At times they had only a single loaf of bread and a pot of soup to last a week. The year before Ilya and his brother enlisted, their younger sister died of smallpox. "They have everything," he said of those who owned the mine. "We have nothing."

In whispers, Ilya spoke of unrest, at home and later in the barracks. "The people are tired. Europe leaves us behind, and still, Russia refuses to modernize."

"You mean the tsar refuses."

He did not shrink from my provocation. "And the nobility, yes."

Fire crept from my belly into my veins. It was my papa he spoke of.

"There is no progress without change," Ilya said.

"It is God's ordained order, not my father's," I reminded him.

"We are in a new century." His kind, unflinching face held mine. "Not everyone believes in the absolute rule of a sovereign."

These were dangerous words. I wanted to slap him, to make Ilya pull them back into his mouth and eat them. He had no idea how hard Papa worked to bring stability and literacy to the people, whom he loved.

Ilya saw the color rise to my face. "I support the tsar, Anastasia Nikolaevna," he said quickly, placing a hand on mine. "It's not personal."

My name from his lips, it was more intimate than if he'd seen me undressed. The warmth of his hand on mine . . .

I felt my heart might burst.

But when you *are* the monarchy, it is indeed personal. This Ilya would never understand, never could understand. We do not choose our fates. I pulled my hand from his. "Grand Duchess," I corrected him.

He bowed his head. "Forgive me, Grand Duchess."

———

Forgive me, dear, as I have just thrown you against a wall. Lucky, as you are paper and leather, you cannot break.

But, oh, if I could go back! If I could hold Ilya's hand more tightly instead of casting it off out of pride. If I could tell Papa what Ilya had told me, about the suffering, the unrest . . . but there's no use in such thoughts.

At our next visit, Ilya didn't speak about politics. Instead, we talked of books. My friend had learned to read in the army. His favorite novelist was Tolstoy. I told him I'd read Count Tolstoy but much preferred the French and English novels M. Gilliard and Mr. Gibbes had us read. We discussed the role of the author in society. He believed a writer's responsibility was truth; I believed it was beauty.

When I was with Ilya, I felt the quickening of a part of my soul I hadn't known existed. He treated me not as a silly child or a princess but as an equal. His challenges thrilled me, and I felt he found in me depths that no other person, not even Mama or Papa or Father Grigori, had considered before.

"It is ironic," he said one day. His corner of the ward was quiet. "Since I was a boy, I heard stories of you, prayed for you, spoke your name. For years, your picture hung in our home."

He pointed to an official imperial portrait on the wall opposite his bed. I blushed and remembered the day the photograph was taken, remembered Alexei was in pain and Mama insisted Maria and I wear our pearls and bows, though I put up a great fight. We were only children in the photograph, and I was embarrassed to think Ilya thought of me this way.

"It's as if everywhere I turned, you were there," he continued, "and yet, it's only now that I really see you.

"You look sad," he said. "Have I made you sad?"

"No," I assured him, and found his hand beneath the crisp white sheet.

"It's what we all want, is it not," he said, eyes sparkling, "to be seen?"

"And what do you see?" I asked. "A supposed princess with ragged nails and a lack of social graces?"

"I see a girl who thinks and feels deeply. Who is more than she believes she is allowed to be."

Under the sheet, his fingers wove through mine.

And then the day came when Ilya was gone.

Like any other morning, I came to the infirmary. I can't say why, but my heart beat faster that day, like a bird in my chest. I had brought books from our library: *Wuthering Heights* and *Jane Eyre* and an old exercise book from our classroom. Ilya wished to learn English while he convalesced. But when I arrived at his bed, it was empty, the sheet pulled tight where the mountain range of his body had once been.

I was distraught. Had his health taken a turn? Had he been released? Sent back to the front? For days, food lost its taste, so unlike me that even Papa noticed, but my pride got the best of me, as well as my fear of a scolding—or worse, teasing—if my family discovered my feelings for Ilya. I could not bring myself to ask the head nurse where Ilya had gone, so I bore my pain silently. There was enough real suffering in that hospital already.

And now, of course, we are here. Ilya is gone, and I am a prisoner in my own home.

There are times I swear I hear his voice or glimpse the seashell of his ear pass around a corner. I turn and rush after him only to find another soldier, a Soviet soldier who wishes me imprisoned, or worse. I wonder, did Ilya join the revolt? Is that his grave in our park, his funeral march whose strains reached my ears? "I support the tsar," he told me, but there are many whose suffering has been twisted by others.

Wherever he is, my Ilya, I wish him well.
Now I have told you, and I am not sure if I feel better.
Yours,
Anastasia

Until her name passes Evan's lips, I don't realize I've been holding my breath. Even ninety years later, Anastasia's longing hangs in the air, like perfume after its wearer has left the room. There's a part of me that feels wrong for reading Anna's private grief. It feels a lot like trespassing. But that's why she left these diaries in a trunk in her attic, isn't it? She knew one day they would be found. And as Ilya said, it's what we all want: finally, to be seen.

Is it what I want? Katie's words on the playground come back to me: *You're not yourself when you're around him.* I still haven't heard from her, and this annoys me for so many reasons, but one of them is the fact that I desperately want to tell her about my aunt's story.

I sweep the frustration aside and clear my throat. "It's so sad," I say, of Anastasia's words. "Couldn't she have found him? Her father was the tsar—at least he still was then."

"She was royalty at a precarious time for the monarchy. A common soldier wouldn't do. If she had married, her husband would have been chosen for political reasons."

A scarf lies on the floor beside me, a gift from Katie's last trip to China. "But that's stupid," I say, wrapping the silk around my knuckles like a boxer preparing for a fight.

"That's a monarchy."

"It's unfair."

"Unfair, yes," Evan reasons, "but some people believe there are things more important than love."

"More important than love?"

"You don't believe there's such a thing?"

"No." I square my chin. "No, I don't."

"Peace, prosperity, geopolitical security?"

"Ilya was just as worthy as some stupid prince or duke. Worthier, even. He saw the girl, not the princess." I'm preparing for his infuriatingly reasonable response. "Maybe he wasn't the person everyone would have picked for her; he wasn't rich or educated or politically connected—"

"I agree."

"That's some patriarchal bull—wait, what?"

"I agree," Evan says matter-of-factly, lips twisted into a smile. "You thought I wouldn't."

"No," I huff. "You're just all . . . rational and logic-y. I didn't figure you for a romantic."

"'Logic-y.' What's that worth in Scrabble?"

A small stuffed whale Ryan once won at the fair becomes an easy missile. Evan ducks, throwing up his hands.

"Logical," I say.

"You know, nerds need love, too. 'Love is life.' Tolstoy."

My cheeks flame. "I never called you a nerd!"

"I never said *I* was in love. . . . And you were thinking it." A full-blown smirk dances on his face now as he opens the journal again to read. "June fifteenth, nineteen seventeen . . ." He pauses. "And, you know, if you throw one more thing at me, I'm going to have to quit because of workplace harassment."

I had told Evan that the Romanovs' house arrest didn't sound so bad, but as the entries creep toward August 1917, anxiety settles like dust over Anastasia's words. The move the empress had feared becomes reality. The provisional government orders the family away from Tsarskoe Selo.

We've been instructed to pack our things, Anastasia writes. Whatever does not go with them—clothes, toys, photographs, books, personal effects, and diaries—will be sent by steamship to England. If their cousin King George will not save their lives, at least he will save their belongings.

30.7.1917

How does one choose what to take when leaving her life behind? What is valuable then?

Some of our belongings have been confiscated; the new government says the property of the emperor is the property of the people. Most of our clothes will go to England, as well as the furniture, some books, and you, dear diaries. I pray we'll meet again, but Mama says we must focus on what is needed for the future rather than on the past.

They tell us we leave tomorrow, by train. Those in charge
will not reveal much, Papa says, but that we are headed for
Tobolsk.

I bid you adieu, dear diary, and surer travels than ours.
Wish me—and your successors—good luck. I believe we'll
need it.

God keep you until we meet again,

Anastasia

"Tobolsk," I say. "Where's that?"

Evan's face is once again grim.

"Siberia."

When Evan leaves to help his grandmother with an errand, I am
determined to find historical sources that will confirm details
in the diaries. Through an internet search, I stumble on an article from the *New York Times*, March 1918. "Captivity Affects
Romanoff's Mind," reads the headline. An introduction to the
article says it draws from an intercepted letter written by the
tsarina to a friend and from a report by one of the Red guards
stationed with the family. It describes the family's residence in
Tobolsk: four small rooms and four large rooms, the largest only
five yards by three, "furnished in the simplest manner," with
no water, no electricity, no bathrooms, and heat from primi-
tive brick stoves. The ground floor is occupied by a company of
soldiers. "Where are the spacious reception rooms of Peterhof

and the Winter Palace, with their surcharged magnificence?" the article asks, almost wryly.

> The Princesses possess in all only four costumes, and are obliged to be contented with those. As regards their jewelry, they were forced to leave it all in Petrograd . . . There is little to say about [their] life. . . . Tatiana spends much time reading French literature, particularly novels, as do others in the family. Olga is much interested in housekeeping. . . . The Princesses can move freely about the town, without special superintendence, but, naturally, not without being followed step by step by the secret police, who perform their duty as discreetly as possible. On the contrary, the heir-apparent is closely guarded.

The article quotes the former tsar as observing, "My life has always been that of a prisoner." I wonder if this is how Anastasia felt also. Her words echo in my mind: *We do not choose our fates.* And Olga's: *Fake it.*

There's a part of the story I've avoided reading: accounts of the actual murders in Yekaterinberg. I know enough to know they will be grisly. The books from the library sit in a tower on my desk. From the bottom, I grab one called *The Romanovs: The Final Chapter*. A chilling title. Only it wasn't, I think to myself, every Romanov's final chapter.

For the next hour, I read gruesome details about a twelve-man firing squad shooting men, women, and children at point-blank range. I read about bullets ricocheting off walls and boots stomping heads and limbs, about bayonets and rifle butts disfiguring faces beyond identification, about moaning and smoke and "rivers and pools of blood" amid chaos. It is stomach-churning and terrible, and it is not fiction. Steeling myself, I search the internet for photos of the "House of Special Purpose," what the Soviets called the Ipatiev House, the building in Yekaterinberg where the murders occurred. One comes up, black and white, of the basement where the family and their servants were killed. Striped wallpaper is pierced by bullets; plaster has crumbled from the wall in front of which the family stood. The room is smaller than I imagined.

After the massacre, the bodies were loaded onto trucks and driven into the surrounding forest. A party of drunk local workers in peasant carts, supporters of the new Bolshevik government who happened to meet the assassination party on the road, helped the soldiers strip, douse with acid, and attempt to burn the bodies before throwing them down an abandoned mine shaft, followed by hand grenades. Details of the murders were recorded in two major accounts: one by the Soviet executioner himself, Yakov Yurovsky, published decades later; and another by investigator Nikolai Sokolov published in 1924. Sokolov was hired by the White Army, supporters of the tsar, after it retook Yekaterinburg—tragically, just a week after the murders—to determine the fate of the family. He used forensic evidence and local testimonies.

Reportedly, one of the peasants who met the soldiers in the woods, disappointed that he didn't get to kill the tsar himself, joked, "Why didn't you bring them alive?"

He wasn't aware that at least one of the Romanovs possibly was.

13

August 21, 2007

"Sleeping Beauty awakes."

My mother stands in the middle of the kitchen, grasping one sneakered foot behind her. Training for a marathon requires limbered quads.

"Morning," I croak, and empty the last lukewarm dregs of a pot of coffee into a mug. Usually, I avoid the stuff, which my mom makes strong enough to fuel a rocket, but this morning, I need it. Last night was another late one, spent outlining my history paper and then replaying in my mind the fight with Katie, blow by blow. It's been three days since I've heard from her. Typically, she'd have texted by now—some irrelevant but endearing olive branch, like a video of a cat playing piano. Instead, last night I got a text from Tyler: *Can u and k8e make up already?* I wondered what she'd told him. That she feels sorry? Or that I'm the one who's supposed to be apologizing?

"Do I need to do laundry?" my mom asks. She's eyeing what I'm wearing: a T-shirt Katie and Tyler gave me last year with the words *It's Lit* over an illustration of the Brontë sisters, a deep respect for puns being a cornerstone of our friendship.

"No," I answer my mom, "I just hadn't worn this in a while."

"Hmm." She switches feet. "Would you like some more sundresses? They look so good on you." She ruffles my hair as I shuffle past.

At the table, my brother's hunched protectively, like a prison inmate, over a bowl of Cheerios. Despite his name-calling the other night, reading Anastasia's diaries, I'm feeling a sudden spot of tenderness toward him, *the little swine*. I give him an eye roll, an attempt at solidarity, but he slurps milk from his spoon and sneers, "Where'd you get the shirt, Nerd Outfitters?" *Poof.* Tenderness gone.

"Later," Griffin says, chair squawking as he stands. "I'm going to Amanda's."

"When will you be home?" Mom asks, but he's halfway out the door. "Good choices!" she calls after him, and I can see him bristle, but I can also see that he's left his cereal bowl on the table. Sighing, Mom rinses it and puts it in the dishwasher. I grit my teeth. If I left my dishes on the table, I'd hear about it.

She leans against the counter. "How's Ryan? Lisa said he's been training a lot."

"Yeah, his coach has really been on him. Are there any Cheerios left?"

Mom shakes an almost-empty box—not even the real Cheerios but the organic ones that taste like cardboard—and hands it over the counter. "She said you left your gray sweatshirt there."

Honestly, I'm surprised Mrs. Hart and my mom haven't installed a dedicated hotline for their discussions of Ryan's and my relationship.

Three spoonfuls of Os drop into the bowl, followed by a mountain of oat dust. "I don't have a gray sweatshirt," I say. "It must be Izzy's." Ryan's sister. Not a skier like her older brother, she's a freshman at Keene High.

Mom picks up a sponge to scrub at an invisible spot on the counter. "Why don't you invite him for dinner before he goes back to school? Or we could have a cookout, invite all your friends. An end-of-summer party!"

She says this with such excitement you'd think end-of-summer summer parties are something I'm in the business of throwing.

I cringe. "Yeah, maybe."

"Great. Talk to Ryan. We'll find a date." She kisses the top of my head and sniffs. "New shampoo?"

"Nope. Same one you've been buying me for years."

She smiles. "Okay, I'll be out today. I have a showing this afternoon and a board meeting at six. You and Griff good for dinner?"

"Yep." I'll scrounge for snacks.

"Oh, and you've picked your outfit for the family photo? Pastels, we decided."

"We" decided no such thing, and there's no use in me choosing an outfit anyway, as she'll change her mind three times before the shoot.

"The white washed us out last year." She squints. "Think blue."

"Bye, Mom."

We've known each other for less than a week, but some of Evan's quirks are already familiar to me. Tugging his hair through his fingers only means he's thinking, but he's doing it so ferociously now on our doorstep that I worry he might pull some out.

"You okay?" I hate that question myself, since it's most often asked when I just want to be left alone with my thoughts, but something is clearly bothering Evan.

"There's a piece of this puzzle I can't make fit," he says, barreling through the door without a hello. He smells like a waterfall, the squeaky freshness so different from the punch of Ryan's Right Guard that I find myself inhaling maybe more deeply than is normal.

"Your aunt didn't tell *anyone* she was Anastasia?" he continues. "No one in your family knew?"

"Good morning."

"Oh. Yeah. Good morning."

"I've asked my parents," I answer his question. "I mean, in a roundabout way."

He frowns. "Why not ask them straight out?"

"'Mom, Dad'"—I affect an air of casual curiosity—"'any chance Aunt Anna was actually Anastasia Romanov—you know, the Russian princess supposedly murdered in 1917? Also, Queen Elizabeth—secretly my grandmother?' They'd pack me off to a loony bin."

This is an exaggeration, but I don't know how to tell Evan that it's also more complicated than that. That every part of my life is smudged with someone else's fingerprints—my parents', my teachers', my friends'. Writing has been the only thing ever wholly and completely, crystal-clear mine. And now the diaries. I'm not ready to share them yet.

He concedes. "I see your point. Maybe once we have more evidence . . . But what about her other family—husband, in-laws, nieces, nephews?"

"Dead, dead, and you're looking at her. Her husband died in the sixties, and she didn't have kids. My family was all she had; that's why my dad took care of her. I can ask my uncle, but I get the feeling he didn't pay much attention." Uncle Dale's an airline pilot and always traveling. The reason we had Aunt Anna to our house every Thanksgiving and Christmas was because he and Aunt Mae were in Tahiti or Mexico or Barbados.

"Trust me," I say, "I wish we had more to go on, but I was reading last night, and the facts do line up. She was the right age. And the details about the clothes and the jewelry . . . I found an article—"

"Circumstantial," Evan cuts me off. "We need witnesses." He paces in our tiny entryway. "If your aunt was Anastasia Romanov, she had to have told *someone*."

"Maybe she didn't. Think about it: if the Bolsheviks knew a Romanov had survived, someone their enemies could rally around, they would have been looking for her. She must have been terrified."

Evan looks skeptical.

"Something *that* risky . . ." I press. "I'm not sure I would have told anyone either."

"But you would have kept a trunk full of diaries about it? *That's* risky."

"True," I admit, "but clearly, she hid them."

Evan stops his pacing and turns to face me. "You could live a lie almost your entire life, pretending to be someone you're not?"

Something in the question makes me pause before answering, "Come on, we all keep secrets. This was just a really big one."

"We *don't* all keep secrets." His brow furrows, and his expression darkens. "Is there something you're not telling me, Jess?"

"No!" I assure him. He's misunderstood. "I'm not keeping anything from *you*. But, yeah, there are things I don't . . . tell the whole world." I shrug. "I mean, here I am sitting on one of the biggest historical finds of the twenty-first century, and I haven't told a soul!"

"Potentially," Evan says. "*Potentially* sitting on one of the biggest historical finds of the twenty-first century." But his frown has relaxed. He sighs. "We know she made it to America," he says, breezing past me toward the stairs. "Maybe she felt safer here, safe enough to tell someone who she really was."

On a Post-it note, Evan has printed the Russian words for "America" and "United States."

Америка.

Соединенные Штаты.

We scan journal after journal for them. As they've always been for me, the letters are still a blur of strokes and swoops, only they're starting to feel more personal, less like an alien script and more like a note left on the kitchen counter by someone you love. And then I see it.

Америка.

And again, a second time down the page. Америка. Back and forth, I skip between the page and Evan's Post-it, confirming each letter.

"America!" Evan startles as I spring from the floor, clutching the journal. It's the most ornate one thus far, with leather corners and covered in beautiful, intricately patterned paper. Even the edges of the pages are marbled with paint.

I thrust the journal into Evan's face, so close his eyes cross. Taking it from me, he squints down at the page.

"There." He points to a word beginning with a letter that

looks, to me, like an uppercase *H*. Our arms brush as I drop beside him on the carpet. "New York," he says excitedly. "And Chicago and . . ."

I smile. "Just read it."

1.4.1922

America bound—and just barely! Last night, turned in certain that the RMS Baltic would depart without me and that all of our scheming would be for naught. Then this morning, greeted Ashbourne in the lobby for breakfast. "Well, my dear," he said, and I knew from the satisfied smirk on his face that his contact had come through. "We got this by the skin of our teeth." Into my palm he pressed a crisp, folded piece of light blue paper. A passport. I began to open it. "Not here!" he hissed, and dragged me to the nearest ladies' room.

Do you know, my dear, that the name Anastasia means "resurrection"? Door barred, I laid my eyes upon my own rebirth:

My name is Anna Dolores Haswell. My birthday remains the same—my only request. "Lake Bluff, Illinois?" I asked, upon reading my place of birth.

"Illi-noy," Ashbourne corrected me.

"Illi-noy," I repeated.

"As good as any Yank." He smiled. "Your practice has paid off." So has the gift for impersonation that once so annoyed my nanny and tutors.

I'm told the small town north of Chicago is "distant enough, respectable enough, and unknown enough" in New York to offer believability without raising questions. When asked if he himself had ever visited, Ashbourne laughed. "No, my dear, why ever would I go to Lake Bluff, Illinois? That's precisely the point."

And "Haswell?" I asked.

"Well, 'Haase' won't do," he said, and sniffed. "They hate the Krauts."

I had one hour to slip into my new self.

The Baltic is larger than the yachts I've sailed on, even the Standardt. Once the world's largest, I'm told. At the dock, Ashbourne and I embraced. I dare say there were tears in his eyes when I offered him my handkerchief, the one he'd had embroidered with my initials—my real ones. "Well," he said, "I suppose I should take that." Removing the pocket square from his vest and tucking the handkerchief close to his heart, he smiled. "Here's where it shall remain." Emotion misted my own eyes. I will miss the old scamp.

Have just now made it to my stateroom. Will write again this evening. Now, I explore. I hear there is a first-class reading and writing room!

Next time I step off this ship, it will be in America.

Yours,

Anna Dolores Haswell

"Anna," I say.

Evan and I exchange glances.

"How long was the trip to New York?" I ask.

He scans ahead. "Looks like ten days."

On April 10, the hulking RMS *Baltic* sailed past Lady Liberty, up the Hudson River, and shuddered to a stop at the White Star Line pier. Into at least a dozen trunks and valises, Anastasia repacked her belongings. She would miss the man who'd outfitted her for a debut into New York society: *Sweet Ashbourne,* she wrote. *Thinking of him, wandering Crispin Court, smashnosed Georgie drooling and wheezing at his heel, gives my heart a twinge.*

After a nerve-racking exchange with an immigration officer, who against all likelihood had a cousin in Lake Bluff, Illinois, Anna Haswell alighted safely in New York City. My great-great-aunt had arrived in America.

From there, Anna made her way to the Waldorf Astoria, where a room had been secured in advance. In her coat pocket, she carried something far more valuable than the furs, silk, and jewels that the porters ferried to her fourteenth-floor suite: a letter of recommendation from Sir Cyril Ashbourne of Knightsbridge introducing Anna Dolores Haswell, beloved niece of a dear and longtime family friend, a "lovely girl unwise to New York City's ways but nevertheless refined in her morals and attitudes."

Unwritten but equally important, Anna possessed an invitation to dine at the house of Mrs. Caroline Schermerhorn Astor Wilson, a doyenne of the Upper East Side and apparent gatekeeper to Manhattan's highest society. "Carrie," Sir Ashbourne told her, owed him a favor.

Intrigued by Anna's mysterious benefactor, Evan and I summon Google and search Sir Cyril Ashbourne. We find no hits but a list of Barons Ashbourne, a wealthy banking family active in British politics. We make a note to look for him in earlier journals.

There is an extensive record, however, for Caroline Schermerhorn Astor Wilson. The socialite's Wikipedia entry identifies her as a prominent heiress of the time. We find links to an obituary, books, and even a *New York Times* article breathlessly detailing the most distinguished guests out of three hundred at her 1904 East Sixty-Fourth Street housewarming party. "Carrie" was the real deal.

"Corroboration?" I suggest.

"We know she existed," Evan allows.

As we continue reading, we still don't know how Anastasia made it from the bleak reaches of Russia to glittering, cosmopolitan New York City, but it does seem that her royal upbringing served her well. Within weeks, the diaries show Miss Anna Haswell of Lake Bluff, Illinois, hobnobbing with the crème de la crème of Manhattan.

Quickly, the entries become a dizzying recital of social engagements: tea at the Plaza with Ailsa Mellon; a charity dance at the Van Cortlandts' on Fifth Avenue; boating on the lake in Central Park; drives to the North Shore in a friend's new roadster; luncheons at the Colony Club; a costume gala for the New York Public Library. It's a nonstop merry-go-round of parties.

Still, despite Anna's impressive ability to infiltrate America's upper crust, there are times she seems disoriented by the sleek, modern city and by her new friends' "more relaxed social mores." Her sheltered childhood had not prepared Anastasia for Jazz Age New York.

13.05.1922

Tea today at the Palm Court, arranged by Mrs. Wilson, for an introduction to her niece. Not the brightest star in the sky but sweet.

Lisbeth Barclay appeared on our way in and invited me to dine with her family evening after next. "Oh, you must come!" she gushed, clutching my hands. "It won't be any fun without you there." As if we've been friends since the nursery, though we've only just met. How odd, this American familiarity.

Afterward, to the library. I don't expect any of my acquaintances step foot in there other than for charity balls, but the quiet of the reading room soothes me.

Tomorrow to the milliner. I'll need a new hat if I'm to dine with the Barclays. Perhaps the new cloche style. Green silk, I think. It's my color, according to Ailsa.

16.05.1922

Of note:

A "big cheese" is an important person.

A "baby" is a sweetheart.

The "cat's pajamas" are neither feline nor related to nightclothes.

"Swell" is all right.

Still unsure what "necking" means . . .

23.05.1922

Discovered the most extraordinary invention!

Invited again to the Barclays. After dinner, the younger guests retired to the drawing room, as Jay Barclay was eager to show off his new talking machine. On a side table there rested a large mahogany box. "Dickie, you'll find this a gas," he said, opening the lid. (He is always looking to impress Richard Van Cortlandt, which puzzles me, as I find the latter to be utterly brutish.)

Inside the box was a panel of knobs and dials and four glass bulbs, and when Jay turned these knobs, a man's voice came out. "But where's the disc?" Betsy Wintour asked, examining the device from all angles. Behind her, Lisbeth clapped her hands. *"There is none!"* Jay turned the knob again, and this time, music!

We once gathered around the gramophone in Mama's room, listening to Tchaikovsky, Wagner, Rachmaninoff . . . but this machine is different. The Radiola, Jay says, plays music from the air. And music, yes, but like none I've heard before. A circus of sound, all jangle and noise. "What is it?" I asked.

Ailsa gave her chirping laugh. "It's jazz, dear. It's what all the fashionable girls are listening to these days."

"You mean the 'flappers,'" Jay replied, hiking an imaginary skirt to his knees.

"I hear in Chicago they call it 'boogie woogie.' Is that right, Anna?" Lisbeth giggled. I smiled. I have no earthly idea. I know what Mama would have called it: vulgar. And yet, I believe I rather like it.

Finally, Jay called for a taxi downtown. Escaped with a "headache." Enough excitement for one night. Am glad to be back with you. Only that song sticks in my head. Perhaps there is music in the air here.

Yours,

A

We google some of the names we come across. Ailsa Mellon was another prominent socialite, the daughter of Andrew Mellon, but the rest turn up only random estate lawyers from Wichita or white page listings from Wilmington, North Carolina. And no mentions anywhere of someone named Anna Haswell.

At first, Anna seems both enthralled and put off by this fast and blingy new world. But change is funny; it happens slowly. Over the three diaries we read, she grows less and less shocked by her peers and more and more like them. She absorbs their slang, their music, their fashion, and their attitudes like a sponge soaking up water—or gin. Even the way she writes the dates on her entries changes.

Late 1922 and 1923 are glamorous, drunken, dizzying as Anastasia disappears into the city's cabarets and emerges as Anna. The diaries begin to read like outtakes from *The Great Gatsby.*

After Delmonico's, to Chumley's in Ailsa's Rolls. Dickie, of course, was in the cups by midnight. Not surprising, as he had us on the giggle water from three o'clock.

El Fey for dancing last night. Some real hoofing. Home at three. Aspirin and eggs for breakfast.

Lunch with Betsy, then juleps at Dickie's. Maybe I was all wet about him. He's asked to take me out in his breezer this weekend.

Yet as many parties as Anna attended, as many invitations as she got and names she dropped, something strikes me: these aren't friends as much as accomplices. There's no intimacy. I think of Katie and the ten thousand late-night convos and impromptu sleepovers we've had over the years, the inside jokes and *u up?*s and doing something just by doing nothing together.

With a pang, I pick up my phone to see if there's a message from her. Nothing. While I'm still mad, I'm also starting to worry we might never talk again.

Without the trust of a true friend, it's not surprising that the diaries show Anna didn't reveal her identity to anyone, at least not in New York. Maybe it was less painful that way—after losing everything to expect nothing—but it must have been lonely. The diaries were the only confidant Anna had. No wonder she kept them.

December 14

Quite a night, and I'm all balled up about it. Lucky to be writing from bed and not a precinct of the New York City Police Department.

I'll write it, and perhaps you can help me make sense of it.

To Chumley's tonight after dinner with Ailsa, Jay, and Dickie. Jay and Ailsa positively corked and arguing again. He doesn't like the way she flirts, but it's none of his beeswax.

Dickie suggested we change scene to uptown when, suddenly, a waiter cried, "Eighty-six!"

The cops.

Chaos, everyone scramming for the doors. Thick smoke.

Women crying. Policemen cradling batons. With alarm, I watched one draw a gun from his holster. . . .

I froze. The room spun, the edges of my vision going black. It was Dickie who pulled me toward the door. We tumbled into the alleyway. Sirens wailing. Lights flashing on cobblestone.

"Let's take a ride, shall we?" he said, pulling me to a taxi. A man tried to get in with us, but Dickie waved bills in the driver's face and—_zoom!_—we were off.

"Ailsa and Jay," I asked, catching my breath as the bedlam grew distant, "will they be all right?"

Every cell of my body rang with alarm, but Dickie was cool as a cucumber. "Fine and dandy," he said.

We rattled up Hudson, turned on Fourteenth and then Fifth as I tried to slow my heart.

In the back of the taxi, Dickie's arm snaked across my shoulders. Pulling me closer, he grinned. "Finally, Anna from Illinois sees some action."

I forced a shaky laugh. "It might be action I could do without."

"Seen enough for one lifetime?" He grinned.

Another forced laugh. "You might say that."

He eyed me, the other eye squinted shut. "You've bobbed your hair."

My pulse had slowed to normal, and I told him I had, last week. Did he like it? "Not really," he said, and I must have looked at him cross, because he laughed. "I mean that I liked it better when it wasn't like all the other girls'."

His face was so close I smelled the whiskey in his stomach. We were coming up on Madison Square. His hand had clamped on my knee. In the artificial lamplight, I watched it slide up. And up. "You're not like all the other girls, are you?" he asked.

The taxi turned; my stomach lurched. His hand had reached the beading of my skirt. "Cash or check?" he asked.

"I don't know what you mea—" I started, but before I could protest, his lips were mashed against mine, cold and wet as a fish.

"Dickie!" The clap of my hand on his cheek startled us all.

The driver's voice drifted back: "You okay back there, miss?"

Dickie's face was flushed. He laughed. "Anna Has-well," he drew out the name, as if speaking a nursery rhyme, "of Lake Bluff, Illinois." His teeth shone like sharpened pearls. "You're being kind of rude, don't you think?"

"Rude?" We were only a block from the hotel, but I directed the cabbie to pull over. He glanced back at Dickie, whose eyes met his in the rearview, and braked. The slam of my door echoed down the empty avenue.

In the darkness of the cab, Dickie's face swam like an apparition. "You're not going to thank me?" he asked.

"For what?" Liquor crawled up the back of my throat, sour, burning.

"*For saving your derriere from the police, princess. You know, you may have been hot stuff in . . . Illinois . . . but here you're nothing without us.*"

My heart beat like a drum in my chest. "Thank you," I replied, suddenly sober, and through gritted teeth, "for rescuing me."

"*At your service.*" *His hand made a tiny flourish and waved the taxi on.*

Anthony greeted me at the lobby door. "Everything all right, Miss Haswell?" he asked as he held the door. I must have looked like something the cat dragged in. Fine, I told him. Fine and dandy.

My first kiss.

What to make of it? Tonight I'll make nothing, I suppose. Tomorrow, toast and aspirin. For now, sleep.

Yours,

Anna

"Jerk," Evan says before turning the page. I smile.

January 1, 1924

I am a fool. And more than a fool, a tragic fool.

Last evening, intended to celebrate, along with half of New York society, the dawn of the new year as guests of Mr. and Mrs. James Osgood. I'll waste no more ink on the frivolities—who cares the number of pieces in the brass band or how many bottles of champagne were drunk by midnight? Suffice it to say I found myself, minutes before the significant hour, in a circle of high-spirited and well-lubricated companions.

As it so often does, the talk turned to the tangled romances of my associates. Who has visited whose bed is of little concern to me, especially as these liaisons so rarely seem to involve genuine love. Besides, what experience do I have to contribute but a bleary memory of a sloppy advance?

Perhaps discomfort at the memory of that night was written on my face, for suddenly, Betsy Wintour turned glassy eyes on me. "Anna, you can't tell us you don't have a handsome young man sniffing at your door."

I felt my face flush. "No, I'm afraid I don't."

"Not even a fling?" pressed Ailsa. "A little indiscretion . . . in the back of a taxi cab?"

Betsy giggled. Dickie, hair slicked flat like a weasel, stood beside her. Briefly, his eyes met mine and looked away. He sipped casually, guiltily, from a coupe. What had he told them?

"Of course not!" Jay Barclay brayed, champagne slopping over the rim of his glass. "The tsarina wouldn't lower herself to a fling—unlike some of you wanton harlots." He chortled, and Ailsa rolled her eyes.

My heart flew from my chest like a bird flushed by dogs.

Lisbeth Barclay spoke my thoughts: "Tsarina?" she asked. She was, perhaps, the soberest of our circle.

Tsaritza is my mother's title—or was. Not this butchered version I've read in American newspapers. Never mind that neither was my title; I knew what they meant.

"You didn't know that our Anna is a Russian princess living in exile?" Dickie grinned like a cat who'd caught a mouse.

Struck dumb, I felt I might be sick, the night in the taxi flashing before my eyes: "at your service". . . . "not like all the other girls". . . . "princess" . . . "enough action for one lifetime" . . . I glared across the circle. He avoided my gaze.

But how can he know, when I have told no one, breathed not a word of my secret since my departure from England?

I berate myself for lacking the self-possession to deny his allegation—for that's how his words struck me in the stifling ballroom. Lisbeth clapped her hands with glee. "How romantic!"

"You're zozzled, Dickie," said Ailsa.

Jay muttered, "I thought the Reds got 'em."

"I don't know what you're talking—" I stammered, but the band had begun its countdown to midnight, and the music swallowed my voice.

"Ten!" my neighbors cheered. Lisbeth bounced on the balls of her feet. Dickie took the opportunity to slip a hand around Betsy's waist.

"Nine!"

They turned to the stage.

"Eight!"

And just like that, I was forgotten.

"Seven!"

The unmasking was over.

I have come to a realization that pains me and yet brings sharp clarity, like a fog lifting. Since those events that I won't bring myself to recall here, I have been running, at times borne along by individuals I had no choice but to trust, at others propelled only by my own wits. Reaching this new harbor, I thought I had stopped running. But I have never stopped. This life, this city of bubbles and gleam is a drug. Lulled by diversion, I've sought escape from the hideous truth in illusion. All these months, I thought that I might hide in plain sight. I had forgotten that when your inheritance is terror and loss, there is no escape, not in truth.

And who is to blame for this new betrayal? Ashbourne? Should I be surprised that, in the almost two years since I left him, he might have let our secret slip? Is it unbelievable that, from the bottom of a bottle of fine Madeira, he might have revealed to some untrustworthy confidant his benevolence toward a poor, unseated princess?

Or is it a more calculated play—has the time ripened for those who wish to use me? My life was bought at the steepest price. Of course I am a pawn. I cannot know what will be their next move.

I no longer have faith that those who brought me here keep my best interest at heart, nor that they ever did. The *people with whom I've surrounded myself are frivolous. More than frivolous, they could prove dangerous. I must leave New York.*

Fate has taken from me everything: family, crown, country. Identity is all I have left, and I shall hold it closer now than ever. I will slip away—and in doing so, return to myself.

Always,

A

"Maybe we're going about this the wrong way." At our kitchen table, Evan puzzles over a third cup of coffee—black with two heaping spoonfuls of sugar.

Anna had answered our question. Yes, her identity, or some version of it, had been known to some, but she had not been the one to share it, and their knowing had only made her more protective of her secret.

"More coffee?" I offer.

"Trying to cut back."

"You're joking."

"I never joke about coffee."

On the counter, my phone buzzes. A message from Ryan: *U feeling butter?* Absorbed in my reading about the Romanovs and obsessing about the fight with Katie last night, I'd told him I wasn't feeling well. It's sweet of him to check on me, but for some reason, the typo annoys me. No, I am not feeling "butter."

"Do you need to answer that?" Evan asks.

"No," I say, and turn the phone off.

"Okay, we need to establish *facts*," Evan says. He stands and paces. "Maybe the bigger question is not can we corroborate Anna's story, but how could Anastasia have escaped the firing squad to begin with?"

The brutal crime scene from the photo of the Ipatiev House flashes before my eyes: bullet holes crumbling the wall, bloodstains darkening the floor. It was a massacre in a tiny room.

Evan continues, "We know how she got to America, but how did she get from Yekaterinburg and the Bolsheviks to London and Sir Ashbourne, *three thousand* miles away? She says people were helping her. . . . Who, how, and why?"

The heel of his sneaker squeaks as he turns in a dramatic about-face. My partner has a point. So far, our approach to the diaries has been a fishing expedition, casting for clues. We've matched dates, authenticated names, searched for someone she might have told her secret. What we need, though, is a chronology.

"All right," I say. "Anna arrived in New York in 1922. Before that she was in London. Let's retrace her steps, follow her back to the night of the murders."

It's almost five o'clock. We've spent the entire day reading about Anna's time in New York and her eventual flight from the city and the people she met there. When I'm with Evan, hours pass as easily as water slipping down a drain.

We decide to meet again the next morning. The only

problem: tomorrow's a Wednesday, and while my mom and brother are likely to be out, my father doesn't work on Wednesdays. I can do without more of his cringeworthy Dad-isms. I suggest to Evan that we meet somewhere else.

"I know a place. Outside, but it's definitely quiet and excellent for reading."

"A park?"

"Sort of." He gives a funny smile and two cross streets on the other side of town.

When I walk him to his bike leaning against our front porch, he straddles the aluminum frame. He's a nineteen-year-old on a purple kids' bike, but there's something appealing in the way he stands, feet apart, hands on handlebars, head tilted to the side, and it makes me smile.

"You know, you're wrong about something," he says. I'm wrong about a lot of things, I resist telling him. "You said you haven't told anybody about the diaries."

"I haven't." Earlier, what I said about secrets has made him think I'm hiding something. "Evan, I promise, there's nothing I'm keeping from you."

"But you have told someone. . . . You told me."

With a sly smile, he steps on the pedals and is gone before I can reply. At the corner, he lifts his hand in a wave without looking back. He knew I was watching him go.

14

August 22, 2007

Very slowly, I spin in a circle. *Have I gotten the address wrong?* For the third time, I check the scrap of paper on which I'd written the intersection Evan named the day before. According to the bright green street signs, I'm in the right place, but *am* I in the right place, standing at the edge of a small, lonely cemetery? Evan is nowhere to be seen.

A stacked stone wall borders the graveyard on three sides. On the fourth stands an old white farmhouse with crooked shutters, a sagging roof, and a beige sedan parked in the barn-turned-garage. Sunflowers tower above the porch. Although no one appears to be home, at the very edge of the house's patchy front lawn, lying on its side, is Evan's bike.

Here . . . I think? The text flies into the air, and immediately a ping sounds across the graveyard. "Evan?" My voice cuts through silence otherwise disturbed only by birds singing.

Suddenly, a head appears from behind the mottled gray statue of an angel—Evan, grinning. "'Each in his narrow cell for ever laid, the rude forefathers of the hamlet sleep.'"

Striding toward me, he sweeps his arm across the graveyard and its crumbling tombstones, which jut from heaved ground like rows of crooked teeth.

"Chekov?" I guess, squinting to read the title on the book he carries, *Selected Stories of Anton Chekov*.

"Thomas Gray. British."

"Well, that's not fair." The stone wall stands between us. "You come to a cemetery often?"

"I appreciate a bit of peace and quiet, at which these esteemed ladies and gents"—he taps a nearby headstone with his foot—"are professionals."

I grin. "Maybe I'd rather be an amateur, then."

To get into the graveyard, I'll have to straddle the wall and swing my legs to the other side. When Evan unexpectedly extends his hand to help, I freeze, for a split second flustered. We both look at the hand, then, blushing, I take it and jump down, landing on the other side of the wall. A tingle lingers in my palm even after he lets go. "Thanks," I say, wiping the sensation on my shorts along with bits of moss and dirt.

"Come on," he says. "I'll give you the tour."

The cemetery isn't large, about the size of a soccer field. Most of the tombstones are no more than granite slabs splotched and worn by the elements and time. We stroll between them as Evan points out his favorites:

PHILPOT, A VICTIM OF THE FIRE

HERE LIETH THE BODY OF PRUDENCE WHYTE
MOTHER OF REASON AND PROSPERITY WHYTE

UNITY,
CONSORT TO HERCULES
DIED IN THE 66TH YEAR OF HER AGE, 1791

We take turns reading the stones in exaggerated British accents. Two pirate-like skulls engrave one, and a few are topped with small stone lambs. Evan explains those belong to children.

"I mean, it's a little spooky, isn't it," I ask, "hanging out in a graveyard?"

Evan waggles his eyebrows. "Afraid I'm a vampire? *That I vant to suck your borscht?*"

"You're a weird one, you know that, Evan Hermann?"

"I'd say that's subjective, but yes." He smiles. "I do. . . . This is my favorite reading spot. Feels fitting, with all the stories buried here, history literally below our feet." He taps the monument he leans on. "You're a writer. Doesn't that excite you?"

"I don't know if you can call yourself a writer when you don't have any readers."

"Baloney," Evan says.

"Baloney?" I laugh.

"Sorry, picked that up from Sonya, but 'Art is in the doing, not the viewing.'"

"Tolstoy?" I ask.

"Hermann."

We find a rusted cast-iron love seat beneath a sprawling maple in the corner of the cemetery. It's small, barely big enough for both of us, and surrounded by knee-high grass where the mower missed a patch, but we settle at either end, attempting to give each other space but failing. The same tingle returns where our arms touch, but I can't wipe this one away.

In the back of my mind, there's a question lodged like popcorn stuck in your molar. The graveyard is an old one, and I haven't seen any recent dates or shiny black markers like the ones at the cemetery where my grandparents and Aunt Anna are buried. On my porch, as we ate PB&Js, Evan had been almost casual about his father's death, but soon after, he'd stiffened and shut down. While I don't want to upset him, I'm curious.

"Is this," I say tentatively, gripping the iron bench, "where your dad's buried?"

From the corner of my eye, I see Evan shake his head. "He's buried in Virginia, with my grandparents." Although I watch his expression, I can't read it.

What would it be like to lose a parent, I wonder. Or to lose your whole family, as Anastasia had? As much as mine drives me crazy, the thought of waking up to one of them not in the world turns the air in my lungs to concrete.

"Do you ever visit him—I mean, his grave?"

"Sometimes. Sonya took me a couple of years ago."

"How did he die? S—sorry," I stammer, "that was rude. You don't have to answer."

"It's okay, Jess." Briefly, his hand rests on my shoulder, and the tingling migrates there, growing to an insistent buzz. "It's a reasonable question."

He sighs and the hand drops. "He was riding his bike when a furniture truck hit him. A futon." He gives a weary smile, and for the first time I hear a trace of bitterness in his voice. "They were delivering a futon."

"Evan, I'm so sorry."

It's not enough; I know words aren't enough. The impulse to wrap his hand in mine is strong, but for some reason I hesitate, and then the moment's gone.

"Yeah. Like I said, I was four, so . . ." He tips his head back and gazes into the branches of the maple tree. For the first time, I notice a tiny, star-shaped scar on his jaw. A crow lands in the tree above us, cawing loudly.

"It's weird," he says. "I miss him, but in an abstract way. I mean, I have these memories. . . . Like, my mom could barely boil water, so he was the cook. I remember sitting on the kitchen floor—old, yellow linoleum—while he made dinner. Hamburger Helper. That was my favorite."

Glancing at his face, I expect to find it twisted with grief, but while his eyes are sad, there's also the barest hint of a smile at the picture in his head. The smile falls. "I don't remember him as a *person*, though, like the sound of his voice or if he was funny or if he played cards, too. Those types of things. He's more . . . the shape of a father."

Heaviness invades my body, the heaviness of how unfair the world can be. "Does your mom talk about him?" I ask.

His brow creases. "I'm not sure," he says briskly. "She left."

Shit. On the porch, when he said it was just the two of them now, I'd thought he meant him and his mom, but he'd meant Sonya.

"When my dad died, we moved here to live with Sonya. And then, one day, she was just . . ." He opens his hand like a magician disappearing a coin. "Gone. *Vamoose. Sayonara*, Mom. See ya never."

Whatever dams had contained the grief before now break; pain runs in rivers beneath his words. "You know the hardest part?" He turns to me, and his eyes are shining, bluer behind the tears he's holding back. "She lied about it."

Talking about his father, Evan's voice had been soft with nostalgia; now, it's sharp as a knife. "I was seven, and we'd run out of milk. Cliché, huh? But Sonya always bought the little jug, even though my mom told her to get the gallon. I'd drink the whole damn thing in a day. Mom said she was going to get more.

"I try to remember if there was anything strange about it, if she said *where* exactly she was going to get milk, as if maybe she'd meant New Mexico." He digs a palm into the corner of each brimming eye. "For a while it was this puzzle, right? Like, if only I could put the clues together, we'd get her back."

The rivers breach the banks. Tears trace pathways down the outside of his cheeks. His eyes squeeze shut.

"At first, I blamed Sonya, for not getting the gallon of milk. How stupid is that?"

He wipes at his nose with a sleeve. His eyes gleam cold. The tears are gone now.

"I've thought about it a lot. . . . She'd been depressed since my dad died. Not getting out of bed, crying all the time. Sometimes she'd look at me and just start sobbing. She must've had a bag packed. Some of her clothes were gone, and this photo she kept by the bed of my dad holding me in the hospital when I was just a few hours old, wearing a blue beanie."

He balls a fist in his lap. It clenches and unclenches. My hand, finally, reaches for it. Evan looks down, surprised at my touch, and turns to face me. "She was planning it," he says with disgust. "She didn't even have the guts to tell me."

"Have you seen her since then?"

Abruptly, as if he can't handle sitting still for one more second, Evan stands. My hand drops. He crosses his arms over his chest. "She's tried."

"But . . ."

"But we have diaries to read."

Above us, the leaves of the maple stir in a breeze. The crow has flown away. It occurs to me that people die, but stories don't. Someone else's just becomes yours, which becomes another person's whose life you've touched, like Evan's dad's story became his mother's became his. Infinite chapters, just new protagonists.

Yesterday, after the New York diaries, I hunted for journals dated between July 17, 1918, the night of the murders, and April 1, 1922, Anastasia's departure for America. We need to follow the timeline of her escape from Russia. Oddly, the first diary dated after July 17, 1918, is from March 1919. It's a large journal, simple and brown with unlined pages. At the center of its first page is printed one word:

Берлин

I'd chased down the translation with the website that let me peck out Cyrillic characters. Now I reach for the journal in my bag and open it to the page. Evan watches, still standing, arms crossed protectively over his chest.

"Here," I say, walking it to him.

He takes the journal from my hands.

"Berlin," he says.

15

11.03.1919

I am delivered. My belongings: the clothes on my back, a dull knife from a Polish potato farmer, two pairs of shoes in equally pitiful condition, and gratitude for the kindness of strangers. Also, this diary, bartered for a link of sausage.

To record my trials until now has been impossible, to relive the horror and risk discovery, not to mention a lack of paper or pen, which were kept from me, I am told, out of caution.

Nothing remains of my past life. My family—snuffed out like candles. My country—behind me. The jewels—sold to facilitate our passage. Even my name is no longer my own. Anna Belyakova, they call me, because it sounds like "white rabbit." Fleeing the jaws of the Bolshevik hounds.

I am ordered to wear a cloak of secrecy, but my survival is owed to men and women—compassionate and *otherwise—whose bravery, nonetheless, should be known by more than God alone. Their names I will never reveal, but the story of how they brought me here I will narrate for you now.*

Over twenty pages, Anna chronicles a trek from central Russia to Berlin. Though she leaves out names and details that could identify the people who helped her, the writing is vivid and rich with description. Emotion bleeds through the words.

She does not talk about the night of the execution, writing only that her memory of those hours is "dark as December night." Instead, her story begins in a small Ural village, where she woke to the smell of manure and wet hay. The wool blanket on which she lay was spread in the corner of a small, covered pigpen. A clean white bandage covered a bullet wound to her left arm. Her coat and dress, caked in blood, sat folded in a pile beside her. On her body, which had been washed, were the coarse pants and tunic of a peasant boy. Raising a hand to her throbbing head, she gasped; her hair had been cut to the scalp, and a crusted wound ran from her temple to the back of her skull.

In another corner of the sty slept two strange men. The only thing that allayed Anastasia's immediate terror was a flickering memory that they had been the ones to carry her here.

Disoriented and aching, Anastasia took stock as the men slept. For how many hours or days she'd been in and out of consciousness, she wasn't sure. Only hazy sounds and images came to her through "a black fog." She sensed, however, that she couldn't be far from Yekaterinburg.

The men were also dressed in peasants' clothes. As Anastasia crept closer to examine the older one's snoring face, a single eye flew open.

"Up, up," he barked, waking his companion. I scrambled to the corner where I cowered. The man crawled toward me, and I saw that his nose was crooked, as if it had been broken many times. Pressing a dirty finger to his lips, he whispered again and again, "You are safe. You are safe."

Silently, he signaled to the younger man, who disappeared and then returned shortly with a bowl of table scraps: gristly pork and thick, fermented porridge whose smell turned my stomach. "Eat," the men urged. I did and promptly vomited into the straw.

That night, Anastasia and her companions slept in the pigsty. The men were not unkind, though they barely spoke to her, or to each other, and never once looked her in the eye. The following day, the threesome moved, Anastasia limping from a swollen right foot, to a village southwest of the first house—the direction she could only deduce from the movements of the sun, as no one told her where they were going. At the second safe house, she was shoved wordlessly through the back door of a small cottage, received by a short, fat woman with breath that smelled like onions. Still, Anastasia did not speak, and no one forced her to.

Only at the third house, reached by the fat woman's onion cart, did anyone speak directly to the grand duchess. There, an old man hid her in his root cellar.

Already bent by age, he knelt in front of me and touched his brow to the floor. "May God bless your family," he said, tears forming in his eyes. Still, mine remained dry. It would be nearly two months before I could cry for my mother, my father, my sisters, my brother, as if their killers had stolen my tears along with their lives.

Later, the old man's wife asked Anastasia to pray with her. They knelt in the dirt before two modest icons and a commemorative photograph of the tsaritza from the tercentenary celebrations. The woman showed her Alexandra's signature on the back.

Choking on grief, I folded my hands, but I could not pray. As the woman did, I stared at the icons, wondering what kind of God could allow his servants to be slaughtered when, BANG—a loud slam from above! Shrieking, I fell to the floor, covering my head. The woman, panicked, smothered my screams with the filthy potato sack on which she'd knelt. The farmer had slammed a door on his way inside from milking the couple's goats. She stayed with me through the night, rubbing circles on my back and muttering prayers beneath her breath, but she did not ask me to kneel with her again.

So, Anastasia traveled, from farm to farm, village to village, dressed mostly as a boy. Sometimes she was the son of whomever escorted her, other times a younger brother. Once, to a nosy neighbor, she was the nephew of a friend, on his way to Moscow, hopeful to be of service there to the Party. When they referred to her, in the third person, as if talking of someone other than the girl traveling with them, it was always as Anna Belyakova: *We will meet Anna Belyakova tomorrow in Smolensk. Tell him Anna Belyakova is eager to see him at dawn.*

Via this underground railroad of unlikely sympathizers, Anastasia was ferried across the country by farmers, shepherds, miners, manual laborers, and their devout and sometimes dour wives, daughters, and sisters. They traveled by foot, on mules, on carts, and twice, for longer distances, by train, though rail was soon abandoned for more modest and inconspicuous means of transport. They slept in barns and stables, pigpens and root cellars, and a few times, outside, with nothing but their clothes to fend off the night's chill. In each place, Anastasia dreamed of blood and death, waking to fresh terror. Sometimes she wet the pallet on which she slept.

Summer turned to fall turned to the first snowflakes of winter, with never more than three nights in one place. The places and faces blurred, though the danger the travelers faced remained clear and ever-present. Word had been received that the Cheka, the Bolsheviks' new secret police, lurked in every town.

If, temporarily, I ever forgot the risk we faced, I was quickly reminded. Once, after a particularly sleepless night, I dozed fitfully, curled beneath a pile of burlap in the back of the hay cart in which we traveled. The wheels creaked to a stop as the driver paused to ask directions from a passerby. "The city, which way is it?" "Kazan?" a voice replied. "Don't you see the kremlin? That way."

Kazan! I had seen it once, with my family just a few years before, when we'd sailed the Volga River for the tercentenary. How I longed for something familiar, some scrap of memory to connect me with that time. . . . Without thinking, my head rose from the cart. Might I recognize the kremlin in the distance, this particular scrap of sky?

Feeling the weight in the cart shift, my bodyguard turned, his eyes narrowed to venomous slits. He hissed like a snake to remind me: I was not only risking my own life, but his as well. Quickly, I shrank back under my cover. Never again did I raise my head from the cart, that day or any other.

Her rescuers never told Anastasia their names, and she never asked. If she had known their identities and was ever discovered by the Cheka, everyone who had helped her would be in danger. This not knowing did not seem to bother her.

I was learning to move as a ghost, and ghosts do not use names. Nor would I ask why they helped me. I couldn't bear the answer: because your family is dead, and you are all that is left.

With the Russian winter howling at their backs, Anastasia and her network of escorts steadily headed west. They skirted Moscow and didn't stop until they reached the newly declared Belarusian People's Republic. The arrival was a lucky thing, as her shoes had by then given out, though she wouldn't mention it to the people who risked their lives to help her.

In Belarus, she rested for three weeks in the attic of a large, fine house. Her clothes and shoes were replaced by her wealthy host, and from there, the journey slowed, with shorter distances covered each day and less urgency to move. Only then, from overheard whispers, did "Anna Belyakova" fully understand the danger that had been driving her from safe house to safe house while in Russia: several times, her handlers had been sure the Cheka were at the door.

From Belarus, Anastasia crossed into Poland, where at the border, she and her Russian-speaking escorts had a harrowing experience. The Polish border guard did not like her companions' accents. (Belarus, Evan explained, was then caught in a struggle between Poland and the new Soviet Russia.) For nearly an hour, a middle-aged guard with stinking-hot breath questioned her. When he realized his fortune—it was not a boy but a girl he had trapped in his unheated hut—he threatened to strip-search her. It was only by bribing the soldier with a pearl necklace that she made the crossing unmolested.

Back in Tobolsk, before the Romanovs' transfer to Yekaterinburg, Alexandra had directed her daughters to sew the jewelry they had managed to keep into the linings of their corsets and dresses. Whether to protect the valuables from guards or to fund an escape, Anastasia had not been clear at the time, but at the border crossing, she realized that her escorts had been using these gems, torn from the dress she wore the night of the murders, to facilitate the party's passage, trading jewels for food, shelter, and transportation. Beside a pang of grief, Anna felt gratitude for her mother's foresight.

By the time Anastasia reached Germany, winter was giving way to spring. On my phone, Evan and I map her route as best we can from the sketchy geographical details. In eight months, she traveled over twenty-two hundred miles; that unfathomable number shimmers before us. And all of this hardship and heartache condensed to twenty pages.

I am delivered, Anna wrote in Berlin.

"Why Berlin?" I ask Evan.

After World War I and its own revolution, Evan explains, Germany was preoccupied with reconstruction. A country in turmoil isn't a bad place to hide. Plus, he added, the Weimar government's attitude toward the new "Soviet Federative Socialist Republic" ranged from lukewarm to hostile.

"So, she was safe," I say.

"Safer, maybe. If the Germans discovered the tsar's daughter in their midst, it's not impossible they wouldn't have secretly surrendered her to Lenin. And there were plenty of Soviet spies."

Anastasia's last escort was a German sympathizer to the tsarist cause whom she called by the fake name "Werner"— in Evan's pronunciation, as if spelled with a *V*. Werner had a widow's peak and an effeminate air and deposited the depleted grand duchess at a decaying boarding house on Ritterstrasse in the Kreuzberg neighborhood of Berlin. The newly rechristened "Anna Haase," according to faked identity papers (*hase* meaning "rabbit" in German, though they'd dropped the "white" part) was from Darmstadt, Empress Alexandra's family birthplace. She would work as a housemaid near the Kurfürstendamm, a once bustling and glamorous shopping district. It was a job, Werner told her, which she was exceedingly lucky to have.

He dropped her in the middle of the day, when the boarding house was at its quietest, introducing her to the landlady as his sister-in-law, recently widowed—and thus, she overheard him whisper, grieving and not to be disturbed. With a sniff and a once-over, Frau Becker, who sucked her teeth and smelled of sauerkraut, showed them to her room. Located under one of the house's eaves, the room's ceiling slanted so low that, in one spot, Anna had to stoop to walk under it. The room contained a narrow bed, an old washstand, a wardrobe, and a bare overhead bulb.

From the single window, ten minutes later, Anna watched Werner's figure recede down the street. They would come for her, he said, when the time was right. In the meantime, he told her, "Forget who you are, and become who you need to be."

And so, she wrote, *I pray to disappear.*

16

After recounting her journey from Yekaterinburg, Anna's Berlin diaries become sparse and tense as a tightrope. Nowhere to be found is the mischievous, tree-climbing girl of the earlier journals. In New York, we know that carefree spirit surfaced again, for a time, but in Berlin, Anna Haase is as gray and grim as the Reaper himself.

Six days a week, she worked as a maid in a house whose master and mistress she described, respectively, as "grouchy" and "bovine." The work was backbreaking. She was grateful, at least, for the German her mother taught her, not that she used it much. The only person, other than Frau Schultz, with whom Anna spoke was Johanna, a quick-talking young boarder from Potsdam who also worked as a maid near the Kurfürstendamm. Sometimes, they rode the U-Bahn together, bonding over Frau

179

Becker's limp cabbage and the caustic soap they used to scrub pots and pans.

Mostly, the life Anna describes was solitary, days filled with work and nights with sweat-soaked terrors. Clearly, she was depressed.

Woke at four thirty. Bathed, dressed, walked to the U-Bahn. A sparrow had found its way into the station.

Cleaned the floors. Frau Schultz showed me a spot that I had missed on the silver teapot. The wart on her chin trembled with glee, as if banishing a smudge might make sense of a world turned upside down.

Returning home, the sparrow lay dead on the platform, its wing broken.

Exhausted. Pray no terrors tonight.

No sleep again. Went about the day as if in a fog. Sawdust bread and an egg for lunch. Rice and onions for dinner.

Sat across from a scarecrow in a baggy suit on the train—a soldier, from the defeated look of him. He pulled his lips into a gummy smile, but to return it was beyond me. Too busy picturing his face as the last thing Ilya saw as he lay dying.

I think of him still. Did they send him back? Did he survive? And the question that grates my heart to shreds . . .

Did he become one of them?

Birthdays, anniversaries, and the name days of her family were especially dark days that brought bitter attacks of survivor's guilt. Eventually, she gave up on dates at all, as if the passage of time ceased to matter. Still, despondent as she was, Anna continued to put words on the page. Maybe this was comforting, or maybe it was a chore. Maybe, speaking from experience, it was both.

The short entries make for fast reading, and before we know it, Evan and I arrive in the summer of 1919: a year since the murder of her family. We know because Anna marks the day ominously in her diary, with a large black *X*. She obsesses endlessly over the idea that a mistake was made and that another, more deserving, sibling should have lived instead. It's unclear whether she's questioning God or her rescuers; mostly, she seems to be questioning herself.

This darkness threatens to swallow me. What if Papa had not abdicated? What if we had refused to go to Tobolsk, refused to go to the cellar? What if I had thrown myself in front of the bullets? If I had understood that Ilya was warning me?

As Evan reads, I'm sad to wonder if he has his own list of what-ifs. *What if his father had taken the bus that day? What if they hadn't moved to Keene? What if he hadn't drunk so much milk?*

"It's heartbreaking." I barely realize I've said it out loud.

181

Surprised, Evan looks up. He sighs, is quiet for a moment. "'The gleanings of an empty heart.' . . . Pushkin."

"But she doesn't even sound like the same person." I'm picking at the hangnails my mother's always begging to cure with a mani-pedi. "'I pray to disappear'?"

I'd thought I knew what Anna meant when she wrote it in her diary: the safety of anonymity, but also the ability to forget herself for an hour or a day, to leave behind the loss and hurt of her own life with a different identity. I'm familiar with the relief of disappearing into a story, a character—but what I'm starting to fear is that the kind of disappearing my great-great-aunt was talking about was the final kind. This isn't the Anna I know.

"Anastasia Romanov was spirited," I argue. "She was tough. Where's the girl who rushed at the crowd that insulted her father, who pinched her sisters in church?"

"Maybe *Anastasia* was that girl," Evan says, "but Anna . . ." He fades off.

Evan knows more than most that grief can change a person—it changed his mom—and, from our conversation earlier, I'm pretty sure he doesn't want to explore that topic.

He confirms it by continuing to read. Within a few pages, though, something interesting happens: just as I've started to fear my aunt had lost her will to live, a stranger appears, another young woman at the boarding house on Ritterstrasse—an emigrée from St. Petersburg, like her.

"Who's the new girl?" asked Johanna at dinner. Frau Becker grunted. "Ein Russki."

A Russian? My heart leapt! "Have you met her?" Johanna asked me. "Nein," I answered, covering my excitement with a cough.

After dinner, I resolved to introduce myself, knocking lightly at her door. "Kto tam?" she called from within—in Russian! I nearly cried to hear it. There was muttering and then, in German, "Who is it?"

On the doorknob, my hand hesitated. Would she recognize me? But I'm a great deal thinner and my hair shorter than it was as a child, and surely sorrow has etched new lines on my face. I entered.

And received a great shock—it was as if I gazed into a mirror. The woman is my age, not more than twenty, with a long nose and chestnut hair. But what struck me was the expression she wore—tiredness and loss; I recognized it as my own. She looked as if she'd been crying.

"Zdravstvuyte," I said, despite myself.

Her face brightened, just slightly. "Zdravstvuyte," she replied.

"I'm Anna," I told her in German, and held out my hand. For a moment, confusion clouded her features. Perhaps, I thought, she couldn't really speak the language, but then she laughed, the smile now stretching ear to ear. "I am also

Anna," she said. *"Anna Vasilievna Rostova. Sehr erfreut."* *Pleased to meet you.*

Werner has cautioned against friends. "Loneliness is your refuge," he said. But she cannot be a Bolshevik spy. Her teeth are too straight.

Despite Werner's warnings, as the entries continue, "Anna Haase" and Anna Rostova quickly become inseparable. They walk in the Tiergarten, browse a used bookstore on Zimmerstrasse, go for *kaffee und kuchen* and for swims at Wannsee Beach. They learn to make each other laugh. Johanna joins the two at times, and the pair became a trio. *It feels like a betrayal to say it*, Anna muses in an entry from late September—dates have magically reappeared—*but it is like having a sister again.* I realize it's the first time in her life that Anastasia truly had friends; sadly, it might have also been the last.

New Anna was drawing Anastasia back from the brink. The only problem was that she had her own dark days. As the two became close, Anna Rostova shared her story. *Like most in these times*, our Anna wrote, *it's a tragic one.* Though not as tragic as her own.

She was born the daughter of a count, a former colonel in the Imperial Army, and a mother, who died in childbirth, but she is now, like me, an orphan. Her father, after military service, was the director of a girls' school outside Tsarskoe Selo, a school that I know and whose students were on occasion invited to performances at the imperial theater.

In a house on a street I also know, Anna and her father lived in the shadow of Tsarskoe Selo. Until the revolution. He disappeared in the last days of December 1917, likely seized by the newly formed Cheka. For months, Anna waited for him, but in vain. Finally, as her money and hope dwindled, she placed herself in the care of an acquaintance of her father's, a man named Volkov, who billed himself as her savior. He was a controlling man, who manipulated and used his new charge for his own devices as he peddled falsehoods about his relation to the tsar across Russia and then Europe. It was Volkov who brought her to Berlin.

She hated him, Anna tells me, but he was all she had left, a fact of which he constantly reminded her between fits of verbal abuse. Only now has she found the courage to slip his grasp and forge a new life for herself. I know something of the latter, I told her. She smiled sadly but, of course, can only half understand.

I feel a great weight crushes my friend's soul. Our stories are different, but our pain is the same. She knows these depths of despair, what it is to be washed ashore, sputtering and gasping, a castaway from one's own life. Because of this, she is not easy—prone to sulky silences and bouts of self-pity—but

185

she is intelligent, kind, and curious, this other Anna, and l can love her because l understand her. We are two of a kind.

As Anna became a confidante to her new friend, a desire grew in her to share her own past. *So we both might have company in our grief,* she wrote. Still, she heeded Werner's warning. Reports had emerged of Germany's own fledgling Communist party. The fear of Bolshevik agents and sympathizers kept her silent.

Then, on an unseasonably warm day in late October, the friends took a walk in the Tiergarten.

October 19, 1920

l have done it. l have told her, and an iron fist has released its grip from my heart.

A difficult day for our friend, her father's name day. We sat for a while in the rose garden, and she told me of their final trip together, to the famous library at the university in Kazan, a pilgrimage of sorts for her papa, a scholar. l almost told her l'd seen that ancient city myself before, twice.

"Oh, Anna," she said finally, breaking down, wiping tears from her eyes, "how do l go on? Everything l knew, everyone l loved is gone."

With autumn here, the roses give up their petals. l watched one fall, a dusty mauve, like the roses that once filled my mother's room.

"You cannot call me Anna anymore," l said resolutely.

She looked at me, perplexed. "You cannot call me Anna any-more," I repeated, "because that is not my name."

I told her who I am.

At first she thought it was a cruel joke to distract her from her grief. When she saw that I was serious, her face turned to confusion to amazement and, finally, to sadness. Her hands flew to her mouth. "Oh!" she cried. "Oh."

For so long I've heard of her papa, of their mushroom-hunting in Vyborg; of skating on the pond near her house; of her spaniel, Gogol, and the hours spent in the nursery of her father's library. Now I can share with her my own memories.

She was in shock, of course. And admitted there had been questions: how I greeted her in such perfect Russian at our first meeting (my aunt, I'd told her, had married a man from Smolensk); how a common maid spoke such high German; why I so rarely spoke of my youth in Darmstadt.

I implored my friend not to reveal my secret to a soul, not even to Johanna. "Never," she promised. She understands the danger. And I trust that my confidence is deserved.

Oh, my dear, it is sweet relief. For the first time in a long time, I am free.

"She told someone," I whisper.

Evan nods.

I repeat, louder, "She told someone!"

The wind has picked up. Suddenly, as if it shares my

excitement, a gust stirs the grass and shakes the leaves above us. It catches my hair, whipping it around my face, and ruffles the thin pages of the journal Evan holds in his lap. It's the sort of wind that feels like a sign, and I laugh, and am further surprised when a yellowed slip of paper darts from between the pages of the diary and is caught on the breeze.

Comically, Evan and I lunge for the paper, but somehow, it manages to evade our grasp and to float, innocently, to the ground. We look at each other, dumbfounded, and Evan bends to retrieve it.

The scrap is thin and delicate as a butterfly's wing, and he handles it gingerly, pinching the corners between thumb and finger. "A newspaper article," he says, squinting at the small print. "In German."

"I don't suppose you speak German, too?" I joke.

"And French and Spanish and a little bit of Swedish, though I'm not proficient yet."

I gape. He shrugs. "You might say I'm a polyglot."

"Well, what does it say, Mr. Rosetta Stone?"

He squints again. "'My, you have a lovely face color!' No . . . 'complexion.' Sorry, my German's not as strong as my Russian."

He displays a black-and-white advertisement for Nivea face cream, and a Cheshire cat grin. Playfully, I smack his shoulder.

"All right, all right." He flips the advertisement over and scours the page. One eyebrow arches dramatically.

"What?" I plead. It's unfair that he gets to understand

everything before I do.

Haltingly, he reads the headline aloud. "'Young Woman Claims Royal Blood.'"

My breath catches. "That's her!" I squeal. "It's an article about her. She didn't only tell New Anna."

Bouncing off the bench, I lunge for the article as Evan, laughing, holds it up and out of reach so that we're nearly wrestling for it. "You don't even know German!" he protests as I bat at him. When I realize I'm holding his bicep in my hands, I release it.

"READ," I command.

According to the article, on the night of February 27, 1920, a young woman was pulled from a city canal following an apparent suicide attempt and admitted to the psychiatric ward at Elisabeth Hospital. She suffered from hypothermia and a fractured wrist and told rescuers that they had made a grave mistake: they should have let her die. What made the story newsworthy, however, was that the woman claimed to be one of the grand duchesses Romanov.

I hang, breathless and crestfallen, over Evan's shoulder as he reads the last line: "'She will not say which one.'" The excitement I just felt has smashed against the reality that, if this article is about my great-great-aunt, she tried to take her own life.

I pray to disappear.

The silence of the graveyard hums around us. "Was it her?" I no longer want it to be.

Evan scans the article again, combing fingers through his hair. "We can't jump to conclusions. The woman isn't named. There were dozens of impostors."

I have an idea. I swoop on the diary. "She jumped on the twenty-seventh," I say, flipping to the back, looking for entries near that date. I find one.

"Read," I instruct again.

February 26, 1920

Herr Schultz is sick. I know because my morning began with cleaning his piss pot.

In the afternoon, Frau sent me to the Markthalle for the weekly shopping. Outside the vegetable stall, suddenly a bang, like a gunshot. I fell to the ground. Only a pallet that had fallen, but I was paralyzed, shaking like a leaf. A woman stooped to help, but I could hardly hear her for the ringing. When will the fits end?

February 27, 1920

A fight broke out today in Wedding. Heard the Schultzes talking at breakfast.

Unlike her, but Frau gave me the rest of the day off. Spent the afternoon walking the Tiergarten. In the snow, reminds me of home.

Worried for Anna.

February 28, 1920

A newspaper on my seat on the train today. There's a new political party, or an old one with a new name. One of its leaders has given a speech at a beer hall in Munich. I have no stomach for politics, but the people are nervous. I can feel it in Frau and Herr Schultz.

"Hitler," Evan said. "She's talking about Hitler."

"Shit," I say. Of course, the time period had occurred to me, but it hits me what's unfolding not just for Anna but around her. Her world isn't the only one being turned upside down.

"But don't you see?" I ask. "There's no break in the timeline. If Anna had jumped, there wouldn't be an entry for February 28. There might not be a diary at all. . . . It's not our Anna," I say, relief washing over me.

"It's not our Anna," Evan agrees, "but that also means it's not our Anna. We're back to no evidence but the journals. And why would she keep the article?"

"If someone showed up at a mental asylum claiming to be you, wouldn't you be curious?"

"Definitely."

"Maybe investigate?"

February 29, 1920

The newspaper from the train. I brought it home to share

with Johanna, who likes to follow the news from around the country.

I am anxious for Anna. Three days since we've seen her, and her bed still unmade. Johanna says not to lose sleep, that she's only found an admirer, but I worry the wicked Volkov has tracked her down.

My intention was to check the police reports when I saw it: there on my desk, in plain sight since yesterday—"Young Woman Claims Royal Blood." The headline to a small article on the third page.

A woman who says she's my sister has appeared! Could it be?! All these months I've wept and gnashed my teeth that I was the only one to be saved, but is this true? Werner, he demanded my secrecy—could he be keeping one himself, keeping us apart in order to protect us?

Tomorrow I will find out. I will go to Elisabeth Hospital and demand to see her. Oh, OTM!

Yours,

A

It hadn't occurred to me as Evan read the article, but the woman claimed to be *a* Romanov princess, not necessarily Anastasia. Could it be she *wasn't* the only survivor? But the other missing body was believed to be Alexei's. . . .

There are two pages left in the journal, two pages of tight, scrawled script.

March 1, 1920

Dearest diary, there is no end to fate's turns.

This morning, I presented myself to the psychiatric ward of Elisabeth Hospital, to identify the unfortunate soul who had been pulled from the canal. The nurse who greeted me was skeptical. She smirked. "You mean Her Royal Highness?"

Imperial Highness, but I did not correct her. Possibly my cousin, I said; she had a history of hysteria.

"What color hair?"

"Brown," I said. Olga's is lighter, more blond than the chestnut of the rest of us, but brown would cover it.

"And the eyes?"

"Blue," I replied, though Tatiana's can appear gray, like the sky before a storm.

The woman placed a brief call on the telephone behind the desk, covering the mouthpiece with her hand as she spoke, then curtly nodded to a second nurse.

"Every family has one," the woman said as she led me through a heavy metal door. We went down one lonely corridor and then another. Moaning and shrieking from behind closed doors. "Where is her room?" I asked. In the basement, the nurse replied.

Deeper into the bowels of the hospital we went, with each floor the howls growing louder, my agitation more intense. Bile rose at the back of my throat. Nails cut my palms. The thought of one of my beloved sisters in this dank hell . . . but

I would not lose myself now.

Finally, when I thought I might turn and run, the nurse stopped before a door. "Good luck," she said. "She's stopped talking." And she opened it.

One step into the room and my heart shattered.

Anna.

Her eyes widened, but there was a look of resignation in them, as if she had been expecting me—waiting, wanting even, to be caught in her lie. A sob lodged in my throat. Her mouth hung slightly open. She had been drugged.

Leather straps secured her slender wrists to the metal bed. "Are those necessary?" I asked, holding my eyes on hers.

"Suicide risk. For her own good," said the nurse.

I nodded.

"Is it your cousin?" she asked, impatient. "Seems to know you."

"Nein," I said. "I don't know her." A tear slid down the patient's cheek. "But she resembles the princesses to me."

The door closed behind us. Anna had not spoken a single word.

I write this in the rose garden of the Tiergarten where I shared my secret with this pitiful creature. There are no flowers now but also no one to disturb me. Again, I am alone. Perhaps I've come here to torture myself, but I wish to gather my thoughts—and you, dear, are my best listener.

What can I say of this broken girl I once called "friend"? What of her story do I believe now? Was there a Volkov? Is she truly an orphan? I can say—and I believe this in my heart—that whatever deceptions she may have spun, her pain is real. In this, I believe her. In this, I recognize myself. It is hard to forgive. She is a liar and a thief. But she is also a survivor. And so, I forgive her, and implore you to as well.

Yours,

A

The diary ends there.

As we leave the cemetery and wander toward my car, Evan stops suddenly. "I'm remembering something," he says.

"I thought you remembered everything."

"Most things . . ." He turns to me. "The most famous impostor was a woman named Anna Anderson. After her death, DNA proved she was a Polish factory worker named Franziska Schanzkowska, but a lot of people believed her: scholars, Romanov family, biographers."

"That's weird," I say. "A third Anna?"

"Maybe . . . but what I'm remembering is that she was pulled from a Berlin canal."

I stare at him. "Could Anna Rostova have been Anna Anderson? Could Anastasia have met her most famous impostor?"

195

Evan shrugs. "It's possible. She was pretending to be an orphaned Russian aristocrat, met Anastasia, realized she'd hit the jackpot, and upped the ante?"

"Huh," I say. One more twist in this story and my head could explode. We reach my car, and I turn to Evan. "Why do you think she did it?"

"Anderson?"

"Any of them, I guess. Were they con artists, thrill seekers, delusional, traumatized?"

Evan sighs, leaning against the driver-side door, hands stuffed into the pockets of his jeans. "All of the above?"

"Would you forgive her?" I ask. "Like Anastasia did?"

He puckers, thinking, and I notice his lips are pink, like he's been eating Popsicles. A Cupid's bow cuts a deep V in his top lip. "Probably not," he says. "I don't understand how people lie."

"Like, how they do it?"

"Yes. Or why."

"You've *never* told a lie before?"

He tips his head back, thinking. "No," he says definitively.

"Not even a fib?" He shakes his head. "I think you're lying now."

He shrugs. "I guess I believe in the truth."

My phone beeps with a text message from Ryan, wanting to know if we're still meeting at the movies in ten minutes. I have to tell Evan I'll see him tomorrow.

A pained look clouds his face. "I can't tomorrow," he says. "I found a job."

My palm smacks my forehead. "Shit! Evan, the money. I'm so sorry." When he hadn't asked for payment, I'd forgotten the fee we'd negotiated—or maybe I'd hoped Evan was just invested in a different way. But now he's gotten a job, and I feel both guilty and disappointed that it means we can't meet tomorrow.

I start to calculate what I owe him in my head: forty-five dollars a journal, and we've read at least twenty of them. Twenty journals—with a panicky jolt, I realize we're more than halfway through the trunk . . . and that I owe him nine hundred dollars. I only have four hundred.

"It's okay," Evan says.

"I'll bring it when I see you."

"Really, it's not important. I'll see you Friday." That's two days, but it feels like an eternity.

He tries to open my door for me, but he's in the way, and I have to duck under his arm to slide into my seat. We pass chest to chest. My chin reaches just above his shoulder: perfect hug height. Maybe he's too short, or I'm too tall, but when Ryan and I hug, I never know where to put my head.

Another text from him dings on my phone, flustering me. "Okay," I say through the open window. *Ding.* And another. I turn the key in the ignition. "I'll text you," I say—*ding*—"It's a date"—without thinking. As I'm pulling away, I cringe.

Mozzarella sticks, garlic bread, two whoopie pies, a half-eaten gyro, and one pizza—with mushrooms—litter the table of a booth at the back of Athens Pizza V as Lila rambles about some drama over her top eight MySpace friends.

When I showed up at the Cinema 6, she and Josh were there, too. Ryan hadn't mentioned they were coming. Lila and I wanted to see the new Harry Potter, but despite Josh's surprise that "Hermione grew tits," we ended up at *Rush Hour 3*. As cars exploded and Chris Tucker and Jackie Chan bickered onscreen, I found myself in the stall of the Cinema 6 bathroom, trying to get bars out of the movie theater's crappy cell reception. If she might have been the Anna my aunt met in Berlin, I wanted to look up Anna Anderson. What I found confirmed our suspicion: Anderson had been pulled from a Berlin canal on February 27, 1920. The brushstrokes of her life: in and out of hospitals; believed by some, reviled by others; finally, after her death, disproven. So, Franziska Schanzkowska, pretending to be Anna Rostova, met Anastasia Romanov, pretending to be Anna Haase, and then pretended to be Anastasia, later becoming known as Anna Anderson. It made my head hurt enough to send me back into the theater.

There was a quote I found, though, that I jotted down on the back of my ticket stub with a pen borrowed from the popcorn guy. It was from Grand Duchess Olga Alexandrovna, Nicholas's sister and Anastasia's aunt. Olga met Anderson once and said of the encounter, "My intelligence will not allow me to accept her as Anastasia, but my heart tells me that it is she." In later years, Olga changed her mind, but I understand what she meant.

At Athens Pizza, I'm thinking of the ticket stub in the back pocket of my shorts as Lila switches topics. "I mean, Adam Levine is so much hotter. Don't you agree?" She's looking at me, chewing on a straw.

"Definitely." I think Adam Levine is the lead singer of Maroon 5, but I'm not sure.

"Don't get me wrong. I mean, I wouldn't kick Justin out of bed, but it's just . . . his hair . . . it's all, like . . ."

"Pubey," Josh says, laughing, and Lila throws the nub of a garlic stick at him.

My social battery is running low. I wonder if it's blinking red on my forehead, the way I feel.

"Well, both of them can sing," Lila says, twisting the straw. "It was *such* bullshit they wouldn't play 'Makes Me Wonder' at prom. Like we don't hear f-bombs all the fucking time." She squints. "Jess, were you there?"

"Ryan had a race that weekend." In fact, I'd been glad for the excuse to skip prom in favor of my five hundredth viewing of *Ella Enchanted* with Katie. In the bathroom at Cinema 6, my resolve had cracked. I'd texted her: *How's the play?* Her reply was one word: *Good.* I'm not sure if this is progress, or if I want it to be.

Lila cocks her head. "Ry, did Isabelle go to prom?"

I'm also not sure how Lila draws a line between me and Ryan's sister, but she knows full well that she's one of only a handful of freshmen who have ever attended our high school prom. Izzy is a girl who sticks to the fringes. Griffin and I might have grown apart, but Ryan and his sister have never gotten along. They're polar opposites. Even at their house, I rarely see her. Ryan gets the basement, and his sister gets the upstairs; that's the treaty. I like Izzy, though, and when I see her at school, usually with the same two girls, both slight and bespectacled like her, I make a point to wave.

"No. Izzy's a loser." Ryan scoffs at Lila's question before folding a slice of pizza into his mouth.

"No, she's not," I say.

Ryan's brow wrinkles. "Yeah, she is. She has, like, two friends. All she does is read fucking vampire novels and bake cupcakes."

Josh snickers.

"Hey, I like *Twilight*," Lila pipes up.

"Her birthday party was the most depressing thing I've ever seen: Izzy and two Mathletes watching Disney movies with zit cream all over their faces."

Heat rises to my cheeks. "Maybe she isn't a queen bee, but *some* people value quality over quantity when it comes to friends."

My statement lands like a cannonball. Lila has stopped

Frenching her straw and turns round eyes on Ryan, who now stares at me, slack-jawed.

"She's your sister," I argue. "Maybe you should stick up for her rather than judge her."

Ryan's frown deepens. "You talk shit about Griffin all the time."

"That's different. He's a jackass."

"And Isabelle's a nerd."

"What's wrong with nerds? Maybe some nerds are cool. Maybe nerds are happier." My head is pounding, blood rushing against my eardrums. I'm not sure why I'm so angry.

Lila's and Josh's eyes ping-pong between us.

Ryan raises his hands like this is a stickup. "Whoa, dude. Sorry, I didn't realize you and Isabeast were besties."

A faint smile twitches at the edges of Lila's lips, and I realize she's waiting for me to lose it, to flip the table like King Kong and make a scene. This is entertainment, something she can tell the Betties.

"I'm not a 'dude,'" I grumble, "and we're not 'besties.' I just don't like it when you exaggerate." But the wave of my anger has receded, leaving only the sandy shore of embarrassment. "Isabelle's cool. She's just . . . quiet." I flick a greasy mushroom from my plate.

"Sorry I brought it up," Lila says under her breath.

Josh points to the last piece of garlic bread. "Anyone gonna eat that?"

~

"What was *that* about?" Ryan has parked the Blazer in front of my neighbors' house. They're old and seem to always be asleep, so it's a place we make out. We won't be making out tonight.

"What was *what* about?" I reply.

"About my sister. You were, like, pissed."

It's humid, and the pleather of the truck's seat sucks at the backs of my legs as I fidget. "I'm not pissed. It's just . . ."

It's just that maybe I'm more like Izzy than you know. Maybe Katie was right; I'm not myself when I'm with you. Maybe I haven't been myself a lot.

I think back to the day on the picnic table in the Harts' backyard, and to all the days since. *Ryan: You like to ski? Me: Yeah, sure.* When you date someone who goes to a different school in a different town in a different state, you're met with the rush of a blank slate. Why not be the cool, outgoing person you want to be rather than the shy, sometimes anxious person you are?

Everyone feels that way sometimes . . . don't they?

Turning, I search Ryan's face. "Do you ever feel like, I don't know, it's all an act?"

Desperately, I want him to say yes; to say yes, he understands, because a lot of times he's just acting, too, and what a relief it is finally to be able to talk about it! But he squints, as if he's trying to read very, very fine print. "You mean Isabelle's *pretending* to be a dork?"

I turn to face the window, worried I might cry.

202

"Why would she do that?" he says.

"Never mind. I'm sorry. I think maybe I'm just getting sick again."

"Another cold?" He grimaces.

"Yeah, sure." Two little words. But words have weight.

Inside, I text Katie again. *U up?* No response. Maybe what I need to say is, *Ur right.*

17

August 23, 2007

"How about these?" I extend a pair of leather loafers polished to a mirrorlike sheen.

"Uh, no."

Ryan and I are wandering the Famous Footwear on Route 12 for a pair of dress shoes. He hates shopping, but he needs a new pair to take back to school, and he leaves in nine days. This afternoon, he showed up at my house with chicken soup, asking if I'd help him. "Awww," my mom gushed. It was only a can of Campbell's, but it was enough to make me think maybe I just needed to relax.

"Okaaaay, what about these?" I gesture to a reddish-brown pair of lace-ups, something you'd find in *GQ* or *Esquire*.

"Maybe if I was Tyler," he says.

"Ryan . . ."

"Fine." He rolls his head on his neck in a sign of exasperation.

"I'll try them on. Where's the guy who brings them."

The store is almost empty. Just rows of boxes under fluorescent lights and the rubber smell of new sneakers. Ryan cups his hands around his mouth and hollers toward the ceiling as if he's lost in the wild: "Hello? Anybody out there?" I roll my eyes, but it's kind of funny.

"May I help you?" The voice is familiar, and as I turn, my expression must be as startled as his. "Jess?"

"Evan!" Dread crackles through my body.

Ryan looks back and forth between us. "Hey," he says finally, the muscles of his forearm jumping as he shakes Evan's hand. *Is he flexing?* "I'm Ryan . . . Jess's boyfriend." His voice is deeper than normal, and his arm goes around my shoulder, only instead of feeling good, like when he touches me in front of Lila and Doug and Josh, it feels claustrophobic.

"You guys know each other from school?" His hand hangs over my shoulder. Discreetly, I shrug it off.

"Um, yeah, kind of," I answer before Evan can. "We had a history project together."

Evan wears a navy polo tucked into—dear God, no—*pleated* khakis. His eyes, their shifting color now the same as his shirt, seem to register my discomfort.

"Cool," Ryan says. He thrusts the shoebox toward Evan. "Ten and a half. And I guess those, too." He points to the loafers.

"Certainly," Evan says, but he doesn't move. Does he want me to elaborate? To explain to my boyfriend here, in the middle of Famous Footwear, that I'm secretly working with a random, kind of cute—when he's not being weird, or sometimes especially when he's being weird—shoe salesman to translate my dead great-great-aunt's hidden diaries so I can find out whether she was Anastasia Romanov? These are not two worlds that are ready to collide, and I just want Evan to stop being . . . *here*. But he stands there, as if not feeling awkward is his superpower.

Ryan looks at me sideways. "So"—I try some chitchat—"you work here."

Evan looks down at the lanyard and ID badge around his neck, stamped with his name in big, bold letters. "Indeed."

"Sorry to hear that," I joke, as if sarcasm could put some daylight between us.

Evan looks confused. "It's not so bad. There's a 401(k) plan if you stay for more than a year, and we get a twenty percent employee discount." All three of us look down at his pristine white sneakers. "We have a great sale section, too, if you haven't seen it." He points behind him.

"Cool." I sound like Ryan.

"So, you think you could hop along and get those for me?" Ryan says. "Not that we don't want to spend our night hanging out in Famous Footwear." It's flat-out rude, and I start to sweat. *How has this encounter gone off the rails so quickly?* It's why I never wanted it to happen in the first place.

"Right," Evan says. "I go . . . 'swifter than arrow from the Tartar's bow.'" He holds up the shoebox. "Ten and a half."

A mother has come into the store with her young daughter, who tears past Evan toward the kids' section. He follows them to the back of the store, calling, "May I help you with something, young lady?"

I feel warm and a little sick to my stomach.

"Swifter than arrow?" Ryan asks. I shake my head. One of his quotations.

We find a bench, and Ryan removes his smelly blue Adidas, holding one up to his nose and inhaling deeply before coughing and gagging. "*Ahhh, eau de* swamp heat!" He smiles.

"Gross." Exactly the reaction he's going for.

Evan returns quickly, balancing four boxes under his chin. He sets them on the floor by Ryan's feet, where I worry he can smell the "swamp heat."

"I've brought a ten and a half and an eleven, just in case." He gets down on one knee. *No . . .* I realize he's going for the fitting stool. *No, no, no, no, no.*

Ryan looks at me, not even trying to contain his laugh. "I'm good, man. I can put on my own shoes."

I'm not sure who I'm most embarrassed for—Evan, Ryan, me? I feel like I've taken a swig of sour milk and am looking for somewhere to spit it.

Evan picks himself up. "Shall I bring socks?" I can almost swear there is a special stress on the "shall." *Is he messing with me now?*

"Nah, I'll go commando," Ryan replies.

Evan looks as if he might object but then leaves us to deliver more boxes to the woman and the girl, who is now pulling shoes off shelves and screaming that she wants the purple unicorns. I soothe myself by studying the squiggle pattern on the carpet.

"These, I guess," Ryan says when Evan has returned to retrieve the boxes.

"Excellent choice."

"You sure they don't make me look gay?"

I cringe. Evan replies slowly. "I am fairly confident I cannot detect your sexual orientation from this choice of footwear."

Ryan looks at them again. "I don't care, dude," he says, frustrated. "I'll just get both."

"Excellent. Is there anything else I can help you with today?"

"Nope! Thank you, Evan!" I pop up, grabbing both boxes.

"Excellent. My colleague can assist you at the register." I'm already on my way there.

"Who was that weirdo?" Ryan asks, not quietly, as we wait for the manager to finish his call at the counter. "'Shall I get you some socks, good sir?'" Ryan impersonates Evan, affecting a very bad British accent. I don't laugh. "What, he's not, like, a friend, is he?"

"No."

"I think he might have a boner for you."

My heart hiccups in a strange way, but it's already beating erratically. "Gross, Ryan. No, he's just a random I know from this history thing. He's nobody."

The sound of Evan clearing his throat behind me hits like a bucket of ice water. I turn, shrinking from what I already know: he's been standing behind us. "Figured you wouldn't get far without these," he says, holding a key chain from which a tiny red Etch A Sketch dangles. Katie and I bought matching ones in ninth grade, dreaming of the day we could drive. I have never wanted to talk to her more. This morning she responded to my text from last night with a string of twelve Zs and the short message *Sry wuz sleeping.* At least she's responding.

Retrieving the keys from Evan, I mumble, "Thanks. Actually, Ryan drove."

Fire ants are crawling up my legs and arms, my face. *Show me the exit.*

"I'll see you . . . around," Evan says.

Lights have just flickered on at the Burger King across the parking lot, and a bat swoops low after a mosquito.

"Chicken fries?" Ryan asks. We're barely out of the shoe store, but a loop is playing over and over in my mind: *I think he might have a boner for you. . . . Just a random . . . He's nobody.* Had Evan heard it?

Ryan interrupts the replay. "You think he tries on all the women's shoes when no one's watching?"

"What? No, Ryan."

"You know, like that creep in *Silence of the Lambs*?"

"No, Ryan, I do not think Evan is a serial killer."

He bumps my shoulder. "But you don't *know* that."

"Look, he's nice, okay?"

Ryan stops abruptly. "What is going on with you? You've been weird all week."

There are so many shades of weird; why are some okay and some not? "Nothing is wrong with me, Ryan."

"Then why do you keep saying my name?"

"Because it's your name." I keep walking toward the car.

"Fine. Whatever." He follows me. "Doug's having people over."

"No," I say forcefully.

"What do you mean 'no'?"

I stop. "No, I don't want to go to Doug's house."

"Why not?"

"Because," I say, spinning on him, "Doug is a stupid, sexist dickhead who thinks getting wasted every weekend is the highest calling in life."

"What the fuck, Jess? That's my best friend."

I can't believe this is happening, not in the middle of a strip-mall parking lot that smells like flame-grilled meat. This wasn't my intention, but now that I've started, I'm a rock rolling downhill, picking up speed. "Why do you have to be such an asshole?"

"How am I an asshole?" Red has begun to creep up his neck, to the tips of his ears.

"You think anyone different from you is a loser. Like you're the only one who deserves to live." All that self-confidence I once admired in Ryan, what if it's just obliviousness, or arrogance?

"What are you talking about?" he spits.

"Do you think being a jerk makes you cool? Going to parties, not giving a shit about anything—is that what makes people like you?" *You're not yourself when you're around him.* "I don't like who I just was in there, Ryan."

"The only person being a dick right now is you."

Rage coils like a snake in my stomach. I want to push him, to shake him, to pound on his chest—anything to make him finally, truly *see* me.

A tear drops onto my shirt, and then another and another. "It's just sad, Ryan. This act, it's sad and desperate."

I know it's not him I'm talking about now, and I drop to the ground, crouching there with my face in my hands. He crouches next to me. The look on his face has changed; he's not angry anymore, but something I can't read. *Scared?*

"Why are you with me?" I demand. I'm asking him the question Katie asked me.

"What are you talking about, Jess?" He says it quietly, almost guiltily.

"Name two reasons."

"This is stupid."

It's like I've announced a pop quiz for 100 percent of his grade, but I need to know the answer. I wait. He sighs and looks around, then back at me. "Because you're cool and you're fun and you're pretty and we like the same stuff."

His answer is not much better than mine had been. "No," I say, defeated. "No, we don't, Ryan."

I think of all the little things about myself I've nudged under the rug so that Ryan would like me. And the bigger, bulkier things I shoved deep into a closet, the things I felt so sure were flaws but now wonder if they're just *me*. Everyone puts their best foot forward in a relationship, but if you don't watch where you're going, you can walk right off the cliff.

Snot is trickling from my nose, and I brush it away with my arm and stand. "You don't even know me," I say, the energy drained out of my voice. "You know a girl who pretends to be a person you could like."

His Adam's apple bobs. There are actual tears in his eyes. I've never seen him cry before.

"I'm tired," I croak, "of being someone I'm not."

It's over. Two little words balance on my lips. They have mass; they have inevitability.

More emotions slide across his face, and these ones I recognize: confusion, disbelief, panic. His eyes glisten with the sheen of held-back tears, and I know this isn't his fault, not really. I've never let him know me.

"But I love you, Jess."

I have loved him, haven't I? Or have I just been so afraid he couldn't love me?

"I'm sorry." The words tumble, and they're more real than any I've ever put to paper, because they can't be deleted.

~

We don't speak on the way home. When Ryan opens the car door and I step out, I am the one crying. He stands stiff as a tree trunk as I hug him and mumbles "I'm sorry" before turning and getting in the car to drive away. Why is he the one apologizing?

"What's wrong?" my mom asks as I come through the door.

I wasn't expecting her to be there. "Everything." I pound up the stairs. Her shadow lingers outside my bedroom for a moment, a smudge of darkness in the light coming through the crack at the bottom of the door. I know she is contemplating whether to yell at me for slamming the door. Finally, the shadow moves away.

18

August 24, 2007

There is a sadness that comes after typing the words *The End*. But there is also the exhilaration of the blank page that follows. While I wake feeling like a wrung-out dish towel from a night of sobbing into my pillow, a vague giddiness buzzes in my head as the morning sun throws bars of light across my floor. A sharp panic at having broken up with my boyfriend of two and a half years is also, oddly, accompanied by a strange sense of relief.

I stare at the ceiling. There is only one person who can help me sort through this all, and I can't let her be mad at me any longer. But before I apologize to Katie, I have to figure out how I'm going to apologize to Evan. After the scene at the shoe store, will he want to continue reading the diaries? Will he even still talk to me? Groaning, I pull the covers around my chin and, with shaky thumbs, punch out a tentative text message: *Still on for today?* Send.

I wait. Chew at my lip. Pull the covers over my head. *Ding.* I grab for the phone, but what started as a sigh of relief catches in my throat like a lump of dry bread.

Might have to reschedule.

Evan—my fingers fly across the tiny keyboard—*I'm so sorry . . .* They stop.

A second message has appeared: *Flat tire on the Porsche and Sonya has the car.*

Calling his bike a Porsche is corny, but it means he's not canceling because he hates my guts—at least not *only* because he hates my guts. Maybe he hadn't overheard what Ryan and I said at all. He had been helping the girl and her mother. . . .

Quickly, I respond: *I'll come to you.* Another uncomfortably long pause.

Ok.

I realize I don't even know where Evan lives, but when he gives me the address, I have to read it twice.

The cemetery? I ask. The cross streets are the same ones that he gave me before. *Wait. ARE you a vampire?*

No, but that would be cool. Next door.

So, I *have* been to Evan's house, not in it, but beside it: the old white farmhouse with the sunflowers and sagging roof.

Be there in 30.

Apple pie. Not sour cabbage or pickled beets or boiled potatoes or any of the other vaguely Russian smells I expected from

Evan's grandmother's kitchen. When I arrive, her house smells of freshly baked, cinnamon-spiked apple pie.

"Would you like a piece?" A half-drunk glass of milk sits on the counter, and a small white Pomeranian yips in circles at Evan's feet. "Anton, down!" he scolds.

The exterior might be slightly ramshackle, but inside, the house is cozy—a medley of throw pillows and flea market paintings, tchotchkes everywhere. In a small side room sits an old sewing machine with a project thrown over it. As Evan washes and hand-dries his plate, I inspect a calendar of Maine lighthouses, courtesy of TD Bank, hung beside the refrigerator. Everything in this house feels like a clue to Evan Hermann, but none of it fits the idea I have of him in my head.

Minutes earlier, I stood on his front steps wringing my hands, but when Evan answered the door, the knot in my stomach loosened; he seemed fine. This might, however, be explained by the five hundred dollars I handed him as I came through the door—the rest of my babysitting money and a hundred dollars I'd gotten from my mom, telling her I was going to buy a sundress. "First installment," I said, pressing the roll of twenties into Evan's palm. He considered it for a second and then stuffed the money into his pocket. I know that paying Evan is right and that I insisted, but my heart fell an inch when he took it, and when I realized maybe he's all right today because, when it comes down to it, I'm just another job.

Evan puts the rest of the half-drunk milk in the fridge.

"I'm not sure when Sonya will be home. If we want privacy, we should probably work upstairs."

His bedroom, unlike the downstairs, is uncluttered, with a way-too-big-for-the-room antique bed pushed into a corner. Gauzy curtains keep the morning light from bouncing harshly off the room's stark white walls. Aside from a poster for the Boston Symphony Orchestra tacked above the bed, the room's only notable feature is a vintage record player atop an old painted chest of drawers.

I drift toward the player. "You have records," I say. My dad loves to lecture Griffin and me on the virtues of vinyl.

"'Music is the shorthand of emotion.'"

I wait for the attribution.

"Tolstoy." He smiles.

Evan opens the closet door to reveal a tall bookcase wedged into the space where pants and shirts should hang. The bottom shelves are reserved for books, but the top two are stuffed with records. I tilt one out. Chopin. And another. Stravinsky. Most are classical, but there's the occasional Beatles or Dylan. *The Dark Side of the Moon.* John Coltrane. "These are just the greatest hits," Evan says.

"Which is your favorite?"

"You realize that's like asking a mother to name her favorite child."

I laugh. "I do." I feel the same about my books.

He runs a finger along the record sleeves. "This one," he says finally, pulling a record with a colorful cartoon on the cover. Not what I'd expected. *Peter and the Wolf* by Sergei Prokofiev, a "symphonic fairy tale."

"One of the first parts for oboe I learned. Each instrument represents an animal. Oboe's the duck."

This makes me smile. "Will you play for me?"

He seems surprised but nods.

From behind the bookshelf, he pulls a black musical case about two feet long. Inside, a complicated arrangement of silver levers and keys gleam against their velvet setting. From a much smaller case, he takes a reed and drops it into a cup of water on the windowsill. "It has to soak," he explains as he assembles the instrument. When he's done, he pulls the reed from the cup, gives it a gentle shake, and inserts it into the end of the oboe. "Here goes."

There isn't a chair in the room, so I perch on the side of his bed. Deliberately and gently, Evan places the reed between his lips. His chest swells, and the instrument releases its first note: a squawk. He frowns, fiddles, curses a little under his breath, and tries again. This time, a long, plaintive note emerges. Around the mouthpiece, his lips curve into a smile.

The song is one I know, and it does have a nicely duckish waddle to it. As Evan plays, fingers dancing on the keys, he closes his eyes. I'd feared he might look ridiculous with cheeks puffed around an oboe, but he doesn't. Elbows slightly cocked and head swaying, he's confident, entranced—he's in his zone.

When he's done, I whistle through my fingers, the way my dad taught me, and applaud. He takes a courtly bow.

"Seriously, Evan, you're really good! Like, really, really good."

"I'm getting better," he says, and it's not fake humility. He sets the oboe in the case.

"Well, *I've* never heard a better oboist." I grin.

Maybe I'm gushing a little too much, but even if he's not mad at me, I still feel bad about what happened at the shoe store. As I contemplate how to apologize without implicating myself if he *didn't* hear us, Evan surprises me by sliding up onto the bed beside me. "Oh," I say.

He scoots back so he's leaning against the wall. His feet dangle off the side. "Do you play an instrument?" he asks.

Am I supposed to scoot back? I wonder. *If I don't, will it be awkward? If I do, will it be awkward?* Then I realize, *It's Evan; he's awkward-immune.*

I push back on my hands so we're sitting side by side. "No," I answer his question. "I wanted to take piano as a kid, but my mom thought I'd like soccer more."

Across the narrow gap between us, I feel the warmth of his shoulder, his hip, his thigh. There's not the same tingling as in the graveyard; instead, there's a warm, squishy pretzel-like knot in my stomach.

"*Did* you enjoy soccer more?"

I shrug. "I never took piano, so I can't really compare. . . ."

"It's not too late," he says.

My hands are in my lap, and I stare at them, at the fingers that might have sat lightly on black and white keys. "My mom's sort of the master of those kinds of 'suggestions.'" I channel Val's voice: "'You should try it. . . . Your hair would look so nice long. . . . Maybe you could have studied more. . . . You'd hate California. . . . You'll love Harvard. . . .'"

They sound insignificant when I say them out loud, maybe even true. My mom thinks her advice will make me happy—*I've* thought her advice would make me happy. It's hard to explain to Evan all the tiny switches and levers a mom can use, the way all those *should*s and *could*s and *would*s can accumulate until they're greater than the sum of their parts and all those "suggestions" become, simply, *you*.

"Harvard, huh?" he says, and I detect a note of jealousy in his voice. "And how does your mom know so much about you when you're still figuring it out for yourself?"

His question is a dart hitting a bull's-eye. I can't look him in the eye as I respond. "I guess, sometimes it's just easier to take her word for it." It embarrasses me, how easily I've handed over so much of who I am.

Three seconds pass, and then five, and then what feels like an hour. Our arms touch now, the space between us having closed as we relaxed.

"Your hair does look nice long," he says finally, and I smile into my chest.

"Evan, about yesterday . . ."

"Does your boyfriend like his shoes?"

The B-word (the other one). *Should I tell Evan that Ryan and I broke up? Do I think he'll care? Do I want him to care?*

"Actually," I say, screwing up my courage to look Evan in the face, "Ryan's not my boyfriend anymore."

He feigns seriousness. "I hope it's not because of the shoes."

"Ha! No," I say. "It wasn't the shoes. It was something that had been coming for a long time."

"Well, that's good, because he seemed like a real asshole."

My eyes pop, but I'm laughing. "Thanks!"

"He's your ex now, isn't he?"

"Yeah, but sometimes there's no harm in telling a little white lie, you know? Like, 'I'm sorry to hear that. He seemed like a totally-acceptable-to-the-point-I-don't-question-your-judgment-but-not-quite-good-enough-for-you kind of guy.'"

"Is that true?"

I sigh. "Kind of."

"Well, I told you: like George Washington, I cannot tell a lie." He tilts his chin as if posing for a marble bust.

"Lying is a critical life skill."

He crosses his arms. "Entirely disagree."

"I'll teach you." He looks dubious. "Come on." I turn to face him, cross-legged. "We'll play Two Truths and a Lie."

I learned the game at Y camp as a kid. The rules are simple: I will tell Evan three statements about myself; two will be true and one will be a lie. He must guess which one is the lie.

I think for a second. "Okay. One: I broke my wrist as a kid while Slip-'N-Sliding. Two: I can recite all fifty states in alphabetical order. Three: I've started six novels but only finished three."

He eyes me. I hum a game-show tune.

"One," he says.

"No, three! I've started *seven* novels and only finished *two*."

He throws his hands up. "It's mostly true!"

"The best lies are. Your turn."

He groans. "I'm going to be terrible at this. Let's see. . . . One: I've never been—wait, no I have been. Shoot. Okay, let me start over."

"All right, you are really bad at this."

"I told you. Okay. One: Last year I was top eight in a Southern New Hampshire Magic tournament—that's a big deal. Two: I speak six languages."

"You've told me that before."

"Okay. Two: I am deathly afraid of spiders. And three"—he takes the money I gave him earlier out of his pocket—"I don't want your money."

He extends the roll of cash in his palm. "Why? Evan, you've earned it. Take it." I fold the money into his hand by wrapping my fingers around his. They hover there, loosely clasped, as my stomach does a somersault.

"It's not important, Jess. It's not why I'm doing this anymore."

"Then why are you doing this?" I ask quietly.

For the first time ever, I think he's speechless. "'There are chance meetings with strangers that interest us from the first moment, before a word is spoken.' *Crime and Punishment*." He pauses. "I like being around you, Jess."

There is no oxygen in my lungs as my eyes meet his. "I like being around you, too."

He blinks. "Good." The smell of cinnamon clings to him.

"Good," I breathe.

"Should we see what happens next?"

"What happens next?" I repeat, and suddenly, he is leaning over me, and suddenly, I am realizing why my father was so strange about Evan being in my room the other day, because my heart is slamming in my chest, and I think Evan Hermann is going to kiss me—

"In the journals," he says. He is reaching for the messenger bag at the end of the bed. He sits up, holding a diary. "Berlin."

"Berlin." I am an idiot, a suddenly flustered and overly warm idiot who's started sweating in the small, un-air-conditioned room. Of course Evan wasn't trying to kiss me; yesterday, I called him a random and a nobody.

"Yes." I collect myself. "The diaries."

"Dangit," he says, smacking himself on the forehead.

"What?" I ask, and a feeling shaped like hope blooms in my chest.

"I forgot to make one of them a lie."

We're intrigued to find that the first pages of the next diary have been torn out. In their place are two loose pieces of paper, folded and tucked neatly into the front.

"Mysterious," Evan says, waggling his eyebrows. He unfolds the creased pages.

March 1, 1920 (cont.)

We head for Paris.

After the Tiergarten, returned to Ritterstrasse. Barely had the coat slipped from my shoulders when a frantic knocking shook my door. I opened it to find Johanna, in a state of high agitation. "Are you insane?" She burst in, locking the door behind her.

No, it was Anna who was insane. Did she know? I told her what I'd found, where I'd been—

"I know where you've been," Johanna hissed, "and you've risked everything." Astonished, I stood as she ripped the curtain across my window and peered from behind it onto the street below. She turned, and her hands gripped my shoulders like two vises. "If you heard of a survivor, don't you think they will have as well?"

"Who?" I asked.

"Don't be naive," she spat. "There are Soviet agents in Berlin." Then, seeing my terror, she softened. "Anna," she said, "you must go. This has drawn attention."

Werner. Johanna. She'd been watching me the whole time.

I was given ten minutes to pack before being escorted to Potsdamer Bahnhof. One ticket to Paris.

"Where will I go?" I asked Johanna. She pressed a piece of paper into my palm. The train whistled—

Nothing is ever as it seems.

Yours,

A

There's more to the entry on the second page. In Frankfurt, where Anna changed trains, she was certain that a short, bald man with a mustache and round glasses was following her. She locked herself in a couchette. What follows reads like a fever dream, scattered stream-of-consciousness lamenting the cruelty of the world and the evil that lurks within it. The entry doesn't end with a sign-off but with a thin, jerky line down the page, as if, exhausted, she fell asleep pen in hand.

"Why are they torn out?" Evan asks, turning the loose sheets over in his hands.

I think about the pages I've torn from my own notebooks, writing I was embarrassed or sad about. "Maybe what was in them was upsetting," I say. "She wasn't in the best state of mind."

"But she saved them?"

I shrug, thinking also of the pages I've fished from wastebaskets.

We refold the paper and hope that the next entry might help explain.

3.3.1920

Better now. Travel exhausts me, rouses the old dark dreams. I awake shivering and sweating. But two days of rest, and I am myself again.

From Gare de l'Est, proceeded to the address Johanna shared at Potsdamer: 88 Rue du Bac. Paris is quite different than Berlin, more like Petersburg, with its wide boulevards and arching bridges, but I found the address and arrived at 88 just as the sun was coming up. Only, as I came closer, there he was! Barring the entrance to the building, the man from the train. It hadn't been a dream! Round glasses, oily mustache.

Panicking, I turned. He pursued. I quickened my pace. Behind me, his voice a hiss: "Anna." I thought to run, but his hand was on my wrist! I screamed, tried to wrench it free. He gripped it tighter. "Grand Duchess," he whispered. "I am a friend of Johanna's." He spoke not in French but in Russian.

There is so much to take in. It overwhelms me, like drinking water from a running tap. For now, I'll share this, the most important: to my knowledge, I am safe. The man, whom in these pages I shall call Monsieur Gagnon, works with those who delivered me from Yekaterinburg. He has brought me to a house, with a bed and fresh clothes and books and a pen and even this journal, which I have found in a drawer and taken for my own. He has insisted that I rest and assures me that all will be made clear if I agree to dine with him tomorrow.

I do not know whether I can afford to trust Gagnon or whether I can afford not to, but I do know that I am exhausted, that my nerves are badly frayed, and that he has offered me a foothold in a city where I do not know a soul. For now, he is all I have.

Yours,

A

It's been overcast all morning, and outside, the clouds finally release their rain. Fat drops patter the windowpane at the end of Evan's bed. Neither of us move.

"It's kind of hard to believe—" I start.

"It is," Evan agrees before I've finished my statement. His finger holds our place in the diary, though we're only three pages in.

I frown. "I was going to say it's *hard to believe* she went through so much. . . . What did you mean?"

He swallows and appears to be choosing his words carefully. "Just that what Anna's describing in the journals is incredible."

Since the day in the cemetery, something he said has been pinballing around in my mind: *maybe* Anastasia *was that girl, but Anna . . .* In the moment, I'd assumed he meant that what Anastasia had been through had changed her, into Anna. But had Evan been saying he wasn't sure Anastasia and my aunt were one and the same? It needles me. Not just because Evan has his doubts but because he's planting them in me.

"Incredible-extraordinary," I start to say, "or incredible-incredi—"

"Evan?" A woman's voice is followed by the sound of footsteps on the stairs.

Evan springs from the bed and pokes his head into the hall. "Be down in a second!" He seems flustered. "Sonya," he says to me, apologetically.

"Baba, this is my friend Jess." In the middle of the kitchen, Evan helps his grandmother shed her raincoat.

"Call me Sonya," she says. "I hate Baba."

Once again, I realize what I'd been expecting was a cliché: head scarf knotted under stubbled chin, gray teeth, blocky shoes. Sonya is beautiful. With her clogs, long gray hair pulled into a braid, and turquoise earrings, she looks a lot younger than my grandma in Florida. She's no *babushka*, although there's an earthiness about her that allows me to imagine her milking goats on a Russian potato farm. The cliché again.

"Did you get pie?" she asks.

"I offered!" Evan defends himself as she clucks and cuts me a slice.

We sit at the kitchen table as Evan makes tea and Sonya tells me about her bad knees and the construction on Route

9. She asks how I know Evan, and I tell her we met through a project we're working on together. "Always a busy one," she sighs.

Evan sets a mug on the table in front of me. "I'm a man of many interests, Baba."

"'It's not enough to be busy; so are the ants. The question is: What are you busy about?' Thoreau." She winks at me. *So that's where he gets it from.*

"Actually, that's a misquote, and you know it."

She shrugs.

Sonya tells me how Evan was in debate club in high school and editor of the student newspaper. How he insisted on being driven to the local community college twice a week as a junior so he could take Spanish because the class at school conflicted with his AP Calculus. How, as valedictorian, his graduation speech had received a standing ovation.

"Really?" I say, amused. "Let me guess—'Oh, the places you'll go.' Dr. Seuss?"

He smirks. "Hardly."

At Keene State, Evan made dean's list both semesters last year, and they're talking of bringing in a German professor at his request. I wonder if Sonya's recited this resume for a girl before. For some reason, I want to think she hasn't.

"You know he's a card shark, too. Better at bridge than any of us. And if you play poker—ho, watch out! He'll take the shirt off your back."

"Baba, that's not the kind of poker my friends play," Evan says.

"That's the kind of poker all boys want to play."

Evan rolls his eyes, a rare blush forming on his cheeks, and I take the opportunity to ask Sonya about the thing, beyond her grandson's extracurriculars, that I'm most intrigued about. "Evan says you're originally from Russia. . . ."

Her lips press together. "Ah, yes. I was born in Nizhny Novgorod."

"And how did you end up here?"

Evan watches her, looks at me, and I fear that maybe I've once again pried too much, but Sonya answers, "My father was a defector, a journalist. When I was ten, my family moved to Moscow. At seventeen, we escaped through East Berlin; Papa was there to report on a chess tournament."

Gravity seems to tug just a little bit harder at the wrinkles around Sonya's eyes. "Most of my life, we lived where the FBI told us to live. Evan's grandfather and I moved to New Hampshire in 1974. It was quiet, all-American. No one was worried about Russians in their midst."

Evan refills our mugs. I'm sure he's heard this history before. "What was it like growing up there," I ask, "in Niz—" I struggle with the pronunciation.

"Nizhny Novgorod." Sonya speaks with almost no accent, but her tongue rolls the syllables of the word effortlessly around her mouth. She smiles. "Sometimes it feels good to say it. For many years, we couldn't. . . . Russia was beautiful, and it was hard," she says.

When she gets up for more sugar, I notice a hobble in her gait. "First, there was the war—you call it 'World War Two'; we called it the 'Great Patriotic War.' So patriotic we lost eleven million men—twenty-seven times as many as the Americans."

She lets that figure sink in, plunks a sugar cube into her mug. "Then there were the civilian deaths. We were lucky to be alive. No money, sometimes no food. Everywhere, distrust . . . My father worked for the state-run newspaper. We were watched."

"Was he against the Communists?" I ask.

She takes a sip. "He was not *for* the Communists."

"Was he a White Russian, then? For a monarchy?" Here I finally have an actual Russian, someone who wouldn't herself have known life under the Romanovs but whose parents would have. I wonder, what did she think of them?

"Ha. No," Sonya says resolutely. "The tsar ate caviar while the peasants starved. My father was for democracy."

Evan clearly hasn't told Sonya about the diaries. What would she think to learn my great-great-aunt was that caviar-eating tsar's daughter?

"But," Sonya says, shuffling from the table with her plate, which she places in the sink, "*some* of us would leave such things behind us." She brushes her hands against each other as if sloughing off the dirt of the past.

There's tension in the air now, and I regret that maybe I've caused it. I'd assumed that Evan studied Russian because his family was from there, but it seems Sonya is more than happy to distance herself from the country she left.

A cell phone rings in another room, jangly and loud, and Evan jumps to search for it.

"My apologies," Sonya says once he's gone. "I've ruined this nice meeting talking too much of ancient history. I try to look forward." She sits back down.

With Evan gone, there's more I want to ask, about his father and his mother, but that's not exactly looking forward. I'll have to be tactful. "Evan doesn't seem to talk much about the past, either. . . ." I say. "At least his own; he's perfectly happy to lecture on world history."

Sonya smiles sadly. "His mother. He's told you."

"A little bit."

She sighs heavily. "It's hard to know what to do with him. He doesn't understand that she was sick."

"Sick how?" I'm surprised that he didn't mention this.

"An alcoholic," Sonya says, and pieces of the puzzle begin to click into place. "After Mark died, I'd find bottles stashed around the house. Vodka, I'm afraid, if you can appreciate the irony."

Evan's always talking about the facts. How could he have left out this crucial one?

Sonya shuffles from the room and returns quickly with a photo in an old silver frame: Evan and his mother in the car of a kids' carnival ride. Her head is thrown back in laughter, and her hands—long and graceful, like Evan's—are in the air, but he grips the safety bar, staring straight into the camera with gritted teeth. I wonder if it was his father taking the photo.

"This is Stacy," Sonya says. "Stasia, officially," she adds. "She changed it in high school. Knew how to get under my skin. Fascinated by everything our family worked so hard to leave behind." But Sonya chuckles.

So, it was his mother who inspired Evan's interest in all things Russian.

"I suppose it affected her, living the way we did. We moved six times before she was ten. When I told her the truth, she was thirteen; she wouldn't speak to me for days.

"She was my miracle," Sonya continues. "Her father and I, we weren't sure we could have children, but then she arrived, a surprise. I was forty-two. She had Evan at twenty-one. Still so young . . ." She trails off.

We both look at the photo, at the little boy holding on for dear life. "In a way," she says slowly, "I think she thought she was doing better by him by leaving."

"Sorry," Evan says, bustling through the door. Sonya discreetly drops the photo to the table, covering it with her hand. "That was Stuart. He's LARPing at one. I was thinking maybe you—" Evan's eyes slide down to the photograph, and he stops. The expression on his face darkens, the way it did at the graveyard. He's angry.

"Larping?" I ask brightly.

His jaw twitches. "Live-action role-playing. . . . But you probably have a lot to do today."

All I had to do today was read the diaries with him. We've barely begun, but it's clear from his tone that Evan would like me to leave. Prying about his mom was the last straw. "Yeah," I lie, "there's some stuff I need to get done."

When I say I have to go back to Evan's room to get my things, Sonya's eyebrows jump hopefully. If she only knew what we'd really been doing up there.

"Please come back and visit," she says, walking me to the door once I've retrieved the messenger bag and journals. "For dinner. Anytime." I promise I will as Evan sulks behind her.

"I'll leave you to say goodbye." I think she gives Evan a look as she goes.

He stands with a hand on the door, as if he can't close it behind me fast enough. I'd come to repair the damage I'd done to our friendship, but I've only done more.

"Evan, I'm sorry . . . about yesterday and—"

He cuts me off. "I'm not another mystery for you to solve, Jess."

"What? I know that. I was just asking Sonya about your family . . . and then she got out the photo."

"And I don't care what people think of me, including some rich jerk in a shoe store, and including you."

It stings like a slap.

"Look, I get it," he continues. "He's soccer; I'm piano. I don't fit your neat, perfect little life. That's why you lied to your boyfriend about me and why you lied to your dad the other day."

"My 'neat, perfect little life'?" I scoff. *Hardly. I just torpedoed anything remotely resembling that.*

"No," I tell him, "that's not why I didn't tell my dad about you . . . and it wasn't a lie; this *is* a history thing, and I'm writing a paper—"

"Wait, you're doing this for *school*?"

"No!" *Why is he twisting everything around?*

"You tell me now?"

"I'm writing about the Romanovs—it's just an extra-credit thing—but that's not what *this* is about."

"What is this about, then?" he asks. "An extra-special project for your Harvard application? I'm sure the admissions department will be intrigued."

I take a step back. "What does Harvard have to do with any of this?"

"I have to get ready for LARPing."

He closes the door in my face.

My car is parked near the graveyard. Hunched over the steering wheel, I let the tears fall in my lap as I dial Katie. They match the patter of rain on the windshield. It goes straight to voice mail. Her phone is off. Or she silenced me.

I'm crying because I broke up with Ryan. I'm crying because

I miss Katie. And I'm crying because I know the answer to Evan's question. At least part of the answer: what this is about is that I like Evan Hermann.

When I get home, something is burning. Neither of my parents' cars are in the garage, so I think I'm safe to stomp upstairs and wallow in my own misery, when I smell it. Weed.

The rain has stopped, and the back door is open. "Griffin!" I charge onto the porch, expecting to tear my brother a new one, but I'm shocked instead to find my father. His eyes widen when he sees me. Quickly, he stubs out a joint on the wet railing.

"Dad?"

He's waving the air around him. "Hey, Jess," he says sheepishly. "I'm sorry, it's not what it looks—well, yes, actually it is, but you shouldn't—"

"Don't worry," I say, walking to lean on the banister next to him. "I don't. But since when do you?"

"Not for many, many years," he says. "Guess I was curious if it had changed."

We're quiet for a second. "Is everything okay, Dad?"

It's only after I ask that I realize both how terrified I am he'll give me an honest answer and also how much I wish he would do it anyway. Because I want to be honest with him, too. I want to tell him about the diaries, about Evan, about breaking up with Ryan, about Katie being right and that I'm so, so tired of pretending in my life. But I need him to go first.

He looks at me and plants a kiss on top of my head. He smells like pot. "Yeah, sweetie. Everything's fine." What's left of the joint he pinches between two fingers. "Gonna flush this down the toilet."

At the door to the house, he turns. "Hey, Jess . . ."

"Yeah?"

"Don't tell your mom, huh?"

19

August 25, 2007

"Hi."

"Hi."

Evan stands on my doorstep.

I texted him this morning: *I think you need to come over.* When he didn't respond, I told him, *They found the missing bodies.*

"I'm sorry," Evan says, "about yesterday. I overreacted."

Every cell in my body wants to hug him. Instead, I say, "I'm sorry, too."

He nods, smiling.

My dad's in the den. As we walk past, he waves to Evan from his chair. Earlier I told him the boy from the other day was coming over, that there was something interesting in the trunk of diaries I found at Aunt Anna's, and that this boy is helping me translate them. It's almost the whole truth.

Upstairs, Evan and I stare at the computer screen. Over my shoulder, he reads the article that popped up this morning in the news alert I set for anything Romanov related. When he's done, he stands up straight, sighs.

"But they won't be *sure* until they've done the DNA testing," I say.

The article, in a UK newspaper called *The Guardian*, starts out sensational, recounting the events of the grisly murders and the 1991 discovery of the mass grave. From there, however, it reports an announcement by Russian officials in Yekaterinburg that the remains of two more individuals have been discovered not far from the original grave site. The remains, found by an amateur archaeologist and his team, appear to be those of a male aged ten to thirteen and a female between the ages of eighteen and twenty-three, though no conclusive ruling can be made until DNA testing on the forty-four bone fragments is complete.

Evan tugs at his hair. "I don't know, Jess; I think maybe you have your answer."

I swivel in the chair to face him. "*We* have *our* answer. . . . But, Evan, there could be bodies all over that area! There was a revolution going on. And Anastasia was seventeen when she was killed, not eighteen."

"Her sister was nineteen," Evan says calmly, "and there's been disagreement whether it was her body or Anastasia's in the first grave."

I'm starting to get annoyed. The seed of doubt Evan planted

is trying to send up a sprout. "Why do you not sound surprised?" I ask.

"We don't have evidence. . . ."

I cross to the trunk and pick up a journal, brandishing it like Moses with the Ten Commandments. "These are our evidence. What reason would she have to invent them? What did she gain? We don't have motive, either."

"The diaries aren't *proof*, Jess." He's brought a backpack with him. It lies at his feet, and he swings down to open it, pulling out a manila folder. "This," he says, sighing, "is proof." He hands it to me.

"What is this?"

There's an official-looking seal on the folder's front: New Hampshire Historical Society. Why hadn't I thought to look there? Evan had.

"Read it," he says.

Inside the folder is a sheaf of papers, photocopies of older documents: forms, lists, handwritten notes. My eyes settle on the top page.

```
Admittance Report

Name: Anna H. Wallace
Sex: Female
Age: 61
Color: White
```

Address: 213 Oak Street, Keene, New Hampshire

Employment: None

Notes:

Patient exhibits delusions and signs of severe mental exhaustion. Possible candidate for electro-convulsive therapy. Family commitment.

Admitted by: Elsie W. Morgan

Signed: Elsie W. Morgan

Date: March 12, 1963

Received by: Dora K. Lawrence, RN

Signed: Dora K. Lawrence

I look up. Evan wears a pained expression. "My friend Russell has an internship at the historical society; his aunt works there. It has all the old records from the state psychiatric hospital. They're not public, but I had him do a search for Anna Wallace."

"A psychiatric hospital?"

"After reading about the asylum, weren't you wondering if maybe she herself had been in one?"

How long has he had this? "When were you going to tell me?" I ask angrily.

"I just got them yesterday. Russell brought them LARPing. I was going to call you today."

I flip through the papers. Visitation notes from a Dr. Douglas Needham. His handwriting is messy, but I pick out what's important: *Irrational. Idiosyncratic. Neurotic. Episodic depression punctuated by hysteria. Delusions of persecution firmly maintained.*

There is a list, three pages long, recording the dates and times of Anna's electroshock therapy. At the back of the stack is a discharge report from September 1963. Two years after Henry's death. She had been committed for more than five months. *Patient cured. Depression controlled with monoamine oxidase inhibitors and sedatives, as needed. Released to family.*

"Released to family." I flip back to the admittance report. "'Admitted by Elsie W. Morgan.'"

My great-grandmother. Dad didn't tell me any of this, but he was just a little kid, so maybe he didn't know. Or he didn't want me to know—Morgans aren't great at the truth, the whole truth, and nothing but the truth.

"To get someone committed . . ." I say.

"They have to be declared legally incompetent. That's in there, too. She had it overturned, after a while. When she got out."

Tears are stinging the corners of my eyes. "Did you ever believe her?" I whisper.

"I wanted to believe as much as you do."

"*Did* you?"

"Jess, think rationally. A centenarian in Keene, New

242

Hampshire, is Russian royalty and has kept that secret her entire life?"

I'm not ready to give up. Anastasia didn't. "We've been over this," I tell him. "She had enemies. Sonya knows what that's like. . . . What do you think would have happened if the bread lines of Soviet Russia knew there was a living Romanov? Anastasia didn't want to be a puppet in some political game, or paraded around parties as a poor, lost princess. She wanted control over her own life."

"Over her own delusion," he corrects me.

"Has it occurred to you maybe she was just exhausted? Exhausted from pretending? 'Depression' and 'neurosis'—yeah, I'd be pretty depressed and neurotic, too! And maybe she was right to keep it a secret! Maybe she told someone and got committed for it by her own family."

Evan runs his hands over his face.

I shove the folder at him. "My great-great-aunt was Anastasia Romanov. Until there is proof *otherwise*, that's what I choose to believe."

He looks at me, exasperated. "Jess, why do you care so much that your aunt was Anastasia?"

Now I'm the one exhausted. "Evan, I have broken up with my boyfriend, my best friend isn't speaking to me, my family is falling apart, and I'm not even sure who I am anymore. These"—I gesture to the diaries—"are *all* I have."

"They're not all you have." His gaze goes to the laptop on

243

my desk, to the latest model cell phone on my bed, to a photo on my dresser of my family smiling, dressed in matching outfits. He runs a hand over his face and looks me straight in the eye. "You could have the truth."

My mom has tried to fix them a thousand times, but the stairs in our house are old and creaky. They whine as Evan trudges down them. From the hallway outside my bedroom, I listen for the click of the front door closing behind him.

I answer on the first ring.

"How you doing, kiddo?"

It's Katie. After a blubbering, jumbled voice mail in which I inform her that I've broken up with Ryan, that I caught my dad smoking pot, that there's a whole new guy she's never even heard of, and that I really, really, *really* need her to call me back, she does. Turns out she hasn't been avoiding me, not entirely; she's just been in back-to-back performances all week.

She thinks it's Ryan I'm most upset about. "I know you hated him, Katie," I say.

"'Hate' is a very strong word. To be honest, I barely knew the guy. . . . It kind of seemed you wanted it that way."

"What do you mean?" Behind the locked door of the bathroom I share with Griffin, my knees are tucked up under my chin. I'd come for more tissues and never made it out.

"I mean you seemed pretty happy to create your Ryan bubble."

244

"Katie, I asked you to hang out with us all the time!"

She barks a laugh. "Yeah, but you didn't mean it."

I'm struck dumb. Mostly because she's right. All this time, I'd wanted to think the distinct boundary between my friendship with Katie and my relationship with Ryan was Katie's fault, but the arrangement wasn't just one I'd settled for; it was one I created. The truth was, I didn't want Katie and Ryan hanging out, because I was afraid of being busted for pretending to be someone I wasn't. I *had* been busted, by Katie.

"Look, I'm not mad at you, Jess—okay, maybe I was a little mad at you."

"You gave me the finger on a playground."

"Well, in that instance, you deserved it. . . . I just wanted you to realize that *you* were enough, that you didn't have to be this other girl you thought Ryan would like." Katie hadn't been mad that I'd betrayed her; she'd been mad that I was betraying myself.

"But, look," she says. "I can hate him if you want me to."

"No." I laugh, blowing my nose. "But thank you."

"Eh," she says, and I can imagine her dismissively waving a hand in the air, "that's what friends are for. More importantly, *who* is this Evan character?"

I tell Katie everything: about Evan, about the diaries, about the bodies that were just found, right up to the asylum records and our fight—if that's what it was—yesterday. Then I groan. I dread seeing Ryan, if not before he leaves for Mountainvale,

245

then eventually at one of our families' get-togethers. I dread going back to school myself, with Lila and the Betties and the inevitable gossip about how *Jess Morgan* broke up with Ryan Hart. More than any of that, I dread the thought that this might have been the last chapter for me and Evan.

"Katie, what am I gonna do?"

"Well, Jesshire Cat, you're gon-na . . . 'put on a happy face.'" She breaks into her best *Bye Bye Birdie* rendition.

"Jess," Katie says when she's done singing.

"Yes, Idina Menzel."

"I am sorry for flipping you off."

Katie has apologized. There's a first time for everything.

20

August 26, 2007

"Okay, now I'm going to have you stand here." By my shoulders, the photographer physically moves me two inches to the left. "And you can stand here." If she wasn't a woman and wearing a very expensive camera around her neck, I think Griffin might sock her one.

The photo shoot is in our backyard, which has already been set up for the annual Morgan family reunion. I'd forgotten about it. Every last Sunday in August. *Yay.*

My dad's cousins will be driving in from Massachusetts. Uncle Dale and Aunt Mae are coming, too, from Manchester. And their two sons, Ken and Neil, who play hockey at Boston College.

First, though, the family photo shoot. *Double yay.*

The photographer's assistant buzzes around us, holding a light gauge to my dad's forehead. "A little in the shadows," she says, nudging him forward. This morning, after he returned from a suspiciously long doughnut run, I gave him a good sniff. No pot smell, so that's good.

We stand awkwardly in front of a large shrub. Mom smooths my hair, pulls it over my shoulder, reconsiders, tucks it back behind my ear. Evan said I look nice with long hair; this makes my chest hurt. I haven't heard from him. "Let him come to you" was Katie's advice. It's not working.

"When is Ryan coming today?" Mom asks.

Ugh. In forgetting about the reunion, I'd also forgotten that Ryan comes every year. He loves my uncle's dirty jokes. It's been almost three days, but I still haven't told my family about the breakup. Mostly, I'm surprised Mrs. Hart hasn't called my mom with the news. It means Ryan hasn't told his mom, either.

"He can't come," I say. Partial truth—he can't come because we're no longer dating.

"What? That sucks," Griffin whines.

I roll my eyes. "You'll have Ken and Neil." Griffin worships our cousins, too. A couple of years ago, Neil got drunk at Ken's graduation party and puked into a potted plant. Griffin hasn't stopped talking about it.

The photographer kneels and holds up her index finger. "All right, everyone!" Behind her, her assistant is smiling way too big, as if to show us how it's done. "Pretend like you like each other!"

Cheese.

As a kid, I loved Morgan family reunions. Hands sticky with watermelon, potato salad on picnic blankets, and Wiffle ball until the sun went down. Now it's a special kind of torture.

Ken and Neil don't come, which means it's just Griffin and me and my second cousin—*Tallulah*—who is nine and the hyperactive byproduct of my father's cousin's third marriage to an artist from Vermont. Griffin and I park ourselves at the beverage station in an unholy alliance and sip cold Cokes—the evil full-sugar, full-caffeine kind that my mom buys only for parties, making sure everyone within earshot knows this rule.

"So, how's your summer going?"

"It's going," I say cautiously, unused to questions from my brother that aren't just veiled ways of telling me that I suck. "Yours?"

He shrugs. "Where's Ryan?"

"Training." *Probably.*

Griffin nods. "He trains a lot. Probably why he's so good."

"Yup. Hey, I'm gonna say hi to Uncle Dale."

"Bring me a deviled egg."

"You've already had four."

"Is that too many, Mom?"

"Fine. You get one."

My uncle stands by the food table. A thought has occurred to me: I know my dad thinks Uncle Dale shirked his responsibilities when it came to Aunt Anna, but she was his great-aunt, too. Maybe he knows *something*.

"Hey, Half-Pint." The nickname really hasn't fit since my growth spurt in eighth grade, but I've never pointed it out. Uncle Dale is short, and I think it makes him feel good to talk about someone else being shorter.

We chitchat about my summer, about Ken and Neil, about college applications, and then I cut to the chase. "Hey, Uncle Dale, this is *really* random, but remember Aunt Anna? I helped Mom clean out her house this summer, and I'm just wondering if you know anything about her. She's a little bit of a mystery to me."

"A mystery. Huh, that's one way to put it. Tough old bird, hung on to that house forever." He drains half the Corona he's holding. "Let's see . . . she was married to Dad's uncle Henry. Gram never liked her, you know—our grandma, Henry's sister. He and Anna were an odd match, I guess, what with the age difference. Wasn't common in those days for a man to marry an older woman."

"How much older?"

"Five, six years. Gram might have been overly protective. Their mom died when they were little. Scarlet fever."

Trying to unlock my great-great-aunt's mystery, I realize there's plenty about the rest of my family I don't know. "Do you remember where Anna was from?"

"Boston, I think. That's where she met Uncle Henry. Although now that you say it, she did have that funny little accent. Kind of came and went. Guess she came from some-where! We all did!" He tips his bottle as if to salute America's rich immigrant history.

"Well, not all of us," I mumble, recalling our ninth-grade unit on Native Americans, but I don't have time to educate Uncle Dale on American imperialism.

He scratches the balding spot at the back of his head. "You know, if you're interested in the family history, I've got all the photos and papers and stuff."

What? My father never mentioned a trove of family memo-rabilia. Of course, I'd never told him I was looking for it.

"You know, deeds, birth certificates, letters. I've got all that crap in a box somewhere. You could check it out." His beer is empty. He eyes the beverage table. "Some cool stuff in there, actually. You might like it. Someone's gotta take it all when I croak."

"Can I come tomorrow?" Manchester's less than an hour and a half's drive.

"Sure," he says, surprised. "I'm flying, but I'll let Mae know you're coming."

"Thanks, Uncle Dale."

He slaps me on the shoulder, a little too forcefully so that I lurch forward. "No problem, Half-Pint."

My mom approaches, and together we watch Uncle Dale wander, unsteadily, toward the bar. "I hope he wasn't telling you one of his terrible jokes." She smiles conspiratorially. "He's sad

Ryan's not here. He asked about him. . . . Everything okay with you two? We haven't seen him in a while."

"We got in a fight."

"Oh, sweetheart," she says. "I'm sorry. You'll work it out."

I hesitate. "Maybe I don't want to work it out."

"But you and Ryan are great together!"

"Are we?" I ask harshly, turning to face her.

Her brow furrows. "Sweetie, people fight; it doesn't mean they don't love each other." She reaches to brush a strand of hair from my face. I turn my head.

"Are you talking about me and Ryan, or you and Dad?"

Her hand falls to her side. "Your dad and I are fine."

They aren't fine. She knows that, right? All the bickering, her long hours at work, her insistence to "put on a happy face." I glance around. Where is my father, anyway? Off smoking pot again? I guess he has his own means of escape.

"Is this about the boy who came by the other day?" My dad must have told her.

"No," I say. Then, "Kind of."

"Maybe if you just talk to Ryan. . . ."

"Stop, Mom!" I don't mean to shout it. "My life is not some house for you to stage."

At the beverage table, Uncle Dale and my dad's cousin turn.

My mom steps back, confused. "Sweetie, I only want you to be happy, to know you can—"

"What, have it all? But what if my version of 'all' isn't the same as yours?"

Her expression shows hurt. "I was going to say, 'tell me anything.'"

"Valerie, do you know where that other cooler is?" My dad has walked up.

"Not now, John," she hisses. He looks between us and leaves.

The shape of a father. I don't know, like Evan or Anastasia, what it is to lose a parent, and I'm lucky for that, but I know something about having one slowly disappear. I resent my mom's meddling, but I'm mad at my dad, too, mad that he's given up.

My mother studies my face. "What is going on with you, Jess? I feel like I know you less and less these days."

"Maybe," I say brusquely, "you never knew me to begin with."

It cuts her, I know it, and as I walk away, there's already regret at the back of my throat. But I'm tired of pretending to be the daughter my mom wants me to be. Can't she just love the person I am? Introverted, yes, but observant. Bookish, maybe, but imaginative. Awkward, a lot, but for the first time in my life simply trying to be honest.

"Whoa," Griffin says as I storm past the deviled eggs. "Didn't know you had it in you."

21

August 27, 2007

The Morgan family archives are three large cardboard boxes
of photo albums, birth announcements, marriage invitations,
loose Polaroids, and bundles of letters not much more orga-
nized than the journals jumbled in the trunk had been. The
same approach to going through them seems to fit, then: dig in.

After the family reunion, I spent time I should have used
to work on my history paper scouring an ancestry website. I'd
unearthed two census records listing Henry Frank Morgan as
head of household with his wife, Anna, middle initial *H*, and
a death certificate for him. My legs went rubbery when I read
the date on the certificate: July 17, 1961—the anniversary of the
Romanov murders. A coincidence, surely, and a horrible one.
No wonder Anna became a recluse; she must have felt cursed.

Another hour searching for Anna Wallace, Anna H.
Wallace, and Anna Haswell turned up only unrelated records

from the 1890s and Walla Walla, Washington. What I am looking for in these boxes, I'm not exactly sure, but I trust that something will jump out at me, a new clue.

Unfortunately, distraction is easy. There are photos of my dad at his high school graduation, sporting feathered bangs and too-tight bell-bottom pants. Then there are grainy, sepia-toned shots of my grandparents. In one, my grandmother, Rosie Morgan, in full Jackie O mode, holds my dad as a baby. Uncle Dale, three years old, stands to the side with shorts jacked to his waist and a tongue stuck out as far as it will go. Next to him is Elsie Wallace Morgan. Gram, my great-grandmother, the one who had Aunt Anna committed. She wears horn-rimmed glasses and her hair in tight pin curls.

"So, what exactly are you lookin' for?" asks Aunt Mae. She's been upstairs but now squats next to me in their wood-paneled den with a glass of sweet iced tea I didn't ask for but appreciate. Aunt Mae's from Georgia; she met Uncle Dale as a flight attendant. I set the tea on the rug next to me as she lifts the flap of a box and peers at the dusty ephemera within.

"I'm not really sure. I was hoping to find something about Great-Great-Uncle Henry and Aunt Anna."

"Ohhh." She puckers a lipsticked mouth into an exaggerated O. "That odd duck." My mom says Aunt Mae's a gossip, but maybe in this case, that's not a bad thing.

"I know it's a weird question, but do you remember any connection she had to Russia?"

Aunt Mae ponders a moment before a light bulb seems to switch on inside of her brain. "Yes, I do! There was one time she had the *strangest* reaction to the news show we were watchin'. It was the day after Christmas. Your dad used to get so sore at Dale for not havin' her over for the holidays—no offense—so we invited her for dinner. She always just sat in the corner, barely talkin' to anyone 'cept the dog. I just figured she was senile.

"Musta been the nineties, 'cause that Gorbachev was resignin'. You wouldn't remember, but he was the president of Russia."

President of the USSR, not Russia, but I don't correct her.

"It wasn't exactly Christmassy, I know, but it was history in the makin'. Like the moon landin', ya have to watch! So, we were all sittin' around the TV—I'm sure Ken and Neil weren't; they were probably playin' with toys. I tell Dale we spoil them too much at Christmas."

My brain is screaming for her to cut to the chase.

"And when they showed the flag lowerin'—you know, the red one with the little yella hammer—Aunt Anna just burst into tears. I mean sobbin'!" She looks at me wide-eyed, still apparently stunned by the reaction.

"We couldn't get her to stop! Dale finally took her home and put her to bed. She was pretty old then. Figured maybe she was missin' Henry at the holidays. Or, who knows," she sighs, "that generation saw some awful bad things."

To put it mildly. Of course Aunt Anna would react this way.

The fall of a government that had murdered her family would surely open up old wounds.

Aunt Mae gives a little shrug. "Is that what ya meant?"

I tell her it's exactly what I meant.

"Good." She pats my knee and pushes herself off the floor. "I'll leave you to it, then. Can I get you somethin' else? A snack?"

"No, thanks, I'll only be a little while longer."

"Please. It's so quiet here with the boys gone. I'm happy for the company." She winks and pauses at the door. "By the way, you still seein' that boy, Ryan? I always thought he was a cute one."

It's not until I'm elbow-deep in the third giant box that I find what I'm looking for. Nestled between a photo album and a framed wedding portrait of my great-grandmother is a small bundle of letters bound by a frayed white ribbon and post-marked in the early 1930s. Delicate and yellowed, they remind me of Anna's journals; only I suspect from their chicken-scratch penmanship that they were written by someone else. They're addressed to Elsie Morgan, return address: H. Wallace.

I climb onto my aunt and uncle's leather couch, sitting cross-legged with the letters in my lap, and carefully, pull the ribbon.

Nov. 2, 1930

Dear Elsie,

Will be home Nov. 12. Cold today. Ground froze last night.

How's Jack? Well and happy.

Henry

Jan. 12, 1931

Dearest Elsie,

Greetings from the newest and youngest assistant professor of history at Keene Teachers' College! Classes began today, and by golly, I think I might teach these men something. In all seriousness, considering the hardship our nation faces, I count myself lucky, not only to put food on the table but to love the work itself.

How's Jack? Rotten luck. I'm sure he'll find other employment soon. In the meantime, let me know if I can help. I only need a little to get to Boston on occasion for my research. You'll pay it back in time. In fact, I owe a debt to you and Jack and your kindness over the years.

With love,

Henry

Feb. 14, 1931

Dearest Els,

I have met the most interesting woman.

I freeze and read the sentence again.

I have met the most interesting woman. In Boston for

research. Seized the opportunity to see Franklin—you remember him from visiting me at Saint Anselm? A librarian now at the central branch on Copley. Think he's embarrassed, believes it's women's work, but I'm glad for him, as it's a good job to have and those are hard to come by. Met for lunch on the square, and he brought a colleague. Anna.

Sharp for a woman, Els, like you, and interested in the goings-on of the world. Franklin says she has a story to tell but she has to tell it to me herself, that he's sworn to secrecy and wild horses wouldn't drag it out of him. I am intrigued.

The plot thickens!

Affectionately,

Henry

A *story to tell. Sworn to secrecy.* Anna had vowed in New York not to reveal her identity to anyone. But she had vowed—and revealed it—before.

I also look again at the date: February 14, 1931. Uncle Henry and Aunt Anna met on Valentine's Day. My hands are trembling. I have to be careful not to rip the thin paper as I pull the next letter from its envelope.

Mar. 29, 1931

Dearest Els,

It will surprise you to hear this, but your little brother is in love. The gal from the library. She's smart, Els. Boy, is she smart. Serious, but good fun. We can talk for hours—or sit easily in blissful silence. Imagine that!

I've never known anyone like her, Els. No doubt she's been through the ringer in this life, but she's resilient. And to no small degree, a mystery. I feel I've found a precious puzzle I'm meant to solve. Is this the way it was with you and Jack?

I wait eagerly for you to meet her.

Your besotted brother,

H

The letters continue like this, Henry writing tenderly to his big sister of his new love interest. He waxes poetic about her spirit, her courage, her pluck, her brain, and even hints at a difficult past, but beyond calling her mysterious, he makes no mention of a secret identity. Anna remains Anna, not Anastasia. It seems whatever intrigue Henry's friend Franklin teased, Anna continued to hold her cards close to her chest. A letter from August, however, shows Henry wasn't the only one falling in love.

Aug. 3, 1931

Dear Els,

I have received your letter of July 19 and hear your concern. It is fast, yes, but trust that I know her—and more as time goes on. There's more to the story.

I only want for myself what you and Jack have. Your

"needle in a haystack," you called him once. She is, indeed,
mine.

Yours,

Henry

Aug. 20, 1931

Els,

You must give her the benefit of the doubt. There's more
to her past than you know. Selfish people exist in this world,
sis, people who would take everything from you, even your
name, and Anna has known them. Fiends and backstabbers.

Trust that I know her, Els, even if you don't and, perhaps,
cannot.

Imploring you,

Your brother

Fiends and backstabbers. Could he be talking about the
Bolshevisks, or about her impersonator in Berlin?

After August, there's a gap in the letters—because none
were sent or because they weren't saved, I'm not sure. Was Elsie
simply giving it time, as her brother had asked? More important,
what did Henry know? While his loyalty to Anna's privacy is
endearing, it's exasperating. I understand his sister's suspicion.

There's one last letter, dated March 18, 1932. It has no
salutation.

The thing is, Els, only I know the real Anna. Franklin

261

thinks he does, but he doesn't know the whole of it. Not nearly
the half of it, even.

She's left behind a life, Els. I don't mean a situation that
might embarrass or incriminate, but that she's had to shed
her past as a snake sheds its skin, to survive. You fear she
misleads me. I myself was skeptical until she shared with me
her testimony, but only someone who has lived such suffering
can tell its full story.

I have already said too much. But I will marry her, Els,
and I ask for your blessing. She has come into my life as a gift
of providence, and she will stay in it as my wife.

Faithfully,
Henry

Testimony. Anna told Henry she was Anastasia, and he
believed her. Corroboration. Her own husband, a respected
professor.

Evan might have his doubts, and I might have my pride, but
I can no longer wait for him to come to me.

22

August 28, 2007

We meet at the graveyard. I've brought the bundle of letters. In my hand, as we sit on the bench beneath the maple tree, they feel like vindication. Anna told Henry she was Anastasia.

"Are there more?" he asks.

"Not that I found. And, from the sound of it, he wouldn't have told Elsie the full story in a letter."

"I suppose that your fiancée is a deposed Russian princess whom everyone believes is dead is the kind of news one delivers in person."

"Elsie is the one who had her committed," I remind him.

Evan surveys the gravestones, kicks a rock underfoot. "It's still highly improbable, Jess. The new remains, the DNA—you have to be prepared that she wasn't Anastasia."

"Improbable, but not impossible. Until we have the facts . . ."

He sighs. "We can't jump to conclusions."

"Will you help me?" I hadn't planned to, but I reach for his hand. "Will you help me translate the rest of the journals?"

Evan looks down at my hand holding his, a little bewildered, and gives my fingers a small squeeze. His eyes are now lake-colored, the kind of blue that goes all the way down. "Of course," he replies. "You deserve to know how the story ends."

"Thank you."

"Besides, 'Nothing is so necessary for a young man as the society of clever women.'"

I smile. "Dostoevsky?"

"Tolstoy."

"Someday I'll get it right."

We had left Anna in Paris, heartbroken by her friend's betrayal, shaken by the discovery that she had been watched by Johanna all along, and reeling from yet another harrowing nighttime escape. She prepared to meet the mysterious Monsieur Gagnon, who promised to answer her questions—and ours.

From the first line of the diary's next entry, it seems he delivered.

4.3.1920

There is no other way to tell it, so I shall tell it straight. God forgive me.

After a grueling day of waiting, as promised, M. Gagnon arrived for me at six o'clock sharp. Our destination, and the setting for our dinner, was an outwardly inconspicuous but inwardly opulent townhouse in the 1st arrondissement. My host, it is clear, is a man of means.

In addition to myself and M. Gagnon, six guests were in attendance. As my escort and I entered the salon, the room fell silent. All six turned to face me. To my shock, each man solemnly bowed his head, a gesture I have not seen in many years. It formed a lump in my throat.

My company—men of apparent rank—were reserved and exceedingly polite, though over dinner of boeuf en croute, they watched me from the corners of their eyes, as if I was a rare and curious bird. One particular guest, a younger man, observed me especially closely. I had the unsettling feeling that we had met before. Had he been following me in Berlin, like Johanna? Had my disheveled mind forgotten one of the many individuals who ferried me across Europe? At the beginning of the evening, the man had been introduced as "Monsieur Sergeyev," though by now I knew that this was a false name.

After dinner, we were led to a fine drawing room. Cognac for the men and sherry for me. I did not tell them I had never tasted a spirit before in my life. I needed courage for what was to come.

By a window, Sergeyev stood solitarily gazing at a fine rain that had begun to fall on the street below. How did I know his face? I reached far back into my mind, into cobwebbed corners and dusty cupboards. The faces of the men from the pigsty the night of my rescue floated before me, but neither of them belonged to him. Sergeyev's face was too narrow, his features sharp. I reached back further . . . and then I grasped it.

A cold feeling overtook my body. But it couldn't be! My hosts had given me no reason to fear my safety.

Shaking, I slipped from Gagnon's side and crossed to where Sergeyev stood. Outside, the rain now fell in sheets. "Monsieur." It shook me to the core, and was a risk, but I knew I must ask.

"Grand Duchess," he replied.

He did not blink, and under his steely gaze, my resolve nearly faltered, but I pressed on, as I have always done. "It is my sincere hope that the question I am about to ask will not jeopardize my position as a welcome guest under this roof."

His chin tilted upward.

"Monsieur Sergeyev, were you in the service of the Red Army in Yekaterinburg?"

A thousand red-hot coals burned in my chest as I waited for his answer. "Yes, Your Imperial Highness."

I gasped, eyes wide, but he grasped my hand. "But it is not what you think."

It took mastery of every cell in my body to remain calm as an officer of the Bolshevik Red Army related how he had saved my life:

Pavel Pavlovich Sergeyev served in Yekaterinburg under

Commandant Yakov Yurokvsky, the rat-eyed monster who, in July of the year my family was murdered, came to oversee the unfolding of the Ipatiev House's "special purpose." I abhorred the commandant and his pattern of cruel indifference.

What Yurovsky and the presidium of the Ural Regional Soviet did not know, however, was that Pavel Pavlovich served two masters. In fact, he had been carefully installed by the anti-Communist White Army operating out of Omsk, to keep an eye on the imperial family and to ensure, at all costs, the survival of at least one of its members. Sergeyev was a plant, and the night of the murders the only thing that stood between us and the complete destruction of the House of Romanov.

"But how?" I asked him. "How did you save me?" Nausea as images of that horrific night flashed through my mind:

(We are woken in the night. Doctor Botkin and the servants, too. Jemmy barks in my arms as I carry him down down down. I count as we go. Twenty-three stairs.)

A dark cloud passed over Sergeyev's face. He sighed and turned to the glistening street below. "A sacrifice was made."

"A sacrifice?" I did not understand him.

(Mama asks for a chair. One for Alexei, too. A bare light bulb and a window crossed with iron bars. "Line up for your photograph.")

Sergeyev's answer was a whisper. "A girl," he said, "a peasant girl, about your age, your height and your build."

(A death sentence is read. "What?" my father asks. "What?" he repeats.)

"Yurovsky had given us each a name. The other Red Army officers, they didn't want to shoot a woman—or a child. I volunteered."

(A crack of thunder. A cloud of red.)

"When the shooting began, we were to aim for the heart. We were at close range. There was confusion, as anticipated. The others, they were only boys."

(Smoke. Gunpowder. Screaming. Vomit.)

"My bullet grazed your arm. You fell. Quickly, I moved to stand over you. The others were screaming. The bullets, they were glancing off the jewels sewn into the women's clothes. Yurovksy commanded us to finish it with bayonets and butts. 'Get their faces,' he said. It was chaos." His voice wavered. "For fifteen years, I have been a soldier. Never have I seen anything like it."

(Mama slumped in her chair, red blooming like a flower. Alexei beside her, arm twisted unnaturally beneath him.)

"You groaned."

(Wet thud of metal piercing flesh. Maria cowering at the wall. Olga's face smashed in by boots. I try to say their names, but no sound comes out.)

"The first blow knocked you unconscious. It was easier this way."

(Tang of blood. Darkness.)

"The site had been prepared, a mine shaft in the forest. Our men would meet us on the way, a bunch of drunken peasants. In the cart, they carried the body of a girl who gave her life for yours."

(Hands grasp. A jerk. Pine needles. Sap. Burlap pressed hard against cheek.)

I doubled in horror. "Gave it?" I asked. "Or you took it?"

Sergeyev's jaw tightened. I thought I would be sick on my shoes. He faced me squarely. "Her life for yours. Your Imperial Highness." He spoke as someone with nothing but scorn for those who have never made such impossible choices and yet judge those who have.

A streetlamp had been lit outside. It illuminated his face. I saw it now in a different light. The mask of death.

"Grand Duchess, can you hear me?"

"Yes," I said. "I am here."

Sometimes, the memories pull me under, boulders chained to my feet.

There was only one more question I could muster for Sergeyev. The other men in the room, they kept their distance from us, but their chatter had quieted. They knew what he was telling me, and they watched.

"Why me?" The question escaped strangled from my throat. It's the question I have asked myself every day since

awakening in a pigsty, stinking and dirty and alone.

For the first time since I'd approached him, I saw real pity in Sergeyev's eyes.

"Why me?" I asked again, more forcefully. The question I couldn't bring myself to ask: Why her?

When the White forces learned of Lenin's order to exterminate us, they had only days to plan a rescue. A secret communication was sent to the tsar: If it was possible to save a child, which child? His answer should be communicated to Comrade Sergeyev in the Red Guard.

That evening, as my father passed the soldier in the narrow hallway of the Ipatiev House, the comrade stopped him, extending a small wooden toy carved by one of the local women as a gift for the imperial children. Before the new commandant, these kindnesses had once been allowed. "One of your children, Comrade Nicholas," Sergeyev said to my father, "does this belong to them?" My father, looking the Red soldier in the eye, took the wooden horse in his hand and responded, "Yes, it is Anastasia's."

"But why?" I asked Sergeyev again. Did Papa say why he had chosen me?

" 'She has always been the bravest.' "

It is a responsibility greater than any person should ever bear.

The clock in the drawing room struck eight o'clock. "I

would like to go to bed," I told Sergeyev. An exhaustion devoid of feeling had overtaken me.

"There's something more," he said. I could not take more, but he continued. "You were once kind to my brother. He never forgot, Your Highness, until the day he died."

It was then that I saw it, in the light from the street, the tiny but distinct dimple at the tip of Sergeyev's nose. I knew why his face looked so familiar, why its proportions plucked a chord deep within me. . . . It was not a face I recognized from the darkest night of my life, but from its happiest days. "Ilya," I whispered. His brother nodded.

Evan's eyes are glued to the page in his hands. Finally, he raises them and turns to me. "Wow."

My head swims with emotions, the same ones Anna probably felt—grief, betrayal, horror—but another as well: hope.

"She can write," Evan says.

"The body they just found. . ." I take the diary from his hands. "It wasn't hers. A girl between the ages of eighteen and twenty-three, that's what the scientists said. A girl of the same age, height, and build. A peasant girl."

The brutality of that possibility settles over us. Evan sighs, runs his fingers through his hair.

"That means Anastasia wasn't buried in the woods outside Yekaterinburg," I say quietly. "It means she survived."

After learning the gruesome truth of her rescue, Anna wrestles in the diary with what it means. She remembers her conversations with Ilya in the Tsarskoe Selo hospital, and how he so delicately tried to convey to her what the Russian workers and peasants felt: that while the tsar thrived, it was they who suffered and died for his empire. The anonymous peasant sacrificed for her survival becomes multiplied, in her mind, by millions.

"We starve," he told me, and in his eyes, I saw that he did know hunger. "We die," he said, and it was happening in the beds around us. I told him, as Mama had told me, "Papa feels your pain. He loves all Russians as if they were his own children."

It sickens me now, this blathering response to his very real suffering. The naive justifications of a child. I knew nothing.

Anna's grief over Ilya's death is palpable. From his brother, she learned how he died: After his recovery in the infirmary, the young soldier had been reassigned to a reserve regiment garrisoned in Petrograd. The same regiment that, on February 26, 1917, was dispatched by the tsar to quell an uprising in Znamenskaya Square. As other soldiers in his regiment mutinied, Ilya was killed by a stray rock to the temple. Despite his misgivings, he'd been faithful to the end.

Newly reminded of her loneliness in the world, Anna stayed

in Paris, the guest of Monsieur Gagnon. One day shortly after the dinner, he came to the apartment where she stayed. Point-blank, she asked him why the White Army had saved her and what they planned to do with her.

"You speak as if you are a captive, Grand Duchess." Am I not? I asked him. "Of course not," he replied, as if offended. Then, he added, "But when one has so few friends in the world, it's wise to know the value of the ones one does have." It was clear what he meant.

As if to prove his point, Gagnon encouraged Anna to explore the City of Lights, though always with an escort. In her diary entries, she walks the markets of Les Halles, reads in the cafés of Montmartre, strolls the banks of the Seine, spends days lost in the galleries of the Louvre, thinking, grieving.

She continues to keep the diaries that she started up again in Berlin—*the only comfort of my old life not completely lost to me, and I am convinced, my only true friend in the world; without you, dear, I should go completely mad*—but she hides them carefully, including from Gagnon and his minders. Even using false names, Anna knew the danger the diaries might pose if they fell into the wrong hands, and so she slid them beneath a small woodstove in her apartment. Smart, Evan and I agree, though probably a fire hazard.

On one of her outings, Anna stopped at a newspaper kiosk

outside the Rue du Bac metro station. Other than the incident with the duplicitous Anna in Berlin, she seemed to avoid the papers, but a small headline in one of the British tabloids caught her eye: "Exiled Empress Lives Quietly in London." Breathless, she stood in the street reading it.

According to the article, a society tidbit, Dowager Empress Maria Feodorovna was now living in London near her sister, Queen Alexandra. There, she mourned her son, Tsar Nicholas II, whose execution the Bolshevik government had announced via official statement in July 1918. The rest of the tsar's family, including his wife, son, and four daughters, the Bolsheviks maintained, had been transferred to a safe but undisclosed location. ("Liars," Anna hissed when she read this, causing the kiosk attendant to ask if she planned to buy the paper or just mangle it.) After a dramatic rescue mission arranged by the king's Royal Navy, the dowager empress was enjoying a quieter life than St. Petersburg had afforded her, and refusing to talk to journalists.

We expect this development to elate Anna—her grandmother had survived. "Maybe that's how she got to London," Evan observes. The reaction she actually penned surprises us.

So, she is alive, Grandmama. On the one hand a salve, on the other a fresh wound.

Of course she loves us. Papa always insisted so. But the slights behind Mama's back—she insulted the court by withdrawing from it; the family's duty was to Russia, not itself—we heard and felt these, too.

If I am honest with you, my dear, I loved my grandmother as a duty like all of the other ones expected of us. Where was she when they came for us? In Crimea. And if she believes that we are alive, how has she not found me?

After all this pain and sorrow, I fear I cannot bear another heartbreak, and Grandmama has never been one for mending broken hearts.

I wonder how this tale of desertion sits with Evan.

The next afternoon, Anna's presence was requested immediately at the townhouse where she met Sergeyev and learned the full tragedy of her story. Nerves and excitement overwhelmed her as she was rushed out the door by an impatient Gagnon.

When she arrived at the townhouse, in a small library off the drawing room, a well-dressed man in a leather chair awaited her. At his elbow perched a porcelain teacup, so precariously that Anna noted in her diary she feared he might smash it to smithereens. Long-faced with a mustache and thin salt-and-pepper hair combed over a balding head, the man had a nose like a beak.

Gagnon proceeded with introductions. "May I introduce the Right Honorable Lord Hardinge of Penshurst, former

275

British ambassador to Russia, viceroy of India, and soon-to-be ambassador to France."

"How do you do?" I asked, mustering all the civility still within me. The man snorted. It is clear to me Lord Hardinge is not to be my friend.

The ambassador stood. He circled, slowly inspecting me as a trainer at our stables might once have inspected a new foal. His gaze felt like hands. After a minute, he stopped, pulling a photograph from the breast pocket of his vest. He held it to my face, beady eyes flicking back and forth, back and forth, between the photograph and myself, myself and the photograph. Awkwardly, I stood.

"May I see it?" I asked. He handed the photograph over to me. Immediately, I recognized it. "This was taken on the Standardt. The sun was in my eyes."

"Yes," he replied, "that's clear enough."

The ambassador's purpose is evident; he has been sent to inspect me, to verify my identity. "May I ask who inquires?" I said. "Is it the dowager empress?" He remained silent.

A visual inspection did not satisfy him. The Lord Hardinge proceeded to barrage me with questions: about the configuration of our rooms at the Alexander Palace; about the pattern of the imperial china; about cousin Elisabeth, first and second cousin on Mother's side and second cousin twice over by marriage on Father's, who, yes, died on a visit to our hunting lodge in Spala at the age of eight; about the birthmark on my sister's thigh (a trick question, as she had none). He asked the name of my dog—Tatiana's dog, I told him, the very one that yipped at my feet as the photograph in his pocket was taken. He even asked about the color of mother's boudoir. Lilac, I told him.

Each query struck me like a bullet. As the interrogation continued, M. Gagnon paced the room and stroked his mustache.

Finally, after no less than an hour of questioning, the ambassador tired. He watched me over the rampart of his nose. Then, as if suddenly bored with his inquisition, he inclined himself toward me from his chair. "I must confess, Miss . . . Haase, that I am weary of this ever-growing list of pretenders."

It was unclear whether I was to take this as an apology or a dismissal. I looked at Gagnon, whose expression had turned sour. Would I be denied my identity, even my own name, once again?

"Take me to my journals," I demanded in a sudden whirl-wind of anger. "They were in the shipment of our belongings sent to England before we were taken to Tobolsk. Bring me to them, and I will tell you what is in them. If I am right, you will take me to my grandmother. If I am wrong, you can leave me on the streets with the rest of the impostors." I challenged his hawk-eyed gaze.

A sound issued from the ambassador's flabby neck, a phlegmy chortle. Rocking to his feet, he said to Gagnon, "I'll be in touch." The latter scurried out after him.

Gagnon had closed the library's heavy door on his way out, but I went to stand behind it, cupping my ear to the wood. I could just make out what the two men said. Their whispered voices were agitated.

"All this trouble for the wild daughter of a naive incompetent and a criminal lunatic." It was Hardinge's voice.

Gagnon replied through his thick French accent, "Well, if that incompetent and lunatic had not been denied asylum by your king, then we wouldn't be in this predicament now, would we? The Romanovs would all be safe and alive eating pease pudding in Shropshire."

"Good sir, they do not eat pease pudding in Shropshire." I heard laughter and smelled cigar smoke. They mingled with my rage.

They are pigs, both of them, but they might prove useful pigs, and I am accustomed now to sleeping in pigsties.

Yours,

A

"Coffee." Evan stretches. "I need coffee."

It's almost sunset, and the graveyard has taken on a peach glow. "Food," I say. "I need food." In the excitement of sharing Uncle Henry's letters, I'd barely eaten before meeting Evan.

He checks his watch. The hair on the right side of his head sticks out at an odd angle from all the tugging he's done over the last two hours. "If you're hungry, I have a dinner date in fifteen minutes."

I'm confused and also—I hope not clearly—jealous. "You have a date?"

"A standing one." He's pleased with himself. "Tuesday night's poker night. With Stuart, Amit, and Russell. Afterward, we go to Lindy's for pancakes."

"Afterward . . . Did I make you miss poker night?" I'm a jerk. When I called about the letters, I hadn't even asked if Evan had other plans.

"I don't mind. This was better."

My cheeks feel warm. "You know, I've been wondering something: How is it that you're so good at poker? Poker requires lying."

"Don't believe anything Sonya tells you," he says, slinging the messenger bag of diaries over his shoulder and pulling me from the bench. "I lose every time."

"So, Evan is hanging there, half of him on one side of the fence . . ." I am laughing so hard my side is cramping. ". . . and half of him on the other, his belt loop caught on the chain-link fence, and he looks like he might upchuck. 'Son,' says the cop, 'we can do this one of two ways: the easy way or the hard way.'"

Across the table inlaid with restaurant memorabilia, Amit and Russell collapse over their chocolate chip pancakes. Russell's laughter sounds like an owl hooting.

In the long banquette at the back of Lindy's Diner, Evan's friend Stuart is telling the story of last year's campus-wide Halloween "Humans vs. Zombies" game, which had been broken up by the police. Stuart, of LARPing fame, is a sophomore like Evan but looks about fourteen. He has a high, nasal voice, which he uses to imitate others when he's telling stories.

Amit is a junior majoring in computer science with a minor in philosophy, and Russell is a sophomore and the procurer of my aunt's psychiatric files from the historical society. Whether he knows they were for me or not he doesn't let on. He spends the first fifteen minutes of dinner making the case that, if time is the fourth dimension, then technically he should be able to travel back and prevent Red Sox owner Jack Frazee from trading Babe Ruth to the New York Yankees in 1918.

There are no two ways about it: Evan's friends are Nerds with a capital *N*. They celebrate their nerdery. They revel in it. They jump in and do the backstroke in it, swimming cap on, nose plug in. They aren't uniform in their nerdiness. Each one has his thing, and I can tell they humor each other's quirks. Plus, they're sweet. Russell has a girlfriend in Boston, and Amit has a new "female acquaintance" he met on something called a "subreddit," but I have a feeling they don't typically slay with the female crowd. I suspect they like having a girl around, especially if it means they can give Evan a hard time.

"So, what did you do?" I ask, relishing this glimpse at an Evan less serious than the one I know, one who trespasses on the college president's lawn while pursuing a "zombie" with a marshmallow blaster.

"He took his pants off, of course." Amit is one of those loud talkers who occasionally bang their fists on the table to make a point. I wonder briefly if Katie and Amit might hit it off. "That's why they call him Evan the Terrible."

"*You* call me Evan the Terrible, Amit," Evan interjects.

"What did Sonya say?" I try to imagine her shock—and riotous laughter—at a police officer showing up at her door with a pants-less Evan in tow.

"You've met Baba?" Russell wonders. He's tall like Evan but with hair to his shoulders and wire-rimmed glasses.

"Well, well, she does exist," Stuart squeaks, and the others chuckle.

I must look confused, because Amit explains, running a forkful of pancake through a puddle of imitation maple syrup, "We were starting to imagine something Norman Bates–esque."

"She's delightful! She offered me pie."

"Technically, *I* offered you pie," Evan corrects me.

"Jess gets baked goods, and we don't?" Amit cries.

"Evan's never invited us to his house," explains Stuart. "For all we know, he lives under an overpass."

"Well, he didn't really invite me, either," I say quickly. "I kind of invited myself." I glance at Evan.

"Baba doesn't really *love* visitors," he says.

"Yeah, yeah, yeah," Russell chimes in. "All those years in 'witness protection.'" He makes air quotes.

"No, it's true!" I protest. "Her father defected from the Soviet Union."

"Maybe if you halfwits knew how to behave yourselves"— Evan balls up a syrupy paper napkin—"you would get some apple pie." He lobs it at Amit.

"Apple?" Amit cries, as if wounded. "That's my favorite!"

I am laughing so hard I don't notice them until they are almost standing over us.

"Jess?" It's Lila . . . and Ryan.

"Lila," I say, taken off guard. "Hey."

Ryan won't meet my eyes. Scarlet creeps up his neck. "Hey."

It's a miserable moment, and suddenly, I regret yelling at him in the parking lot of a Burger King. I regret not fully explaining why I was hurt and that it wasn't all his fault, because I'd never really let him in. I do not, however, regret breaking up with him.

"Who are your hot friends?" Lila asks. Her voice has that singsong quality it gets when she's drunk. It's not nine o'clock yet.

I look at the guys, who have no idea what's going on. "This is Amit, Stuart, Russell, and . . . Evan." My voice falters at his name. I'm scared Ryan will recognize Evan from the shoe store.

Lila smells it, like blood in the water: uncertainty, weakness.

"Evan." She tilts her head so her hair falls over one kohled eye. "Is that the guy I saw going into your house the other day?"

She asks it casually, but she knows she has me pinned. Ryan's eyes flash to me, a look of confusion.

My heart starts beating fast. "Um, yeah, probably. He's helping me with a project."

"Your 'family project'?" There's an actual sneer on Ryan's face. The red continues to creep up his cheeks. Has he been drinking, too?

"Yeah, that one." I finally find some strength in my voice.

"The one for extra credit in Ass-tin's class?" Lila is smug. "I heard about that. You got an A-minus, but it wasn't good enough for you."

There's a cruel sparkle in her eye. This feels personal. But why? Have I hurt Ryan that bad, and why would Lila care so much?

"It was a B-minus, actually. And no, that's not good enough for me. Some of us have goals, Lila. Other than taking over the Curl Up and Dye on Route Nine." My own eyes have narrowed to slits.

"What does this nerd with a foot fetish know about your family?" Ryan is definitely slurring his words. He shoots daggers at Evan, while Lila looks confused by the foot comment.

Evan clears his throat. "I don't believe you know the nature of my personal expertise," he says, "nor my carnal inclinations, though I do appreciate a good loafer when I see it."

Amit chortles.

"He's not a nerd," I state.

"In fact," Evan says—he turns in the booth to face Ryan—"I am." He holds out his hand. "Evan Nikolai Hermann. Pleasure to make your acquaintance."

He's not helping.

"Look, nerd," Ryan says, like the villain from a bad eighties movie. He bends so his face is inches from Evan's. "I'll tell you when I'm talking to you."

Where am I? Worse than the eighties, this feels like drag races and fisticuffs. I have to act, but since Ryan and Lila appeared, something's been bugging me.

"Where's Josh?" I ask. "Or Doug?"

Ryan and Lila are friends, but I've never known them to hang out alone. In my experience, they travel as a pack. The gears in my brain are whirring. Ryan's panic the other night when I confronted him in the parking lot, Lila's behavior now, the flirtation, all those "training" sessions, taking his grandma to dinner, the sweatshirt that wasn't mine . . .

Lila isn't mad at me because she feels sorry for Ryan that I've broken his heart; she's finishing me off because she wants Ryan for herself, because she already *has* him.

"Wait, what the fuck?" The words spring from my mouth. "What the fucking fuck?" Stuart quickly slides out of the booth so I can stand in front of Ryan, whose eyes have gone wide. *Busted.*

284

"You." I poke at his chest. "I almost felt sorry."

His breath smells of cinnamon, and not the pleasant cinnamon of apple pie but the artificial burn of Goldschläger, the bottle his parents keep at the back of their liquor cabinet.

"You've been cheating on me. With *Lila*." I don't know which is worse: that Ryan has been lying to me or that he's been lying to me about being with Lila. All this time I'd been folding myself into a human pretzel to be the person I thought he wanted. And *this* was it?

"He loves me," Lila says. Her arms are crossed over her chest, and her face is white, sweaty with booze.

"I'm sure he does," Russell cracks from the table. From my peripheral vision, I see Evan give him the *cut it out* look. He senses my bubbling rage.

A waitress slips over to refresh our coffees. "You okay, hon?" she asks me directly, her eyes flitting to Ryan.

"Yep," I say, meeting her gaze. "I've got this. Thank you."

Happy, she winks and sidles to another table to see if they wanted hash browns.

"Lila . . ." Once the shock has worn off, I'm not even mad, just exhausted. "You can have him."

Before they leave, Russell, Amit, and Stuart invite me to next week's poker game, although I don't have the vaguest idea how to play. "I'll teach you," Evan says.

"Maybe I want someone who wins to teach me," I tease.

"Oooooooh!" Amit and Russell hoot.

Now Evan and I sit on the hood of my car in the diner's parking lot. Stars wink from the sky, diamonds in a field of velvet. Lying back against the windshield, I tilt my head to see them better. Evan tries to recline next to me, and the metal of the hood makes a *thunkety-thunk*. He springs from the car. "Sorry!"

I laugh and roll my head to look at him. "It's okay." I sit up. "I'm the one who needs to apologize." He looks perplexed. "I'm sorry my ex-boyfriend was a jerk just now. And I know you don't care, but I'm sorry I was rude at the shoe store, because I do care what you think of me."

The pained look on his face says he regrets the other day's choice of words.

I'm on a roll. "I'm sorry I freaked out about the hospital records, when you were just making sure we had all the information. And I'm sorry that I ever judged you. . . . I guess I'd just gotten so used to judging myself."

What draws me to Evan is that there's never any pretending for him. He'll always make the terrible joke, linger a beat too long, say "shall" when any normal person would say "will" . . . because that's *him*. And it gives you the courage to be you.

In sixth grade, MASH was Katie's and my favorite game to play on the school bus. This was before I'd met Ryan, so he didn't enter into the picture. After the house and the car and the number of children, we'd create a list of those qualities we most wanted in a spouse: pretty eyes, smart, nice, sense of humor, good butt (that was Katie's). "Think of it this way," she'd say, glitter pen poised above the page, "what is it you're most looking for in a soul mate?"

This—to wholly, unapologetically, with every proud fiber of their being be the person they are—is the most attractive trait I've ever found in a person.

"Two Truths and a Lie?" I ask Evan. He's sitting on the bumper now, and I slide down next to him. With fall around the corner, the evenings are getting chilly, and it's nice to feel his warmth next to mine.

"Oh no," he says, but then he takes in my pleading face. "All right."

I start. "One: I'm also deathly afraid of spiders." He grins. "Two: Three times I've competed in the Kentucky Derby." I am counting on my fingers. "And three: I like you, Evan Hermann."

He's surprised but maybe not surprised. "Like, you *like me* like me?" he says. I nod, and he takes my chin in his hand.

We kiss tentatively at first, in an unpracticed way, and then like we've been doing it for a long, long time. His fingers brush the nape of my neck; they play me like an instrument.

The lights in the diner flicker off and then on and then off again. The waitress.

"Wait," Evan says, pulling away for a moment, "that wasn't the lie, was it?"

"You are terrible at this game."

"You have *not* competed in the Kentucky Derby?" I roll my eyes. "And it's not one of those half-lies, is it, where it's a lie because you've only competed once?"

"Are you going to make me regret this?" I ask.

"No," he says definitively. "Because I like you, too." Full stop.

23

August 29, 2007

As much as I love Sonya, I'm glad she's convinced Evan to live on campus this year, even if dorm beds are, apparently, the size of a postage stamp. Not that I mind, as Evan and I lie on the narrow twin. We have the tiny cinder-block room plastered with his music posters to ourselves. Stuart, his roommate—who's responsible for the rest of the room's decor: empty Cup O'Noodles, dirty clothes, and a plastic helmet that I *think* has to do with LARPing—is out.

Our legs intertwined, Evan and I read the journals between long breaks where I come to realize physical chemistry has nothing to do with someone's experience in the making out department.

The Paris entries continue. Two weeks of Anna wandering the banks of the Seine next to greasy Gagnon, with whom her relations have become icy. While Anastasia's feelings about reunification with her grandmother are complicated, that Grandmama sent someone to verify her identity pulls her toward London.

When will you take me? I ask Gagnon. "Soon," he says. "Lenin, unfortunately, is gaining power, and the time is not yet ripe." How will we know when it is? I ask him. And what does that mean? He evades an answer.

At least, she knows, she can't stay forever in the apartment on Rue du Bac, which she now realizes has been sponsored by the ambassador. Evan and I have looked him up. Indeed, Charles Harding, 1st Baron Hardinge of Penshurst, was Great Britain's ambassador to France from 1920 to 1922.

Gagnon says that it may take time for Anastasia to obtain an audience with the dowager empress—Maria Feodorovna refuses to believe that the family was put before a firing squad as much as she refuses to meet the many impersonators who have surfaced in the wake of that news. "Bring me my diaries, then," Anna tells him. Gagnon promises she will be reunited with these.

We move from one journal to a second, procured at a *papeterie* in the Opéra quarter. Finally, about ten pages in, Anna learns that she will travel to London the following day by train. We fear the travel might once again stress her.

Many years ago, on my seventh name day, Shura gave me a wooden doll. The doll was painted with vibrant colors: pink circles for cheeks, a cherry-red scarf, brilliantly flowered apron. It smelled of balsa.

But the doll was not special because it was beautiful; it was special because it held a secret. If one looked closely, one would find a crack in the wood around the doll's mid-section. And if one twisted the doll, one would find that it came apart into two pieces. Within the doll was a smaller doll, painted just the same as the first: bright red scarf, pink cheeks, flowered apron. That doll also had a crack around its middle, and if one twisted it, another doll was revealed. And so on and so on, until one reached the final tiny doll, with no crack.

It was a matryoshka doll, Shura told me, and I kept it by my bed until one Christmas when Mama said we were sending our toys to less fortunate children than ourselves.

I remember this story now because I have found another doll inside the matryoshka.

It was my belief that Ambassador Hardinge had been sent to Paris by my grandmother. I was mistaken. It was not Grandmama who sent for me at all but Sir Cyril Ashbourne. I have never met this man in my life; he is now my charming host.

Evan drops the diary to his chest. Finally, we'll meet Ashbourne, Anna's benefactor and, potentially, the person who betrayed her secret.

"Keep going!" I nudge his leg with my foot. He nearly distracts us again, but I refuse to kiss him until we find out what Ashbourne wanted with Anastasia.

Even on the page, Sir Cyril Algernon Ascot Fitzroy Ashbourne of Knightsbridge, London, is, as his five names suggest, larger than life. According to the diaries, the English gentleman, then approaching his sixties, was the second son of a train conductor. He made his fortune first in copper and then in motion-picture magazines during and after the First World War, "the money behind the money," he told Anna cryptically. He wore an old-fashioned beard with an extravagant mustache and favored bespoke suits paired with voluminous silk ties. An overweight bulldog named Georgie trailed him around Crispin Court, his sprawling Knightsbridge mansion. Besides the mansion, he owned a sixteenth-century country estate in Surrey and spent two months each spring in Paris. This was how he came to know the owner of the 1st arrondissement townhouse and of Anna.

On my phone as Evan reads, I look for Crispin Court. There's nothing on the internet about a house with this name, but I do find an article about damage to city districts during World War II bombings; Knightsbridge is mentioned. On a

National Trust list of historic houses, I find a reference to the country estate in Surrey.

Quickly, Anna comes to realize that her eccentric host has something of an obsession with the Russian empire—the tsars, in general, and the Romanov dynasty, in particular. He has studied the language enough to read it and speak it passably. He peppers her with questions about the minutiae of royal life— what they dined on for breakfast, the type of duck that swam in the ponds at Tsarskoe Selo, who tailored the tsar's clothes, and really, who was that Rasputin chap? It's the same way Lord Hardinge grilled her, only Ashbourne's interest seems motivated less by suspicion than by hobby-like fascination. He's an oddball but a lovable one, and Anna grows fond of him, as she realizes his interest is well meaning; he does intend to reunite her with her grandmother—as well as, if the opportunity presents itself, her throne. Alas, he tells her vaguely, the situation is "delicate," and the dowager empress travels frequently. Echoing Gagnon, he informs her regretfully that a reunification may take some time.

In the meantime, Anastasia becomes comfortable at Crispin Court. After being treated for so much of her life as no more than a valuable object, it must be refreshing, I think, to find someone who takes not just a political interest in her but a personal one.

In September 1920, she writes,

It cheers me to sit in the library at Crispin Court, a cup of piping-hot tea and Georgie at my side. Ashbourne and I read or discuss home and the way things used to be, though I try not to linger too much on the memories, lest one get away from me and the rest—all the horrible, grotesque rest—come barreling forth.

It seemed Ashbourne had gotten the daughter he claimed to have always wanted. There wasn't a single thing Anna desired that she couldn't ask for, except one—her journals. Related to the "delicate" situation, it was taking Ashbourne some time, and favors, to get ahold of them. Understandably, this frustrated Anna, as she both wanted her personal diaries back and knew that her knowledge of what was in them would finally convince those blocking her way to her grandmother to step aside. Finally, around Christmas, seven months after Anna had arrived at Crispin Court, her host called her to his study.

23.12.1920

It's been years since I've celebrated Christmas properly. Ashbourne asked if I should like a tree. No, I told him, the days of glitter and sweets are behind me—but I've had a surprise today, and Christmas has come early.

Morning in the conservatory writing. Cold with its many windows, but I enjoy watching the snow collect on the rooftops and on the branches in the park. Snow comforts me in this way, that it transforms the world into something vast and bare and pure, like a blank page.

I had just begun to doze when a bell rang down the hall. Ashbourne, I grumbled. At his laziest. Tchaikovsky played from his study, *The Nutcracker.* "You rang, master?" I teased—it delights him when I do so—but when I saw the thing to which he gestured at the center of the carpet, I gasped.

A trunk. And not just any trunk. Navy canvas with polished wood ribbing. Strong leather straps to keep the lid closed tight, and brass fittings that shone like gold, or once had. My trunk. And on top of it a large, white curled bow.

"My diaries!" I gasped.

"And your books and some of the other belongings that were with them." Ashbourne was nearly as giddy as I was.

"Oh!" I cried, throwing my arms around his lovely frame.

"The ambassador has finally come through on his word. Cost me a pretty penny," he added, not entirely to himself, "but he's brought them just now. An early Christmas gift."

"Is he here still?" I asked, turning in a circle as if I might find him standing behind me. "I want him to see me account for what's in them. I want to prove to him that I am who I say I am."

Ashbourne's smile fell by a degree. "He's not, my dear. He's sent his deputy, but I'm sure we can catch him if you'd like him to be a witness."

The ambassador's absence, I knew, was a vote of no

confidence, but I had nothing to lose and everything to gain. "Yes," I said firmly. "Yes. Call him back in."

For the next two hours, the ambassador's deputy sat as I demonstrated to him my knowledge of the contents of the diaries, Anastasia's diaries. Ashbourne would read a date, and though sometimes I required a hint, I'd recount, to the best of my knowledge, what had happened that day, or thereabouts. My accuracy was not 100 percent, but I doubt anyone should be able to recount with full confidence every last one of her days.

The deputy ambassador sat next to Ashbourne, who translated the journals. The bureaucrat alternately yawned and peered over his interpreter's shoulder, as if he could discern the language if he only squinted hard enough. For Ashbourne and myself, however, it was great fun, like a game. The game of my life.

"You see!" I cried finally, when it appeared the deputy might actually fall asleep. The snow had continued outside, and I was sure he was wondering how he would make it home in the motorcar idling outside.

"I do see, Grand Duchess," the deputy added, smiling kindly. He was not, after all, against me. In fact, I like to think, he is now rather for me (though not likely to ask for an encore performance).

"Tell him." I walked around the trunk to the deputy ambassador, a potato-faced man with small, oddly placed ears and teeth that overlapped like shingles. My voice left no room *for questioning. "Tell the ambassador what you've seen here today. And he will tell my grandmother. There can be no question after this. I am the grand duchess Anastasia Nikolaevna Romanova of Russia, and I wish to see my family."*

The last line of my speech caused tears to prick my eyes. Until now I have not realized how much I do wish to see her. Grandmama and I have had our rocky path, but we are all each other has now.

"I will, Your Highness," the deputy said, grasping my hands. "I will."

And so it shall be a good and happy new year.

Merry Christmas,

Your A

"So, what happened?" I ask, frustrated. "If she was able to prove who she was, why would she leave London for New York? Why have Ashbourne forge her a new identity?"

My head is cradled in the warm crook between Evan's chest and shoulder. He holds the diary above us, sighing as he brings it down to rest on his body. I roll over so that I'm leaning on his chest.

"I don't know," he says honestly.

It's something I don't hear him say often. "Can I get that in writing?"

"For a price." He wiggles an eyebrow suggestively.

"Put it on credit." I hand him the journal.

Christmas comes and goes at Crispin Court. Besides her journals, Ashbourne gives Anna an enameled music box, a fresh diary covered in Florentine paper from Italy, and eight pairs of new shoes. "One can forgive many things," he tells her, "but a bad pair of shoes." Anna gives him an engraved letter opener and a monogrammed leather journal.

As her short, clipped entries show, however, Anna quickly began to grow impatient again. On January 2, the two argue over the moral implications of divorce. Two days later, over the correct placement of a dessert spoon in a place setting. Anna's starting to get what my mom would call "cranky," or, if her story wasn't actually so tragic, "melodramatic."

10.1.1921

I am furious. I am devastated. I am forsaken. Clearly I am damned, if not to hell then to purgatory.

Two weeks and four days since I proved to the deputy ambassador that I am who I say. Nine months since I was promised in Paris to be taken to my grandmother.

This morning, at breakfast—another tête-à-tête with Sir Ashbourne over gluey eggs and those repugnant British beans—I'd had enough. "When will you take me to my grandmother?" I demanded. Having just said something about horse racing, he blinked at the nonsequitur. I continued, blood boiling, "I am not a toy to be kept for your amusement, Cyril, not some pet like Georgie."

Ashbourne is capable of taking the bait, but he didn't. Instead, he sighed. He seemed to crumple like a paper doll, and for the first time since I've known him, betray his age.

"Your grandmother, my dear," he said slowly, "has gone to Denmark." The regret in his voice was palpable.

"On a trip?" I asked. "Well, that's fine. She was born there; she has family there. I'm sure she'll return, and when she does, I demand to be taken to her. No more intermediaries; I can speak for myself."

Ashbourne looked at me sadly. "She's gone there to live."

"Did she know I am here?" I asked incredulously. "Did she know I am here?" I repeated, shouting. Had he been keeping me from her all this time, his plaything, his pastime?

"She did," he said.

A tear coursed down my cheek.

"She did," he said again, rising from his seat at the head of the table to take my hands, "but you are not the first . . . Anna." He wiped the tear from my chin but another took its place. "Sometimes there is only so much an old heart can take."

I tore my hands away. The loneliness and frustration, tamped down to that dark place where I sent all hope and feeling long ago, it flowed out of me, drowning everything in its path. Like a caged animal, I paced the room. "She couldn't have waited?"

"There are some telling her that reports of the death of

299

her son and family are only stories planted by the Bolsheviks to discourage the people. She chooses to believe you're all alive, together, living in exile."

"Alive and together?" I screamed, doubling in pain. "The only way they are 'together' is in a mass grave in the forest of Yekaterinburg. And I should be there as well!"

Back and forth, I rocked as Ashbourne tried to hold me.

"Her hopes have been dashed so many times, Anastasia."

"Her hopes?" I turned on him. "What of my hopes, you old loon? What of the agony I have lived? What of the loss that feels like a mountain burying me alive, being trapped here with a daft old bugger who picks at my scabs for his own amusement?" He flinched.

There was more. I am not proud of what I said to my friend today.

Finally, once I'd calmed and sat sniveling but silent by the fire in his study, Ashbourne spoke. "There is nothing I can do, my dear, to take away the pain that has been inflicted upon you, to correct the injustice of this life. But I might be able to offer you another one."

I looked at him. "What do you mean?"

"Okay," Evan says, closing the diary as I protest, "I know this is getting good, but we have twenty minutes until Stuart is back, and then I have to go to biology lab. . . ."

Tomorrow he has his shift at the shoe store, while Katie and

300

I have a long-overdue sleepover and hang session, so we won't see each other until Friday.

I put the diary on his desk.

"You're home early."

"So are you," I say, reaching for the fridge.

Mom sits at the kitchen island on her laptop, BlackBerry in reach and blinking. "It's five o'clock," she says, indicating the Diet Coke in my hand. "Won't the caffeine keep you—never mind," she says to my look.

We've been tiptoeing around each other since the family reunion three days ago. I know I hurt her with what I said, and part of me wants to apologize, but most of me is glad I finally said it.

"Hey, I was thinking you might need new cleats. Want to get some tomorrow? Luca's afterward?" She offers it chipperly.

"I don't think I'm going to play soccer this year. Actually, I'd like to take piano lessons."

She presses her lips together. "You've played for six years, Jess. If you quit now, it will look like—"

"It will look like I'm not sticking with something I don't enjoy? Besides, I don't care what it *looks* like."

"All right," she says, sighing. "All right. We can look into piano."

The knot in my stomach loosens. She's thinking about something, deciding whether to say it. "What?" I ask.

"I saw Lisa today," she says tentatively.

"Oh."

Ryan's mom. I wonder what he's told her. Probably not that he was cheating on me.

"You know, maybe it's better that you two take a break, have some time to grow as your own people. Your dad and I, we met at nineteen . . ." She leaves the thought unfinished.

"Sometimes I think it's better to know yourself first," she says. "Besides, it'll be harder to maintain a long-distance relationship in college. It's not likely he'll get into Harvard."

It's time to rip off the Band-Aid. "Mom, I don't want to apply to Harvard."

"Because you don't think you'll get in? Jess, if you pull up this grade . . . and then with your extracurriculars and your writing . . ." She starts to gather her papers and drop them into her tote. "And you're a legacy; Dad's a graduate."

"No," I say. "It's not about that. I need some space, Mom. And Stanford and UCLA, they have really good creative writing programs."

"So does Harvard," she reminds me. I bristle. "Okay," she says. "Okay. Those are both very good schools."

"And if they weren't?"

She stops her busyness and pulls in a breath, as if she's caught herself. She smiles. "Then I would tell you you should go where you want go."

"Thank you," I say.

She comes around the island and stands in front of me. "I'm just confused, Jess."

"I know," I say, "and that's my fault."

"Hey." Her hands grip my shoulders. She doesn't fix my hair or tuck in a tag. She doesn't examine my nails or ask what my plans are tonight or tomorrow or forever. She says, "I love you. I love *you*."

I bite my lip and nestle into her shoulder. She smells like me, like the shampoo she's been buying us both as long as I can remember.

"We're trying, Jess," she says, hugging me tight.

My tears create a wet spot on her shirt. "I know," I say. "We all are."

24

August 31, 2007

Stuart is writing a paper, so Evan and I agree to read at my house. We need to connect the last dots between London and Anna's life in New York.

Maybe out of nostalgia, we take the same stations as the first day Evan came to my room, the day we read of Anna's doomed but idyllic life in Tsarskoe Selo. He sits in the rolling chair at my desk. I lean against the frame of my bed on the floor. As Dad requested—again—the door is even open.

At first, Anna's not sold on Ashbourne's idea of New York, but after weeks pass, and then months, her friend presents a case: Anna is welcome to stay at Crispin Court as long as she wishes, but there are some "considerations" related to the "delicate situation" that he has been previously reluctant to divulge.

According to Ashbourne, within the upper echelons of British society was a growing opinion that King George, in some oblique but definite way, had been responsible for the death of his cousin, Tsar Nicholas II. By denying his relative a safe harbor in the storm, the king had doomed him.

Nearly three years had passed since the world had lain eyes on the Romanovs. People had begun to whisper about the fate of the tsar's wife, young daughters, and son. If Anna—Anastasia—made public the horrific details of the Romanovs' last days and hours, the backlash would be swift. To avoid such an embarrassment, might the king send the grand duchess back to her homeland to silence her? It would be an extreme reaction but not an unimaginable one.

Ashbourne's second point was delicate in a different way. Beyond occasional trips into central London for books and odd errands, Anna's life in England was confined to Crispin Court. On March 14, 1921, she wrote:

Ashbourne has urged me again to join the Season when it begins in April. "You needn't reveal yourself," he assures me, "but you must desire friends, my girl."

I tell him I have no use for derbies and debutante balls. I have him and the library and Georgie, and in my new acceptance of the way of things, this is all I need. Besides, I've never learned the art of talking to strangers. "Then you must learn," he tells me. "A young person withers without the company of other young people."

Am I young? I ask him. I don't feel it.

The irony, of course, was that in a little more than a year, Anna would lose herself in the social carousel of New York City in the Jazz Age. Still, fear gripped her. She stalled. The Season passed. Another Christmas. Anna gave Ashbourne a silk tie and gold cuff links. He gave her kid gloves, a fur-lined cape ... and a set of two leather suitcases. In February 1922, they fought again.

Though Ashbourne's concerns seem sincere, I can't help but wonder, knowing what will come, whether Sir Cyril began to tire of his Romanov intrigue. It makes my heart ache for Anna a little more.

Finally, Ashbourne prevailed.

13.4.1922

The lilacs bloomed today. And it's decided. I will go to New York.

After a walk in the park, sat with Ashbourne in the afternoon. Again, we discussed my situation, and I expressed my misgivings:

I'll know no one in America—he assures me his connections are more than enough;

I'll have no income or way to live—he promises to keep me as long as I need and that one day I'll be married; I warn him marriage is the farthest thing from my mind;

I'll need an identity and the papers to support it—since the war, he acknowledges, the Americans have gotten pricklier on immigration, but he is a master of invention and of the favor;

And not least, the people who brought me out of Russia, who followed me in Berlin and kept me like a pet in Paris, surely they will have an opinion on my whereabouts—let him worry about that, Ashbourne says; the group's primary interest is my safekeeping, and there is nowhere safer at this time than the United States.

"My dear," he said finally, "the question is plain: Do you wish to live your life as a chess piece, or to make your own way in the world? Here is your chance."

I think of the simple existence for which my parents longed, of the normalcy they endeavored so hard to create in as lonely a habitat as a tsar's palace. The Romanovs ruled Russia for three hundred years. No one more than we understood the terrible burden of being the chosen. We paid for it with our lives. That furnace is one I do not wish to step into again.

Russia is behind me. There is only what lies ahead, and so I have agreed. I will go to America.

Ever and never,

Anastasia

Evan closes the diary. It was the last page. Anna liked this: clean endings and new beginnings, a fresh journal for each new chapter. She'd start the next journal on the RMS *Baltic*.

I crawl over to the trunk and pick up a journal and then another, looking them over. "What haven't we read?" I ask. Maybe there's one we missed from childhood, although we'd realized early on that the first years, when she was younger, were sparse and incomplete. One after New York, in Boston?

"This was the last one," Evan says.

I frown. That can't be. Tsarskoe Selo to Berlin, Paris, London, and New York—the story can't just end there. Surely there was one telling her love story with a young professor from Keene Teachers' College?

"What about Tobolsk?" I say, digging through the journals, pulling them out one by one. They've fallen out of chronological order, and I start to stack them again in piles by year.

"And Yekaterinburg? We didn't read any diaries from those places." I'm aware of the note of panic in my voice, but I'm not ready for this story to end.

"I've thought about that," Evan says. He slides off the desk chair and joins me on the floor, placing the last London journal in its pile. "The family sent their belongings to England when they knew they were leaving Tsarskoe Selo—the ones she was reunited with in London. And she started new ones in Berlin and Paris. She must have brought them all with her to New York."

We've acknowledged the risk this would have posed, how important the diaries must have been to her to keep them.

"But the diaries from Tobolsk and Yekaterinburg," he continues, "would have been left behind the night of the murders. The family was hurried to the basement in the middle of the night; she wouldn't have had time or reason to bring them with her. They were left at the Ipatiev House."

"Destroyed," I say.

"Likely."

I picture a Red soldier pawing the delicate paper, mocking the pain within. Showing his friend. Burning it. Tossing it down a mine shaft with her family's disfigured bodies—and the body of an innocent peasant girl whose blood is on his hands as much as on those of the Whites who killed her.

Perhaps it's better not to have those diaries now, not to read Anastasia's final, haunting entry, her blindness to the horror and grueling journey that lay ahead. What was the last line, I wonder, before her world ended?

"It's over," I say sadly. I've slumped in front of the trunk, the journals spread around me in their various shades of blue and brown and red and green, their gold foil and ornate paper and their simple, unadorned plainness. They're extraordinary and ordinary at the same time.

Evan sighs. "'And the rest is rust and stardust.'"

"Who wrote that?"

"Vladimir Nabokov."

"Will you do something for me?" I ask.

Evan slides next to me. "Of course."

"All this time, I've never heard the Russian. Will you read to me, not the translation but her actual words?"

He leans toward the stacks of diaries, goes to the earliest one, from 1913.

"*Snova sneg*," he begins. I lean into him and let only the sound of his voice paint pictures in my head.

25

September 1–4, 2007

I spend part of my last weekend of freedom before school starts finally finishing the history paper. Saturday, I sequester myself in my bedroom with my computer, a thermos of Mom's coffee, and all the books on the Romanovs I'd checked out from the library. Even Evan doesn't hear from me; like a black hole, sound doesn't escape the zone.

By Saturday night, the coffee is gone and the paper is done. After a final read, I email it to Mr. Austin at 1:34 a.m. I don't really care about the grade anymore, but I feel I owe it to Anna.

On Sunday, Katie, Tyler, and I go back-to-school shopping. She takes us to the vintage shop and makes me buy the black-and-white dress. I also get two cool sundresses and a punny vintage T-shirt.

Afterward, Evan and I meet Stuart and Russell in Grafton, where dozens of people wearing plastic chainmail and foam swords are gathered for a LARPing event called the Realms. A costumed wizard introduces our "quest," and we must decide our course of action. It's not my cup of tea, but I like the story aspect of it, and I get to watch Stuart battle a guy in a homemade dragon costume.

On Monday, my mother, for once, decides not to labor on Labor Day and, instead, makes us drive to Lake Sunapee. She packs lunches and has my father strap our ancient metal canoe to the roof of his Subaru. In the car, Griffin finally learns I've broken up with Ryan. "*You* broke up with him?" he asks fifteen times. "Way to go, turd blossom."

My parents manage not to fight, but the water is freezing and all I want is to be holed up with Evan, reading the journals in some alternate version of reality where they keep going and going, right up until my aunt looked at me in the nursing home and told me I was a storyteller just like her.

It's Tuesday now, and Evan is taking Sonya to dinner for her birthday, which, unlike Ryan, means he's *actually* taking his grandmother out, not hooking up with his best friend's girlfriend. At Sonya's request, I'm joining them after a long first day back at school. At lunch, I got the cold shoulder not just from Lila but from every one of the Betties. "Geesh," Katie said, "you'd think *you* were the homewrecker." No one said hi to me in the halls except the usual suspects, which means word has gotten out that I'm not Ryan Hart's girlfriend anymore, and in fact, I heard two girls whispering my name in study hall. Who knows what Lila's told them? Who cares? The good news is that I got an A on my history paper. *Highly creative*, Mr. Austin wrote at the top and raised my grade to an A-minus.

To my surprise, Sonya has asked to go to Margarita's, the Mexican restaurant on Main Street always full of college students. Apparently, she lives for the fried ice cream.

"*Féliz cumpelaños* to you! *Féliz cumpleaños* to you!" Evan and I sing as a waiter delivers the deep-fried confection drizzled in chocolate sauce and topped with a single birthday candle. Sonya beams, spoon at the ready. She looks pretty tonight, with her hair in the same long braid and the turtleneck replaced with a blouse and a vest embroidered with flowers. Evan has given her a new teapot to replace her old chipped one; we found it together at the antique shop. It's pale yellow with painted gold flowers and came with four teacups.

"And many more!" We sing and clap as Sonya blows out the candle.

"What'd you wish for?" I ask.

"If she tells you, it won't come true." Evan reaches a spoon for the fried ice cream. Sonya jokingly bats it away.

"I wouldn't have expected you to be superstitious. Hey! Get your own!" I cry as he comes for my chocolate lava cake. "You have your coffee and four sugars."

"Well," Sonya replies zippily, "my wish has already come true."

"Really?" Evan asks. "What was it?"

She says it carefully. "For your mother to call."

I'm sitting next to Evan, so I can't see his face, but I feel him go rigid. Tension rises off of him in little squiggly waves, like anger off a character in a comic strip. A waiter sweeps by with a tray full of steaming fajitas.

"Well, do you want to know what she said?" Sonya asks finally.

"Not especially," Evan replies, but then adds lightly, "but I'm glad you got what you wanted, Baba."

"She's in Chino, California. Sober now and working at a halfway house for women."

"Good for her," Evan says crisply.

"She'd like to see you. Maybe you could—"

"Excuse me." Evan stops our waiter in his orbit. "May I please have a refill?"

Across the table, Sonya gives me a crooked smile and a shrug that says, *I try*.

After dinner, we go back to the dorm.

"Hi, Jess. Bye, Jess." Stuart whips past me with a giant black instrument case on wheels. I hear them roll down the hallway and then an elevator ding.

"Tuba," Evan explains. Stuart's a musician, too.

The Keene Chamber Orchestra is holding a concert in the auditorium of the public library next week, and Evan and I are going. It's my first-ever date at a library, and I find this swoon-worthy. He's promised to invite me to one of his concerts, too.

"Oh." I suddenly remember. "I brought you something."

In my messenger bag are pages from a chapter of my new story. I'm not really sure what it's about yet, but printed out, they feel more real than when glowing from my laptop screen. Evan wants to read them, and although this makes me nervous, I'm excited for someone's take other than Katie's. I know Evan will be honest—then again, I know Evan will be honest.

I lay them on his desk, on top of a copy of *Anna Karenina*, hoping maybe Tolstoy will lend some brilliance by osmosis.

"Thank you," Evan says, kissing me. "I can't wait to read them."

He flops onto the bed, which bounces under his weight. "I almost thought you'd found another diary," he says.

"No. I wish."

As I wrote my paper for Mr. Austin, the trunk watched me from the corner of my room. I wonder how long we'll have to wait for the DNA results on the newly uncovered bodies. Will one prove to be an anonymous peasant girl, about Anastasia's age, height, and build? I know Evan still has his doubts, but I don't need probability, just possibility.

I lie back next to him on the bed, finding the now-familiar crook where his arm meets his chest, knowing that I will never experience the smell of Ivory soap the same way again. My fingers twine through his. He gently bites the tip of my thumb.

I don't like to compare, but just lying with him like this is so different than it was with Ryan. It's the most comfortable spot I can ever imagine. I want to melt into it, into him.

I'm thinking about dinner, though. "I think Sonya had a good time," I say.

"Yeah, me, too." He turns his face to my neck so I feel his breath on my skin.

"What did you think about her wish?" I ask carefully.

"What about it?"

"Are you curious? To talk to your mom?"

He sits up abruptly, and I'm forced to sit up, too. "Curious?" he says. "No. She abandoned me, Jess. She left me without an explanation."

There's so much hurt in his words, and I don't want to prod a bruise that's already black and blue, but there's a hole in him, shaped like her, and I want to help him fill it. I know his mom screwed up, but I also know that she loves him. How could you not? This quirky, honest, kind guy.

"But she was an alcoholic. You were seven. Do you think you would have understood if she *had* told you?"

I try to ask it gently, but he immediately bristles. "Dosto-evsky said, 'It is better to be unhappy and know the worst, than to be happy in a fool's paradise.' Have to say I agree with him."

"I just wonder . . ." I'm not sure why I have to push. ". . . if maybe she saw it in a different way." Evan scoffs. "I mean that maybe she has her own version of the story. You've got this

316

narrative in your head that she left you because she didn't love you, but what if it wasn't exactly like that? What if she thought leaving you with Sonya was the better thing for you? You haven't talked to her in years."

His voice is tight when he says, "For very good reason."

I think of Sonya's glimmer of hope at the restaurant and then her sad resignation. She still believes in her daughter, even after all the hurt, and I'm sure she has plenty of her own. "You believe in the truth; you said it. Isn't not letting your mom give her side of the story a way of avoiding it?"

He stands from the bed. "Jess, I know you like to live in a fantasy world, but facts are facts. For some of us, at least. My mother left me after my father *died*. I was *seven*."

His fists are balled at his sides. I feel awful, so bad, but there's something I'm puzzling through, as well. And I don't want him to miss out on a relationship with the only parent he has left.

From the bed, I take his hand. "Of course, facts are facts. But maybe . . ." I'm stringing the words together in my mind, ". . . truth is something else, like . . . the arrangement of facts in the way that's most real to your heart?"

He drops my hand. "You don't know what you're saying. That's dangerous, the crap of conspiracy theorists and demagogues. The sky is blue, Jess. One plus one equals two. We all agree on these things. We have to."

"But sometimes the sky *is* red, and if my parents are any indication, one plus one equals zero. . . . Look, maybe I'm talking about Truth with a capital 'T,' but what if *that* is just a story we tell ourselves?" A fleeting image of my aunt in her hospital bed, rasping, fighting. "And your mom's is different than yours."

I try to touch him again, but he shakes me off. I've never seen him like this.

"So, everyone's allowed their own personal truth? You know what that is? It's spoiled, Jess."

Spoiled? So that's what this is about. Why he wouldn't take my money, why he was jealous when I mentioned Harvard, why he thinks I was embarrassed to introduce him to my family.

"It's insane," he says.

My anger flares. "Now I'm spoiled *and* insane?"

"I didn't say *you* were spoiled."

"Oh, *I'm* not. Just the way I act?" I say sarcastically.

"And, yes, it is insane to believe your aunt was Anastasia Romanov."

I stand in front of him. "*You* were the one who told me she was Anastasia," I remind him, pointing a finger at his chest.

"Maybe I got carried away. A pretty girl brings you an exciting mystery—"

I ignore that he has called me pretty. "'I'm not another mystery for you to solve.' Who said that?"

"Jess," he grasps my shoulders, "do you honestly believe that your great-great-aunt was Anastasia Romanov, that she survived a firing squad and made it across Russia and Europe to marry your uncle in Keene, New Hampshire?"

"You never really believed." It's my turn to shake him off. "And you don't get to decide my aunt's truth."

"I do, however, get to subscribe to reality . . . 'A lie told often enough becomes the truth.' Know who said that?" He pauses. "Vladimir Lenin."

Bitterly, I laugh. "Your quotes. You know why I think you love them, Evan? Because you can cherry-pick them to fit whatever it is you want them to mean. But a quote doesn't tell the whole story. . . . You're a hypocrite, you know that?"

"Are you done?" Evan says calmly.

My chest heaves with emotion. "Yes."

"I think you should go."

26

May 1, 2008

I've seen Evan twice since our fight, the first time in October, after the dust settled. He was at Brewbakers, of all places, at a table in the back. I'd gone with Katie after school for pumpkin spice lattes. Our eyes met through the glass, and Katie, seeing this, suggested we move along for a smoothie instead.

The second time was harder. January at Lindy's Diner. I was there with Katie and some theater friends. It was a Tuesday. Poker night, I'd forgotten. There they were: Evan, Russell, Stuart, and Amit in a booth at the back. My eyes stayed glued to our table. Only once did I let myself glance up and think, for a second, that Evan had just looked away.

At least a dozen times, I've sat down to write him. Not a text or an email but an old-fashioned letter on unlined, cream-colored paper from my mom's desk. The thick kind, with a watermark. I want to say I'm sorry, that I was hurt and sticking my nose in something that wasn't my business, but each time I start, the feeling of Evan calling me spoiled, calling me crazy, hits me again. I was the hypocrite, of course, the one who'd just found the courage to tell the people closest to her who she really was. Only, those aren't the right words, and I can't find better ones.

In February, my parents separated. Dad moved to a two-bedroom apartment with a pool that he's promised Griffin and me we can use once the weather warms up. The separation, for lack of a better verb, sucks—my brother's taken it especially hard—but I realize we've all been expecting it for a while and, actually, both my parents seem happier. I can't say the same for myself, but I'm adjusting. Some nights I stay at Katie's and fall asleep to *Ella Enchanted*.

Then, last month, Lila confronted me in the second-floor girls' bathroom. She was in tears. I suspected she'd been drinking. She didn't apologize, exactly; she wanted to know how to get Ryan to love her. I felt sorry for her, sorrier maybe than I've ever been for anyone in my life, even Anna, because I knew how she felt. I wanted to tell her everything I'd learned about not pretending to be someone I'm not just because I thought that was what people wanted, or needed, to love me, but then the bell rang for fourth block. The next day she pretended it hadn't happened. Maybe she'd forgotten.

Things with the Harts are complicated, with our families as close as they are. The separation means no one expects us all to have ski trips and barbecues together anymore, but Ryan and I have crossed paths once, outside the movie theater when he was home for winter break. To my surprise, I didn't feel mad or even hurt. Like I did with Lila, I felt empathy. Maybe Ryan's under his own pressure to play a part, to be someone he isn't. I do believe he cared for me, and I cared for him. He wasn't my first love, but he was my first lesson in it.

Now, graduation is around the corner, one more month to freedom, and I can almost feel the California sun on my skin. It's been nearly a year since I found the diaries, and I've forgotten about the news alert I set on my phone when it chimes at lunch.

"You're blowin' up," Tyler says behind me. We're waiting to feed our trays into the dish return slot.

"Always," I joke, extracting the phone from my pocket, and my stomach drops. It's a link to an article in the *New York Times*. I click on the headline: "DNA Tests Confirm the Deaths of the Last Missing Romanovs."

The dateline is from Moscow. Tyler's bumping his tray against my butt to nudge me forward. I force myself to read on.

Eduard Rossel, governor of the region 900 miles east of Moscow, said Wednesday that tests done by an American laboratory had identified the shards as those of Aleksei and Maria.

"This has confirmed that indeed it is the children," he said. "We have now found the entire family."

I read the full article once and then again. People are pushing around me, throwing annoyed looks my way, but I am frozen to the spot.

That's it. Just like that. The official mentions Maria, but the experts have never agreed which younger daughter's remains were at the first grave site. With seven confirmed bodies, it no longer matters. There was no peasant girl. There was no trek across Europe. No Ashbourne, no Johanna, no Gagnon.

Anna was an impostor.

The disappointment has an actual crushing weight, and on top of it is the fact that Evan was right.

But *why*? What did my aunt have to gain from concocting this elaborate story and locking it away in a trunk? She was eccentric, yes, but I can't believe she was merely delusional.

I also can't process this information alone. Tyler and Katie stand by, talking in low tones, and I feel them look over, but I'm focused on the text my thumbs are typing out.

New York Times. You were right. I'm sorry.

His reply comes immediately. *Can I see you?*

27

August 2–3, 2008

"You can't possibly need these." Griffin holds up a pair of fuzzy yellow Tweety Bird slippers. "It's California; it's hot."

"It's Northern California, and I might!" Swiping them from his hands, I throw the slippers back onto the growing pile of stuff in the corner of my room destined for Stanford. I'm just back from a piano lesson—I'm terrible, but that's okay—and he's helping me pack, which means scavenging for stuff I might leave behind, like the small flat-screen TV that used to be in Mom's office.

Since the separation, we've initiated a truce. I used to blame Griffin for making things at home worse, but since we've started therapy, I've realized maybe my brother was just trying to be the crisis that would force my parents into the same room. It helps. I like to think he'll actually miss me this year.

Dad and I leave in a week. Driving out to California, just the two of us, was his idea, and while the thought of six days in a car hurtling cross-country with my dad feels a little intense, I'm glad for the father-daughter time.

Evan will meet us in Las Vegas for a trip to the Grand Canyon. We've promised Sonya pictures; she's always wanted to see it, but she swears Evan going is almost as good. He's been in Chino for three days already, visiting his mother. The week after our fight, he'd told Sonya he was ready to talk to her. Teary, Baba placed the call. There's still repair to do—Evan and I spent an hour on the phone his first night there—but, like me, he's starting to realize there might be more than one side to every story, even his own.

"What about that?" Griffin says, eyeing the trunk that still sits under the window on the far side of my room. I've told him about the diaries.

A shirt lies on top of the trunk. When I go to toss it on the laundry pile, I find myself lifting the trunk's lid. The smell of leather and old paper brings me back to last summer, a kaleidoscope of mystery and discovery, disappointment and change. Sometimes I see the trunk and feel the betrayal all over again, but I can't call my journey through Aunt Anna's fabrications worthless; they led me to Evan. And while I taught him that truth isn't always black and white, he's taught me the importance of telling it.

I know I should do something with the diaries—lug them to our attic or donate them to an eccentric Russian scholar and make them his problem. Maybe I'll take them to Uncle Dale to put with the rest of the family stuff. Whatever I do, it's time to let them go.

"Half-Pint!" Uncle Dale crows from his front stoop. "Good to see you. Hear you're taking off soon."

"Yep. Next week."

"Your parents are gonna miss you, kid."

"So they say," I crack, but I know he's right.

My car's parked in the driveway. Grumbling, Griffin helped me wedge the trunk into the back seat. With Uncle Dale's help, I deposit it in the foyer of the McMansion he and Aunt Mae bought earlier this year. The house has high, airy ceilings and a dramatic staircase with a very large chandelier, and the trunk looks out of place on the shiny new floor.

Maybe Uncle Dale notices my spasm of doubt, because he says, "You know, if this stuff floats your boat, most of Uncle Henry's papers were donated to the college. Just lectures and notes and nerdy stuff like that, but maybe some personal effects. In case you're interested."

My eyes narrow as something occurs to me, something I'd stupidly failed to ask: what kind of professor Uncle Henry was.

"History," Uncle Dale replies. "Apparently some kind of expert on Russia. Even testified before Congress in the Cold War. That's why the college wanted his papers. Took Aunt Anna a while to agree, though."

I've told myself I'm done with Anna's fictions, but there's one mystery I've never been able to solve, and that's *why*. Could the answer have been under our noses all this time?

Back in my car, I check the hours of the Keene State library. The school's archives and special collections require an appointment. Besides, it's Katie's opening night of *Fiddler on the Roof*, her farewell production. She's going to NYU in the fall.

I call Evan in Chino. "Aaaargh!" he bellows when he hears the news. In all of our sleuthing, there was a rock he'd left unturned.

28

August 4, 2008

When I present myself to the young, pinched librarian for access to the Henry Wallace papers, she asks if I'm a student. No, I tell her, but I'm a descendant. This seems to satisfy her.

The room is less grand than the picture I had in my head—something like the great reading room of the New York Public Library, which I'd looked up after Anna mentioned it. Instead of golden desk lamps and long, shining tables, I find fluorescent lights and institutional carpeting.

The librarian gives me the call number for the Wallace papers, which are in a floor-to-ceiling stack on rollers at the back of the room. She turns a big crank, opening space for us to walk between the shelves, and traces her finger along the highest one. "Here," she says, spanning her hands to indicate where the collection begins and ends. I deflate a little; there's much less material than I'd hoped.

Some of the papers have been put in binders, and there are three square, gray archival boxes stacked one on top of another, labeled Wallace, Henry H., October 3, 1908—July 17, 1961. I'd asked the librarian when the papers were donated. With a few brisk clacks of the keyboard, she'd supplied an answer: October 13, 1964.

"I'll leave you to it." She ekes out a prim smile. "A reminder that the library closes at noon today, and materials are *not* to be taken from the room." I only stick my tongue out at her back for a moment.

When I'm alone, I gather from the shelf what I can and deposit the materials on a table, inspecting the binders first. The room is silent, and every turn of a page sounds excessively loud to my ear. The papers are crisp and well-preserved, much more so than the diaries, but a thin layer of dust has settled over the top gray box, as if no one has touched them in quite some time.

Mostly the boxes contain irregular-sized items, much of it scribbled in the same handwriting as the letters to Aunt Elsie. There are notes about lectures, drafts of articles, memos, and newspaper clippings. I wonder if I should be wearing gloves while handling these things. Clearly they are, or were, important to someone. Honestly, I have no idea what I am looking for.

The second box contains visual material: photographs of Uncle Henry (with a monocle!), looking sharp and vaguely ridiculous with the rest of the 1952 Keene Teachers' College history department; antique postcards in glassine sleeves; and a couple of brochures from scholarly conferences, such as the Second International Conference of Educators of European History.

The third and last box holds more papers, one black-and-white marbled composition book, and a stack of official-looking letters with return addresses from the State Department, the United States Information Agency, and the White House. I open the last one to find a typed letter from President Dwight D. Eisenhower thanking Professor Wallace for his valuable service to this country at a time of great political uncertainty.

The letter below it, at the bottom of the box, has one word written on the front of the envelope: *Henry*. It's the handwriting that stops me cold: spidery, familiar cursive—only it's in English. As I turn the envelope over in my hands, they tremble. The letter has never been opened.

Heart beating in my throat, I slide my index finger under the corner of the flap. The glue, old and dry, hardly resists. Carefully, I draw the letter from its paper sleeve.

November 13, 1964

My dearest,

First, you must know that I have penned this letter a thousand times and many years before meeting Dr. Douglas Needham. Now, the doctor believes it to be the first and most necessary step on a different kind of journey, one of healing.

I may say without reservation that you were a good and

kind husband. For twenty-eight years, not every day bliss, but every day a gift. You were honest and kept your promises, which, in my already too-long life, I've found is more than can be said of many.

Most who knew you would say scholarship was your legacy. Indeed, you gave much of yourself to the study of my homeland and to a better understanding of the present through the examination of the past.

However, I know your life's true work, and that was to love, honor, and protect me. I was your dear, lost Anastasia. And I wished it this way.

Now, I am too late, of course—far beyond it. This letter you cannot read. However, while it has been many years since I've placed my trust in a divine hand, it is my deepest hope that wherever your soul now rests, it may read this writing upon my heart. You deserve the truth:

I was born Anna Vasilievna Rostova, only child of Count Vasili Vasiliovich Rostov, of St. Petersburg. My mother died in childbirth, and my father raised me, a loving and doting parent who viewed my intellectual instruction as his highest calling and responsibility.

You know my story, or some of it.

Papa was a colonel in the Imperial Russian Army, wounded in 1905 in the war with Japan. After his retirement from military service, he devoted his life to the study of history and literature, and soon became the director of a distinguished girls' school outside the gates of Tsarskoe Selo. It was there that I matriculated, though my true education was only beginning.

We lived in the shadow of the Tsar's Village, in a home grander than necessary for a bookish widower and his shy but curious daughter. The girls at school held themselves apart from me, as the daughter of their headmaster, but this suited me fine. My closest and only friend was a boy by the name of Ilya Ivanovich, the son of our maid, Ksenia. From a young age, Ilya often came to work with his mother; his father was an alcoholic who disappeared for weeks at a time. As children, I taught him to read, though he taught me much more. Attracted to politics, he was a passionate advocate of change in Russia, about which we sometimes argued; how could I not feel his condemnation of the nobility was a condemnation of me, of all the work and sacrifice of my father? Ilya was killed in the First World War.

Papa was adamant that, in addition to Russian, I learn French, English, and German. By the warmth of our samovar, he read to me the literature of these cultures. Then, as my learning progressed, I read to him. The library was the heart of our home: Herodotus, Thucydides, Plato lined our shelves, as well as the writings of Solovyov, Dostoevsky, Pushkin, and Tolstoy. Books were my mind's playground.

"Riches allow one to travel," Papa often said, "but literature will give one the world." I will never forget the smile that lit his face the day I informed him that I myself planned to become a great writer. He had another saying as well: "History is a story we tell ourselves." It took longer before I understood what this one meant.

Papa felt the winds shifting. Though he did not share this with me, I often eavesdropped at the door of his study, especially on the evenings he hosted friends and associates.

When the revolution came, it swept through the aristocracy like fire through a library. I was fifteen years old when the Bolsheviks seized power. Fear coursed through Petrograd and our small town like electricity through a wire. Soldiers in red-starred caps now poured from the tsar's private train station. Every day, someone Papa knew left home never to return. Every day, a palace I'd visited, an estate in whose park I'd once picnicked or played blindman's buff, was shuttered as if against a storm and abandoned to the looters and the revolutionaries. They stole art, destroyed icons, and burned books as they made the owners watch. If you were lucky, weapons, silver, or jewelry bought you time, or your life. There were stories of homes in the country set afire with families inside them, of princes hiding in boxcars and countesses selling diamonds for flour. "Former people," they called us, as if already we had ceased to exist.

Papa disappeared on December 30, 1917. In the morning, he went out for a meeting. He never returned. I waited for him. For weeks. And then months. I wrote to my grandmother in St. Petersburg, and never heard back. A minor figure of my childhood, she had not forgiven my father—or me—for my mother's death. I found later, from Ksenia's sister, a maid in the city, that she had left for Europe.

Eventually, my alarm turned to grief. Most of the servants had quit or disappeared within days of Papa's disappearance. My governess, Sofia, and Ksenia stayed with me as long as possible, but with it clear their employer was not coming back, and in fear of being branded enemies to their class, eventually they left, as well. Ksenia left me with enough provisions to last for months if I was careful. Most nights I ate potato cutlet or toasted bread with cheese. Eventually, I was forced to venture beyond our gates for food and for news. The Tsarskoe Selo I found was much changed.

It was clear that Russia was no longer safe for me. As well as my mother, I'd now lose my motherland. Already the tsar and his family were prisoners, now in Siberia. Many were dead or imprisoned or had left the country for more welcoming lands—Britain, the United States, France. Every night I waited for the knock of the All-Russian Extraordinary Commission for Combating Counterrevolution—the Cheka—at our door. For the first time, I knew what it was to be wholly and utterly alone.

Except for one person. Count Adrik Vladimirovich Volkov was one of Papa's acquaintances, a widower with two grown sons and a crumbling estate. He had a deep cleft set in a pointed chin, above a neck sagging with age, and the plump lips of a woman. He was an odd man who unnerved me with caustic humor and long silences. Once or twice, when he visited our home, I'd caught his eyes tracking me. Nevertheless, when I found Count Volkov on the lonely doorstep of our house one afternoon in June of 1918, I fell upon him as one would a savior. He would prove to be the opposite.

Volkov was aware of my "unfortunate predicament." He was traveling to London, he said, until the disturbances died down, and he had come to offer—selflessly, he pointed out—to take me with him until more permanent arrangements could be made. "I could use . . ." he said, ". . . a companion."

My skin crawls to recount the way I so easily fell into Volkov's web. We left Petrograd by train a week later, but only after the count picked our home clean of the valuables that had not already been sold, stolen, or given to Sofia and Ksenia. We boarded a train for Minsk.

At first, Volkov seemed kind, even caring. He had known my father in the army and fathered two children of his own. He told me that his wife had died, though I believe now she left him. Still, I remained wary. To save money, we traveled as father and daughter, sharing a couchette. My first night in the compartment, I lay awake and fully clothed, remembering the feel of his eyes in my father's house and the whispers of the girls at the Tsarskoe Selo School for Girls. He never touched me, and for this, I am grateful. However, with St. Petersburg behind us, he began to abuse me in other ways, while also planting in me the seeds of dependence.

Papa had trained me well in the social etiquette of our class. Still, Volkov watched me like a hawk, each meal and interaction an opportunity to criticize my manners, to point out some flaw in my appearance, to question my intellect . . . and so to build in me the belief that no one else in the world would possibly take on such a burden as myself. With each step of our journey, I became less my father's daughter and more Volkov's pawn. He had plans for me.

On my doorstep, Volkov had not mentioned extended stops on our way to London, but by the time we'd reached Warsaw, it was clear why he had brought me, and it was not only for companionship or out of the goodness of his heart. As our accommodations grew increasingly modest, I realized that he had needed the little money I had to get us so far, and that that money was quickly running out.

In Warsaw, Berlin, and Paris, over a period of many months, Volkov established himself within communities of wealthy émigrés, tsarist sympathizers, and even an ambassador, whom he, astonishingly, convinced that he was the emperor's second cousin. In these masquerades, I was his prop, for he believed my presence—the poor, noble orphan on whom he had taken pity—made him a more sympathetic figure.

I dreaded these visits with Volkov's dupes. Once he instructed me to walk with a limp. "But I don't have a limp," I told him. "You do now," he said. With one devout émigrée in Warsaw, I was forced to kneel and pray for three hours; the following day, bruises flowered across my knees. Another sponsor, I am sure, did not buy Volkov's act; nonetheless, he was willing to overlook it in exchange for time—in private—with me. When I fought off our lascivious benefactor's advances, Volkov, spitting mad, called me a fool—the fifty-year-old man, he said, could have been my ticket.

I recall one particular visit with an aged, half-blind baroness in Berlin. In a once-fine Kurfürstendamm salon, she stroked an enormous pet rabbit. So blind was our hostess that she failed to notice the rabbit's soft white flanks shudder, releasing a cascade of tarry black pellets down her skirts. Volkov kept right on spinning his tale of woe.

As he wheedled money from his unwitting marks, I sank deeper into depression. Increasingly, the role in which my guardian had cast me settled deeper into my consciousness: I was an orphan. My father, I had to accept, was dead. Or worse, being tortured in a Bolshevik cell. There was no one left to me in the world. No one but Volkov.

In Berlin, I contemplated suicide more than once, imagining myself and my pain slipping quietly beneath the icy river, but I could never bring myself to jump. A girl had appeared in the city, claiming to be a Romanov grand duchess; she had the courage to jump, only she survived. I read about her in the newspaper, which Volkov bought daily and scoured for details

337

on the imperial family and their whereabouts. Briefly, hope flickered—if a Romanov had escaped, then possibly so could Papa! I followed her story. The girl proved to be a lunatic; they locked her in an asylum, though some believed her.

In Paris, I contemplated escape from Volkov, and even dreamed of enlisting the help of some kindly stranger who might have sympathy for my plight, but I had learned what happens when one trusts strangers, and feared falling into the clutches of someone more twisted even than Volkov. Besides, I had neither the means of supporting myself nor the courage.

Until London. When we arrived in Great Britain, nearly three years after leaving St. Petersburg, finally I mustered the mettle to slip from my puppeteer's strings. For two months, I shaved a shilling here and a pence there from the small sums Volkov dispensed for groceries and incidentals, like the small, leather-bound journals in which I'd taken to writing, hiding them always from my keeper. This diversion, once so familiar an activity, soothed me. The blank page was an escape, a fresh beginning, a listener, and a friend. With a pang, I often thought of the promise I'd made my father, that one day I would become a great writer.

The coins I hid in the seams of my coat, along with a pearl-and-emerald brooch that had once belonged to my mother and which I'd had the foresight to sew into the coat's lining before Volkov appeared on my doorstep. We were staying in Surrey, at a drafty country estate as the guests of one *of Volkov's dupes. One day he sent me to London to retrieve for him a new leather valise.*

And so I slipped into the anonymity of that great city. With his dubiously formed connections, I feared that Volkov would find me and demand repayment for my travel; of these "expenses," he kept a running tally. Knowing, however, that he would never sully himself, or his most valuable possession—his reputation—by visiting the more downtrodden parts of the city, I found lodging at a doss-house on Crispin Street in Spitalfields.

The accommodations were fetid and the company coarse. In my escape, I had retained few belongings: my journals, a large handbag containing one change of clothes, some costume jewelry, and the new leather valise. I carried these with me always, wary of the other women at the lodging house, rough types who eyed with suspicion and envy my unscuffed T-straps and hand-tucked blouse—style being an important element of Volkov's act. A velour coat made my pillow.

On Crispin Street, the roof leaked, and the drafts through the walls chilled me to the bone. At night, I took to luring the wheezing, snuffling bulldog that roamed the house into my bed for warmth. However, the proprietress and her husband were kind, perhaps sensing that I had endured times more difficult than most my age. One evening shortly after I arrived, over a tuppence meal of potatoes and cold meat, I told the Ashes of my desire to buy passage on a steamship to New York.

Naive of my past, which I doubted would win friends in my current surroundings, they thought I was off my head. When I revealed my history and showed them the brooch, however, Mr. Ash promised to escort me the following day to a pawnbroker on Petticoat Lane and immediately after to the office of the White Star Line steamship company near Trafalgar Square.

That night, the girls in the bunk next to mine complained as I sniffled with relief, gratitude, and, for the first time since my father had vanished, hope. Still, I slept with the brooch pinned to the inside of my dress.

Mr. Ash made good on his promise. I am proud to say I managed not to weep when I relinquished the brooch to the oily-faced pawnbroker, who bit the pearls with his teeth. I returned to Crispin Street with a ticket to New York Harbor.

And this night, I better understood Mr. Ash's kindness—and the unmistakable gleam in his wife's eye when I had showed them the brooch. For their efforts, the Ashes expected a cut of the money I'd received for the jewels: 125 pounds—far less than I knew the piece was worth. Having learned for the second time in my life that charity comes rarely without a price, I pressed ten pounds into Mrs. Ash's palm. "Bless ya, lass," she said. The ticket had cost seventeen. The rest I sewed again into my coat with a needle she lent me.

I was hardly disappointed to step aboard the RMS Baltic on April 1, 1922. Europe was no home for me any longer. America, with its large, anonymous cities, was my future. On the ship, though I traveled steerage, my best British English served me well. I had learned something from Volkov after all. When we docked, I disembarked amid a large family from Long Island traveling first class, whom I'd met after sneaking into the ship's reading and writing room.

Nearly all of my resources, emotional and otherwise, had been exhausted on my journey from Russia to the United States. That night, I sobbed in the bed of a Bowery flophouse. The next day, I found a job as a maid at the Waldorf Astoria Hotel.

My experiences with Adrik Vladimirovich Volkov, however, had confirmed my father's favorite saying: riches had allowed me to travel, but literature—or stories—would give me the world. Tyrant that he was, the count had taught me that a good story was, in fact, the most valuable thing in existence.

Often as a child I'd been told that I resembled the youngest grand duchess, Anastasia Nikolaevna, with her chestnut hair and gray-blue eyes. I had seen her a handful of times in my life, once at the imperial Chinese Theatre, where my father and I, along with girls from the school, had been invited for a performance of the ballet Sleeping Beauty. From the auditorium, we craned our necks for a glimpse of the family in their imperial box and then giggled as the youngest grand duchess's mother scolded her for eating chocolates without removing her gloves.

I saw her again later, in 1913, at the tercentenary events with Papa. A frigid February morning outside the cathedral, but even snow and rain could not dampen our spirits as we waited along the carriage route from the Winter Palace. The weather made Petersburg gray as a tomb, but the parade was awash in color: banners of blue, red, and white; Cossacks in scarlet; the Chevalier Guard in silver. As the gilded open carriage of the imperial family pulled to a stop in front of the church, I held my breath. Out stepped the emperor and empress followed by four grand duchesses in long white dresses and dashing sashes. Curiously, beside them, the tsarevitch was carried by a royal bodyguard. Even from a distance, one could see the liveliness of Anastasia. She sidled toward the church as if toward a picnic. There was a spark in her eyes, an ease in her smile. Surely, I thought, she is the favorite.

In Russia, the royal family's photographs were everywhere: on postcards and tins, in commemorative albums, atop boxes of chocolates, and in newsreels. Our nation had an appetite for news of our reclusive rulers that rivaled America's for its motion-picture starlets. Sometimes as a girl I would see Anastasia's picture and think we might be friends, she and I, if our lives ever met.

The last time I saw her was under far different circumstances. Papa had not yet disappeared but grew increasingly distant. A constant cloud of anxiety shrouded my father. The school had ceased meeting, but he was out in the city more than ever before. Under strict orders, I was to stay within the gates of our home, but I had grown lonely in our house, without Ilya there to keep me company, and eager to see what had become of the world outside, the world I heard about only in hushed and urgent tones from Papa's study.

At this time, the Romanovs were under house arrest at Tsarskoe Selo, and I hoped to steal a glimpse of the beleaguered family. I pedaled my bike down Moskovskoye Shosse, past the Cathedral of St. Catherine. Everywhere, Soviet soldiers in long brown coats and pointy caps. I had just come to the pond past the monument to Pushkin near Catherine Palace. The park around Alexander Palace was bordered by a wrought-iron fence. At intervals, Soviet sentries were positioned. A crowd had begun to gather at the fence, and there was shouting. I stopped my bicycle. "What is it?" I asked someone standing by. "Is it them?"

"Da," the man said, a worker by the looks of him. "Blood-sucking dogs." He spat on the ground before him. As he did, the crowd parted, and I saw her again, Anastasia. She was much changed. Her hair, under a cap, was cut short, as someone who's been recently ill, and her skin was sallow. Tsar Nicholas was there, and the grand duchess Olga. To my shock, Anastasia raged at the crowd, her face set in a horrible grimace. That's when I heard the chant: "Hang them."

In New York, I had worked my way to the coat check at the Palm Court of the Plaza Hotel. American men often flirted with me, commented on my hair and, occasionally, my legs—the short new style of dress that the manager encouraged showed them off. At first, I was scandalized by the looseness of America, but soon I enjoyed it. So much freedom I'd never known in Russia.

Then, one day, pressed in one of the journals I had carried with me all the way from Berlin, I found the article about the woman who had claimed to be a grand duchess.

In America, after the execution, conflicting reports of the Romanovs' fate had begun to circulate: they were living in Sweden, in the Vatican, in Japan; all of them had been murdered, down to the family dog, and Nicholas's severed head graced the desk of Vladimir Lenin; a single child had escaped . . .

I was the right age, with the correct accent and a knowledge of Russian noble life as well as the daily workings around Tsarskoe Selo. From Volkov, I had picked up many morsels about the imperial family. And, thanks to my father, I had the bearing and education of a royal. Already, I had found myself fake documents through a busboy in the Waldorf's kitchen; Anna Haswell could work without question. And so, to survive—while I prayed that the real Anastasia had found her own safe harbor—I became her.

At the Plaza, I tested my new identity; if it failed, I would simply say I'd been making a joke. My first marks were my colleagues. They winked and nudged each other, laughing, but soon I found willing ears for my tale. A girl named Liza, who worked as a hostess, introduced me to her uncle, a department store manager from the Bronx who showered me with gifts acquired with a five-fingered discount. One hotel guest, a stockyard owner from Chicago, proposed marriage after knowing "Anastasia" for two days. I gave him the slip before he could leave his wife and children but not before he bought me a sable and paid three months of my rent.

Only when useful did I employ the story of the lost princess, and besides, I found most preferred the temptation of a secret, the deliciousness of innuendo, to the tale itself. However, quickly, I learned the stickiness of lies. More than once I feared myself caught out. To keep it straight, I did what I did best: I wrote. A diary as her, and then another one and another. It wasn't unlike the novels in Papa's library, only I was the author.

The missing Romanovs, and poor Anastasia, were an obsession of this postwar new world, and she became an obsession of mine. Since I'd arrived in New York, the public library had become my refuge. Four days out of seven, after work, I'd find myself stroking the mane of Patience or Fortitude, the twin stone lions who flanked the broad steps of the impressive building on Fifth Avenue, before bounding inside. For hours, I sat in the library's grand Rose Reading Room, ensconced in a book. For information on my protagonist, its collections were a treasure trove. I read everything about the Romanovs

I could get my hands on: newspaper features on the imperial family's life, biographies penned by members of the royal court, memoirs of Alexandra's closest friend and the children's tutor, even a grisly account of the Romanovs' murder published by a White Army investigator. I wept bitterly the day that I read of Anastasia's last hours, as bitterly as I'd ever wept for my own papa.

Whole days went by that were nothing but a frenzy of reading, smudged ink, and cramped fingers. The library's research department, familiar with the "book" on which I was working, was happy to help. I was a woman possessed, the story spooling out before me. Finding the journals themselves became a game, as I haunted dusty antiquaries and stationery shops.

More than a prop, however, I realize now that the diaries had become an escape from the horrors of my own past. I disappeared into them, disappeared into her. She was everything I was—alone, wounded, doomed—and nothing I was. Where I was shy and nervous, she was bold and confident. Where I was frightened and weak, she was strong.

New York was good to me, for a time. Soon, though, I discovered how small that great city could be. I had gotten into trouble, become lazy with my story. One of my most intimates betrayed me to my employer—though, to be fair, I had betrayed her. There was money in my pocket now, enough for an apartment and a new dress when I needed it. I decided to leave New York for a quieter city, one less saturated with champagne and bad behavior. Without telling a soul, l moved to Boston. lt was time to retire Anastasia, to write the last chapter. The problem was that l was now no more Anna Vasilievna Rostova than l was Anastasia. So, l remained Anna Haswell.

When l met Franklin Adams at the library, l liked him immediately. Sweet, trusting, faithful Franklin. Over lunches and shelving books, we became friends. It was my own story, Anna Vasilievna's, that l told him. After so many years, it was a relief to speak it out loud. And a misery.

l swore Franklin to secrecy, as l later swore you. You both proved faithful.

And then l met you. Do you remember? Valentine's Day. If ever there was a sign, l believed that was one. l loved you from the moment l saw you. Worse than the dime-store romances! Never had someone made me feel so alive. You were a scholar, with interests and ambitions. Your knowledge of Russian history rivaled that of my father's. You had awe for the country of my birth, or what it had once been. You had awe for me. And suddenly, l wanted to erase my past, especially the painful parts, to scrap and burn it and start again with only the best chapters. You needed more than the disgraced and abandoned daughter of a schoolmaster count; you needed a princess.

After l told you l was Anastasia, you would hardly leave

my side. I was not a novelty to you but a destiny. The day I shared the first diary with you, I scarcely breathed. Would you see me for the storyteller I was? I meted them out each time we met, and it was as if I was casting a spell, one I never wanted broken. And then you asked me to be your wife, and I realized too late that I had trapped myself in my own lies.

I decided to revise my story, to write myself into the chapters in Berlin. If you felt for the poor young girl who'd lost everything and betrayed her dearest friend, if you could forgive the impostor, as Anastasia had, then perhaps you could forgive me. . . .

You were horrified at this betrayal, shocked that one, even one so wounded and desperate, could do such a thing. For days you ranted about this episode from my past, for years maligned the unscrupulous impostor Anderson, thought my forgiveness of her a sign of my virtue.

For the first time since my father last kissed the top of my head, I was really and truly loved. I could not bear to be unloved ever again. And, so, I decided. To live the fiction.

François de La Rochefoucauld once wrote, "We are so accustomed to disguise ourselves to others, that in the end, we become disguised to ourselves." I feel this is true, my beloved. As the years went on, and we settled into life together, I as your lost princess and you as my sage prince, I <u>became</u> Anastasia.

To lie may be a sin, and there is not penance enough for the *guilt which I feel, but I do believe that, through my fiction, I saved Anastasia's life and she saved mine. I do not ask for pity. For my dissemblance, there is no one to blame but myself. Even Volkov I have forgiven. My love, I pray that, in whatever star-strewn plane you now exist, you may do the same for me.*

> *Ever and always,*
> *Your Anastasia*

A bell chimes overhead in the library. It's twelve o'clock. The library is closing, and the lump that has formed at the base of my throat is as big and round as a walnut.

I am so sorry for Aunt Anna, for all the crushing cruelty she experienced, different from her fictional Anastasia's but maybe only by degree. She also lost her family, her sweetheart, her country, her identity. Her life was a tragedy, a series of betrayals, but the worst might have been the betrayal of herself.

Still, something in me revolts against Anna's words: *You needed more than the disgraced and abandoned daughter of a schoolmaster count; you needed a princess.*

No! I want to scream into the hushed silence of the Special Collections room. *You were enough!*

Tears sting my eyes. Because I know what it is to pretend to be someone you're not, to believe if you were someone slightly different, slightly *more*, you would finally be safe and loved—because that's the fairy tale we've all been told. But I refuse to be that impostor any longer, and I'm angry at my aunt that she wasn't able to do the same, that she could only speak the words in a letter shoved deep into the stacks of a library.

A knock on the room's glass door causes me to jump. Outside, the dour young librarian is tapping a finger to the watch on her wrist. "The library is closing," she mouths. I nod and start putting the papers back into their boxes. Scowling, she turns.

In some way, I feel relief packing this story away, closing the lid on the trunk. Anna's mystery has monopolized my thoughts for . . . a year, I realize, exactly a year today. I'm glad I got a why, but I'm sad, too, sad that it's really, finally, over.

Vibrating in my pocket startles me a second time. I don't have to look to know it's Evan. That morning, I texted him to say I was going to see Uncle Henry's papers. With the time difference, he's probably just waking. Rubbing angry tears from the corners of my eyes, I check to see what he's written.

Did you find what you needed?

Overhead, the bell chimes again.

You needed more than the disgraced and abandoned daughter of a schoolmaster count; you needed a princess.

What had *I* needed? I think, and a numbing shame spreads through my limbs. My aunt believed she had to be Anastasia to be loved, but wasn't that what I'd asked of her as well? Didn't

I want her to be Anastasia and care more when I thought she was? Wasn't I disappointed when she wasn't? I can't fault her; I was her accomplice.

The letter is dated November 13, 1964, a month after the library acquired her husband's papers, three years after his sudden death. Anna must have snuck it into the box to reside with Henry's legacy. Where else could she have sent it? My heart aches to imagine it.

Hers is a romance and a tragedy, but it doesn't have to be without a happy ending. The letter has been here, unopened, for more than forty years. It doesn't belong in a dusty, gray box that no one will touch for another decade. Anna's last chapter should live where it belongs, where the story began—in the trunk with the journals.

No one's entered Special Collections since I've been here; still, I swivel my head to make sure the room is empty. No cameras—not in the library's budget. I crane my neck to see that the librarian has left her post and, quickly, lift my shirt and shove the letter into the waistband of my jeans. With satisfaction, an image flickers across my mind of Anastasia—Anna Rostova—doing the same with a slim journal.

"The library is closing," a disembodied voice crackles over an intercom.

The last binder goes onto the shelf labeled Wallace, Henry H. I pause, thinking: if I was an accomplice, then so was he. I am sure there are things he swept under the rug, tucked in the closet—puzzle pieces that didn't quite fit. *But my heart tells me that it is she.* I get it.

Waving to the librarian, I paste on a smile to hide the fact that I have a forty-four-year-old letter stuffed into my pants. Outside the library, thin clouds have dissolved into pale sun.

Evan picks up on the first ring. "Evan Hermann speaking." He is chipper, likely on his third cup of coffee and sixth spoonful of sugar, but I'm glad to hear it. It means things are going well with his mom.

"Hi. It's me."

"I know," he says. "I have your number."

I smile.

"Did you find the papers?" he asks.

"I did."

For all that it holds, the envelope is light in my hands. The slopes and curls of the script are less enigmatic now that I know the hand that made them, but not all of their mystery is gone.

Was my great-great-aunt's pain any less real because the details of her story were not? I don't think so. Sometimes, I believe, fact becomes truth becomes Truth becomes fiction; it's only in the telling that we finally understand.

"Did you get what you needed?" Evan asks again.

"Yes," I reply.

"Which was . . ."

"The end."

Postscript

I've been thinking a lot about stories lately. We're all made up of them, the ones we tell ourselves and the ones we tell each other, the ones that obscure and the ones that reveal.

The ancients used to gaze up at the night sky and see the glowing, objective facts of stars. It wasn't until they connected the dots, etching constellations into the vastness of the abyss, that the stars became maps for journeys of discovery.

Aunt Anna's trunk now lives in the middle of a dorm room in Stanford, California. I went back and got it from Uncle Dale before my epic drive cross-country with my dad. Mom was right; it makes a good coffee table, when you don't trip over it in the night.

My favorite class is Beginning Fiction Workshop. The professor likes to talk in profound statements that remind me of Evan's fondness for quotations (even though we don't see each other as much as we used to, he's still around).

Show, don't tell, our teacher says. *Keep the scene moving. Kill your darlings. A protagonist should be flawed but forgivable.* It makes me wonder—

Can you forgive an impostor?

Author's Note

Although I've made every effort at historical accuracy in these pages, like Jess, I am first and foremost a storyteller; I am also human. Some facts have been bent to the story, and some details I have surely gotten wrong. Complicating things, many particulars of the historical record around the Romanovs remain disputed.

I owe a great debt to the writers, researchers, and sources who contributed background to this story. Any errors are wholly my own. If you find one, I invite you to share it with me. (You can find me at kathrynwilliamsbooks.com.)

A few things to note:

At the start of the Russian Revolution, both Maria and Anastasia Romanov reportedly burned their diaries. Only their letters survive. These, along with translations of other family members' diaries, were an inspiration, but the voice I've created for Anastasia is my own.

Until February 14, 1918, when it was changed by Soviet decree signed by Vladimir Lenin, the Russian Empire followed the Julian calendar. In the twenty-first century, this put Russian dates thirteen days behind the newer Gregorian calendar used in the West. In some sources, you'll find dates labeled "Old

Style" or "New Style," accordingly. In this book, dates prior to February 14, 1918, are in the Old Style, as Anastasia would have known them. Dates after are in the New Style.

During the First World War, Tsar Nicholas II changed the name of the city of Sankt-Peterburg (in English, St. Petersburg) to Petrograd because it sounded less German. (In 1924, after Lenin's death, the name was changed again to Leningrad.) In this book, I've called the city St. Petersburg, or just Petersburg, for simplicity's sake and because, having known it as such for most of her life, Anastasia likely would have continued using the old name.

A number of news articles that Jess references in the book are real. You can find citations for them on the Sources & Further Reading page. The article titled "Young Woman Claims Royal Blood," however, is a fabrication. While there was a published police report of a then-anonymous woman's jump into the Landwehr Canal, Anna Anderson did not immediately make her claim, and news reports only surfaced years later. Published accounts of Anderson's story also conflict on the date of the police report. The article titled "Royal Remains Finally Confirmed" is a fictional composite of similar articles. Lastly, passages of the real article "Captivity Affects Romanoff's Mind" have been rearranged.

The New Hampshire Historical Society does house archival material from the New Hampshire State Hospital (chartered as the New Hampshire Asylum for the Insane), but most are administrative records. Some patient information is included in the collection, but it is limited and older than Aunt Anna's era. Newer records have been kept confidential for privacy reasons.

The vintage shop that inspired the one Jess and Katie visit did not yet exist in this location in 2007.

Lindy's Diner, in Keene, is not open for dinner, but breakfast and lunch are highly recommended.

The graveyard that Jess and Evan visit is invented but inspired by numerous graveyards like it scattered across New England.

Likewise, Mountainvale Academy is a fictional school based on similar ones.

The Sugarloaf ski lodge arcade room, outside of which I imagined Jess and Ryan sharing their first kiss, did not actually open until 2012 (and is now closed). However, it felt so perfect, I had to keep it.

Sources & Further Reading

If you're interested in the lives, deaths, and world of the Romanovs, as well as their impostors, there are hundreds of books and websites on the topic—fiction, nonfiction, and something in between.

Here are some that were helpful in the writing of this book and that make for excellent further reading.

Articles in the Book

Associated Press. "Captivity Affects Romanoff's Mind." *New York Times*, March 18, 1918, via https://timesmachine .nytimes.com.

Associated Press. "DNA Tests Confirm the Deaths of the Last Missing Romanovs." *New York Times*, May 1, 2008, https://www.nytimes.com/2008/05/01/world/europe /01russia.html.

Harding, Luke. "Bones found by Russian builder finally solve riddle of the missing Romanovs." *Guardian* (UK), August 24, 2007, https://www.theguardian.com/world /2007/aug/25/russia.lukeharding.

Hulem, John. "The Czar At Home—An Intimate Study." *New York Times*, October 2, 1904, via https://timesmachine .nytimes.com.

Website

Atchison, Bob, creator and editor. Alexander Palace Time Machine. 1997–2021. https://www.alexanderpalace.org/palace/.[1]

Books

On the Romanovs

Azar, Helen. *The Diary of Olga Romanov: Royal Witness to the Russian Revolution, with Excerpts from Family Letters and Memoirs of the Period.* Yardley, PA: Westholme, 2014.

Massie, Robert K. *Nicholas and Alexandra: The Classic Account of the Fall of the Romanov Dynasty.* New York: Random House Trade Paperback, 1967, 2011.

Massie, Robert K. *The Romanovs: The Final Chapter.* New York: Ballantine Books, 1995.

Montefiore, Simon Sebag. *The Romanovs: 1613–1918.* New York: Vintage Books, 2017.

Rappaport, Helen. *The Last Days of the Romanovs: Tragedy at Ekaterinburg.* New York: St. Martin's Griffin, 2008.

Rappaport, Helen. *The Romanov Sisters: The Lost Lives of the Daughters of Nicholas and Alexandra.* New York: St. Martin's Press, 2014.

---

1   This website is a treasure trove of photographs, historical reports, public domain books, letters, diaries, previously untranslated sources, and other materials related to the Romanovs.

On Anna Anderson

Anderson, Anna. *I Am Anastasia: The Autobiography of the Grand-Duchess of Russia, with Notes by Roland Krug von Nidda.* Translated by Oliver Coburn. New York: Harcourt, Brace and Company, 1959.[2]

King, Greg, and Penny Wilson. *The Resurrection of the Romanovs: Anastasia, Anna Anderson, and the World's Greatest Royal Mystery.* Hoboken, NJ: John Wiley & Sons, 2011.

Lovell, James Blair. *Anastasia: The Lost Princess.* New York: St. Martin's Press, 1991.[3]

On the Russian Revolution

Smith, Douglas. *Former People: The Final Days of the Russian Aristocracy.* New York: Picador, 2012.

Fitzpatrick, Sheila and Yuri Slezkine, ed. *In the Shadow of Revolution: Life Stories of Russian Women from 1917 to the Second World War.* Princeton, NJ: Princeton University Press, 2000.

Film & TV

Anastasia (animated). Directed by Don Bluth and Gary Goldman, starring Meg Ryan and John Cusack. 1997; USA: 20th Century Fox. Film.

---

2   This book, if you can get your hands on a copy, was originally published in German by Franziska Schanzkowska, aka Anna Anderson, living as Anastasia Romanov, and her supporters.

3   Lovell, one of Anderson's staunchest believers, died the year before DNA tests disproved her claims.

Anastasia. Directed by Anatole Litvak, starring Ingrid Bergman and Yul Brynner. 1956; USA: 20th Century Fox. Film.

The Last Czars. Directed by Adrian McDowall and Gareth Tunley, starring Robert Jack and Susanna Herbert. 2019; USA: Nutopia/Netflix. Miniseries.

War & Peace. Adaptation of the book by Leo Tolstoy. Directed by Tom Harper, starring Paul Dano and James Norton. 2016; UK: BBC. Miniseries.

Acknowledgments

Writing is often a solitary endeavor, but putting a book into the world is a team effort. There are so many individuals and communities who have shaped and supported this book over the eight years since the idea first implanted itself in my brain that I fear my acknowledgments will be incomplete. If you touched this book, know that you are appreciated. Especially . . .

Elizabeth Rudnick, former editor, constant friend, early believer, and agent extraordinaire. At HarperTeen, Catherine Wallace, who patiently refined the story in significant ways, as well as Alice Jerman and Clare Vaughn, who shepherded the book over its supremely important last miles. Corina Lupp and Alison Klapthor for design, and Holly Ovenden for a cover that made me swoon. My copy editors (publishing's unsung heroes), Jessica Berg and Brenna Franzitta, and the production and marketing teams.

Kristyn Keene, Christy Ottaviano, and Kat Rosenfeld, who acted as early readers in various capacities, asking important questions that pushed me and the story deeper.

The staff, students, and community at The Telling Room, who cheered me on, and especially our Young Emerging Authors, who inspire me every single day.

Hewnoaks Artist Colony, which granted immeasurably valuable and beautiful space to imagine a new ending. And the Sewanee School of Letters, which instilled in me a profound respect and curiosity for the way stories work.

The people of Keene, New Hampshire, for indulging my seemingly bizarre photo-taking and random question-asking during a pandemic. Also, the kind staffs of the Keene Public Library, the Mason Library at Keene State College (who are, it should be noted, far friendlier and more helpful than the librarian invented for the book), the Historical Society of Cheshire County, and the New Hampshire Historical Society.

Kilian Herold, for answers about oboes, and Ella Falkovska, for confirming Russian names and customs. Lisa Branch, for obscure forensic queries. Katherine Bowers of the North American Dostoevsky Society and Dr. Carol Apollonio of the International Dostoevsky Society for help on a quotation wild goose chase.

My beloved family and my friends—who I hope will forgive me for being too many to name here—from Richmond, Sewanee, Nashville, and Maine. They listened as I wrung my hands and celebrated at each milestone along the journey. This is no small thing.

Amma, always.

Greg, who has known this book as long as he has known me and who has supported both unfailingly.

And Teddy, who will someday hear all the stories. I love you.